AGENTS
OF THE GLASS

MICHAEL D. BEIL

Alfred A. Knopf New York

THIS IS A BORZOI BOOK PUBLISHED BY ALFRED A. KNOPF

Visit us on the Web! randomhousekids.com

Educators and librarians, for a variety of teaching tools, visit us at RHTeachersLibrarians.com

Library of Congress Cataloging-in-Publication Data
Names: Beil, Michael D., author.
Title: A new recruit / Michael D. Beil.
Description: First edition. | New York : Alfred A. Knopf, [2016] | Series:
  Agents of the Glass | Summary: Andy witnesses a bank robbery and becomes
  recruited to a secret organization that finds and eliminates evil.
Identifiers: LCCN 2015033930 | ISBN 978-0-385-75321-0 (trade) |
  ISBN 978-0-385-75324-1 (pbk.) | ISBN 978-0-385-75322-7 (lib. bdg.) |
  ISBN 978-0-385-75323-4 (ebook)
Subjects: | CYAC: Good and evil—Fiction. | Spies—Fiction. | New York
  (N.Y.)—Fiction.
Classification: LCC PZ7.B38823495 Ne 2016 | DDC [Fic]—dc23
LC record available at http://lccn.loc.gov/2015033930

The text of this book is set in 13.5-point Fournier MT.

Printed in the United States of America
September 2016
10 9 8 7 6 5 4 3 2 1

First Edition

**To Maggie, Isabel,
and good dogs everywhere**

A PROLOGUE JUST FOR YOU:
DO NOT SKIP THIS!

By the time I heard about the explosion at the First Mutual Bank on Seventy-Seventh Street, Andy Llewellyn had already made the decision that would change his life. And mine. And, although you didn't know it until this very moment, yours.

As long as we're on the topic, let's get one thing out of the way right now. You may think that the decision to read this book was your own, but that's not quite true. You're reading it because I—we—want you to read it. In fact, we've gone to quite a bit of trouble to make certain that it ended up in your hands at this very moment. Don't bother asking how we did it; it's the kind of thing that we've become very good at. After all, we've had a few centuries to hone our skills.

Why you? That's simple. Because we see something in

you—something special, a quality that sets you apart from your friends and classmates. We saw that quality in Andy right away, and he didn't disappoint us. That doesn't mean that we expect you to follow in his footsteps. Andy is, well, a special case. Keep reading, and you'll see what I mean. You're a bit more of a calculated risk, but I have a good feeling about you, too.

Of course, you could set the book down right now and walk away, but I don't think you will. I've been watching you for a while now, and I can picture the expression on your face as you read this; I've seen that mixture of fear, curiosity, and skepticism before.

I've also been wrong before, though, as my colleagues are eager to point out. If this is one of those times, and you want to stop reading right now, just set the book down and walk away. I'll take care of the rest. I'd appreciate it if you didn't mention what you've read to anyone else, but to be honest, it doesn't really matter, because no one will believe you, anyway.

It's up to you.

1

There's no doubt about it—Andy's full name sounds a bit stuffy: Andover James Llewellyn. His story, however, starts with an ordinary pickle, the kind that fast-food joints put on their burgers.

"It wasn't even supposed to be on the hamburger," he told Silas at their first meeting. "I told the guy: no pickles. When I opened the wrapper and saw that slimy thing staring at me from beneath those sesame seeds, I thought seriously about taking it back. And I would have if there hadn't been a long line at the counter. I *really* hate pickles. So I used a French fry to push it onto a napkin and wadded it up. I had to throw away that fry, too, because it had touched the pickle."

Five minutes later, he was on his way home, ready to face the fact that it was the Friday before Labor Day, with school starting in five days, and he had precisely zero plans for the long holiday weekend.

"*All* that changed in a hurry," said Andy. "My mom is always telling me that life is like that. It just . . . happens."

He made the turn from Seventy-Seventh onto York Avenue and was walking north, a few steps behind a guy pushing a shopping cart full of bags of cans and bottles. The latest album from Karina Jellyby, his favorite singer, was pouring into his head through his earbuds when the blast hit him. According to the laws of physics, there could only have been a fraction of a second between the time he saw the flash and flying glass and heard the explosion, but Andy insists that, in his memory, they are two distinct events.

"When I close my eyes, I still see the poor guy with the shopping cart flying sideways and slamming into a parked car, and all those cans and bottles being blown clear across the street," he said. "A *blizzard* of glass and aluminum. And I hear Karina Jellyby's song 'Don't Blame Me,' the part where there's just the piano at the beginning."

The explosion knocked Andy's feet out from under him and rolled him between the front and rear wheels of a delivery truck that was screeching to a stop.

"The way I see it, that pickle saved my life," Andy insisted. "If they had made the burger the way I wanted it, I would have finished eating a few seconds earlier and would have been a few steps ahead of where I was, and instead of a cut on the forehead from a chunk of flying glass and some bruises from bouncing off the street, I would have ended up exactly like the guy with the shopping cart—dead."

Instead, Andy was alive. Disoriented, confused, and bleeding a little—actually, a *lot*—but definitely alive. He was lying under the truck, curled up into a ball and waiting for the next explosion, when he felt a hand on his shoulder and heard a voice that sounded miles and miles away.

"Hey, kid, are you okay? Kid?"

Andy lifted his head from the hot, greasy pavement. "Unh."

"He's alive!" shouted the man.

A woman asked, "Are you hurt?"

"I don't think so. Maybe. I can't tell."

"Can you move?"

He wiggled his toes, then clenched his hands into fists as he became aware of sirens blaring all around him. "Yeah. Everything works."

"Good. We're going to get you out of there, but we have to be careful because there's broken glass every-where," the woman said. "You're going to be all right."

"Yeah, I know," Andy said. He admitted later that he had no idea why he said that; at that moment, he didn't know *anything*. "What happened?"

"There was an explosion in the bank. The whole front of the building is gone."

Just then someone came with a push broom and swept all the broken glass aside, clearing a path for his escape.

He commando-crawled in reverse, then, once his head was clear of the truck, stood and turned to face those who had helped him.

Two sets of hands immediately pushed him back down onto the ground. "The way they looked at me, I knew something was wrong with my face, and when the blood started getting into my eyes, I got a little worried. But it was just a cut from some flying glass. I guess I was lucky—if it had been an inch lower, I would have lost an eye."

Five minutes later, after wrapping his head almost completely in gauze, the paramedics loaded him into the back of an ambulance. They were just about to shut the door when the woman who had assured him that he would be all right shouted at them, "Wait! I have his backpack! It was under the truck."

Maybe it was the loss of blood, or maybe he bumped his head and was suffering from a slight concussion, but Andy swears that right then he absolutely believed it was his backpack: same black-and-silver color scheme, same brand.

"Thanks," he said, never pausing to ask the obvious question: Why would he have been carrying his schoolbag on a Friday in August?

The rest of that afternoon was a blur of X-rays, doctors shining lights into his eyes, tetanus shots, and his mother's tears. By the time the nurse brought her into the treatment room, he was sitting up on the edge of the bed, drinking a ginger ale (they didn't have root beer, his favorite), and munching on saltines.

"Hey, Mom."

Abbey Llewellyn immediately broke down in a flurry of hugging and sobbing.

"I'm okay, Mom. Really. It's just a cut. Eight stitches. D'you want to see the piece of glass they took out? It's, like, two inches long."

Like most twelve-year-olds, Andy has a habit of saying exactly the wrong thing at the wrong time, at least where his mother is concerned.

The police investigation revealed that a (still-unidentified) man had wrapped himself in dynamite and walked into the bank to rob it. The teller handed over the money, and the robber turned to leave, but just as he reached for the front door, something went horribly wrong. Because the bank's employees were all on the floor, they had only some cuts and scratches, but the robber and the homeless man pushing the shopping cart weren't so lucky.

The phone was ringing when Andy and his mother walked in the door to their apartment, and it didn't stop until she finally unplugged it an hour later. Everybody wanted to talk to Andy—the NYPD (super nice), the FBI (a little scary), and every reporter in the city. Andy's father let him talk to the cops and the FBI but told all the reporters to . . . Well, let's just say that he told them that they *really* needed to stop calling.

His father had some typically blunt advice for Andy,

who had told him his theory about the pickle saving his life. "You ought to keep that little bit of information to yourself, unless you want to be known as Pickle Boy for the rest of your life. Because that's what the newspapers and the TV reporters will call you."

Howard Llewellyn was right. The editors at the *Daily Torch*, New York's most notorious tabloid, lived for "pickle boy" opportunities. Not that Howard was above a little name-calling himself. As the host of the nightly radio show *Tellin' It Like It Is* (where he went by the name Howard Twopenny), he spent his fair share of time in the gutter on his never-ending search for what he called the LHD—the lowest human denominator.

Andy slept on the top bunk of a set of bunk beds; the lower one had long ago been replaced by a desk and a small bookcase. After all the day's excitement, however, sleep was impossible. For a long time, he lay there while a steady stream of pictures of a shopping cart tumbling through the air, followed by a million cans and bottles and an innocent bystander, played in an endless loop on the ceiling above him. It was the image of that man pushing the cart that haunted him, and the more he thought about him, the clearer the man's face became. He had seen him before around the neighborhood, going through trash cans on Tuesdays, which was the trash pickup day on his street. He was angry with himself for never paying attention to him or being even the slightest bit curious about his life. What had happened, he wondered, to lead the man to a life on the streets of New York—certainly not a conscious choice anyone would make. He had been a teenager once, just like Andy, with friends and dreams, going off to school with his backpack, and—

A backpack! Andy sat up in bed so quickly that he slammed his head on the ceiling—luckily, *not* the spot where his stitches were. Rubbing his forehead, he jumped to the floor and turned on the light. Hanging from his chair was his backpack, but his eyes soon landed on another identical pack parked in its usual spot next to the door.

"A lot of things went through my mind at that moment," he explained later. "Mostly, I was imagining how many pieces I was going to be blown into if it was another bomb. I didn't know what to do, so I just got back in bed and stared at that backpack. My mom must have heard my head hit the ceiling, because in a few minutes she came in to check on me. I think she was feeling a little guilty about leaving. She's a scientist and works for Concern Worldwide, this big international organization—you know, like the Red Cross—and she was flying to Tanzania first thing in the morning. I know I should have just told her about the pack right then, but she started talking about her trip to Africa, telling me that she would call me every day, and how everything was going to be all right, and to listen to my dad while she was gone, even if he was acting like, well, the guy I call Radio Dad. Sometimes, when he's talking to me, it's like he's still on the air, saying the craziest things you ever heard. And Mom will always remind me, 'Take your father with a grain of salt, Andover.' Sometimes, I think I need a whole saltshaker. Anyway, when she left my room, I hopped down from the bed and stared at that backpack, pacing back and forth and trying to work up the nerve to open it up. I finally kneeled down next to it, took a deep breath, slid the zipper a few inches, and peeked inside. And then . . . wow."

Wow, indeed. Two hundred and ten thousand, seven hundred and forty dollars' worth of wow, to be exact, in crisp new twenty- and fifty-dollar bills.

I KNEW THE TWO HUNDRED GRAND WOULD GET YOUR ATTENTION. BEFORE YOU READ ANY FURTHER, STOP A MOMENT AND CONSIDER THIS QUESTION: WHAT WOULD YOU DO IF YOU WERE IN ANDY'S PO- SITION? TWO HUNDRED AND TEN THOUSAND, SEVEN HUNDRED AND FORTY DOLLARS. IN A BACKPACK. IN YOUR BEDROOM. AND ONLY YOU KNOW. IF YOU'RE STILL INTERESTED, KEEP READING.

2

"Two hundred grand?" bellowed Howard Llewellyn, spilling coffee down the front of his custom-made shirt in the process. "And you're going to do *what?* Whoa! Slow down. Let's talk about this. A bag full of money lands in your lap, and you want to give it *back*—even though you nearly got blown to smithereens?"

"Easy, Dad. That's a coffee cup, not a microphone. It wasn't *that* bad." Andy touched his bandaged forehead. "Just a cut."

"Okay, maybe I'm exaggerating a little, but face it, you were damned lucky. Are you sure that's what you want to do? I mean, that's your college education right there." He paused, grinning. "Or a nice car for your old man."

"I'm sure. It's not my money."

"Does your mom know about this?"

"No."

"Really? Huh. I would have bet . . . Well, you do what you think is right. But do me a favor, okay? This is for real. I have a reputation in this town. People have certain, um, expectations of . . . well . . . of Howard *Twopenny*, anyway, and I don't want them to think I've gone soft or something. So if there's a way to keep *my* name out of it, I know my boss would appreciate it."

"I'll try," said Andy as he threw the backpack over one shoulder and started for the door.

"Whoa! Hold on. I'm coming with you. I don't care how safe people say this city is; you can't go walking around New York with two hundred grand in your backpack."

◆ ◆ ◆

Andy returned the money.

His dad patted him on the back outside the door to the Nineteenth Precinct. "You're a good kid. A little crazy, maybe, but . . . Call me if you need me."

"Thanks, Dad. I've got it."

A minute later, he set the backpack on the desk of Detective Greg Cunningham. He had been the first policeman to talk to Andy in the hospital and had given him his card.

"What's this?" Cunningham asked.

"It's . . . um, well, you'll see. Yesterday . . . some of it . . . is a little fuzzy. Somebody handed this to me as they were putting me in the ambulance. I thought it was mine. . . . I mean, it looks exactly like mine, but then when I got home, I realized something was wrong."

The detective sprang out of his chair, looking very concerned. Backing away from the pack, he yanked Andy out of the office. "That came from the bank? On the ground—now! It could be a bomb. Everybody, down!"

All around the squad room, cops threw themselves to the floor.

"No! Wait!" cried Andy. "It's not a bomb. It's money. That's all. I already checked."

"What do you mean, money?"

"The money from the robbery. The explosion must have . . . I don't know, sent it flying, because it ended up next to me under that truck. Look inside. Really."

The other cops slowly got to their feet, eyeing Andy suspiciously. "Everything okay, Cunningham?" one asked.

Cunningham grinned, shaking his head. "Yeah. Sorry, everybody. My bad."

Andy followed him back into the cluttered office, where the detective used his handkerchief to pull on the backpack's side zipper. His mouth fell open when he saw the contents.

"Two hundred and ten thousand, seven hundred and forty dollars," said Andy. "It's all there. I didn't take anything, I swear."

Cunningham had him tell the complete story and then

called in another detective and had Andy repeat it. When Andy finished, they were speechless for a few moments, shaking their heads in disbelief.

Finally, Detective Cunningham spoke: "And you brought it straight to us. I've been a cop for fifteen years, and this is the craziest story I've ever heard. Who *are* you?" He laughed so loudly that a framed picture of the mayor fell off the wall.

"You . . . don't believe me?" Andy was crushed. Here he was, doing what he thought was the right thing to do, and nobody believed him.

"No, no, you've got it all wrong, Andy!" said Cunningham. "I believe your story—I'm just having a hard time believing that there's still someone like you left in New York City. You're going to be *famous*. Wait till the newspeople get ahold of this. You're going to be on the front page of every paper in the city tomorrow."

Andy shook his head vigorously. "No. No. You can't tell *anybody*. Promise? I don't want my picture in the paper or on the news. I just want to give back the money and not make a big deal out of it. It's not like I tackled the robber or something. I was just in the right place at the right time. Well, except for the almost-getting-killed part."

Detective Cunningham had a dazed look on his face. "Wait, *what*? Nobody? Are you sure? People love stories like this. People *need* stories like this. This would go viral in minutes."

"I don't want to be famous," said Andy, holding his ground. "Promise you won't tell anyone?"

"Yeah, sure. I mean, if that's what you want—"

"It is. Promise?"

"You have my word. No reporters."

"One more thing. You know the guy who was killed? The homeless man? Have you found out who he was yet?"

"Afraid not," said Cunningham. "We're still looking for some ID, something he might have been carrying."

"What will happen to him?"

The detective shrugged. "Hard to say. If no one claims the body, it'll be buried out on Hart Island."

"Where's that?"

"The Bronx. There's a cemetery there—it's called a potter's field—for people . . . like him. People who don't have anybody to . . . or can't afford anything else."

"Then we have to find out who he is. There must be somebody out there who knows. He has to have a family somewhere. I'll help you. Just promise that you won't give up looking."

"I'll do some checking around, but I wouldn't get my hopes up, if I were you. A lot of these people . . . Well, these things can get complicated."

"But you're going to look, right?"

Another burst of laughter exploded from Detective Cunningham, sending a coffee mug to the floor. "I like your style, Andy Llewellyn. I promise. I'll look into it."

After walking Andy out of the precinct, he returned to his desk, closing his office door behind him. Checking once more that no one was watching, he pulled the lower right-hand drawer out and reached underneath it. Taped to the bottom was an index card with *Silas* and a phone number printed on it.

Cunningham dialed the number.

"Hello, Detective," a man's voice answered. "It's been a while."

"I think I might have what you're looking for," said Cunningham.

THE NAME ON THAT CARD AND THE VOICE ON THE OTHER END OF THAT LINE? BOTH MINE. I'M SILAS. IT'S NOT MY REAL NAME, OF COURSE—I BORROWED IT FROM MY FAVORITE BOOK. FOR NOW I'LL TELL YOU WHAT I TOLD ANDY: IF THERE COMES A TIME WHEN YOU NEED TO KNOW MY REAL NAME, I'LL TELL YOU. AND IF IT MAKES YOU FEEL BETTER, ANDY WASN'T EXPECTING ME TO DROP INTO HIS LIFE ANY MORE THAN YOU WERE WHEN YOU PICKED UP THIS BOOK.

3

Within minutes of his departure from the police station, Andover Llewellyn was on Silas's radar, and a few moments after that, Silas had his very best and most trusted people hard at work, digging up everything they could find about young Mr. Llewellyn.

Andy had dropped the money off on Saturday morning, and by noon Silas knew enough to make him eager to know more. He was intrigued by Andy, whose mother seemed perfectly lovely and normal. Howard Llewellyn, however, was harder to figure out. If the real Howard was anything like his radio personality, the apple hadn't merely fallen far from the tree. In Andy's case, that apple had hit the ground, rolled down a long, steep hill, and then dropped into a river that carried it out to sea, where the wind and currents carried it to lands far, far away.

As details about Andy trickled in—photographs, report cards, essays he'd written, interviews with friends and neighbors—Silas became more and more convinced that he was a perfect fit for a position that his employers had been desperately trying to fill all summer. The assignment was in a school, and they were hoping to have their man—or boy, in this case—in place when classes started on the Wednesday after Labor Day. That meant that they had just four days to make a decision about him. And then there was always the chance that he would say no. It was up to Silas to persuade Andy to take the job, but first he had to be absolutely convinced that he was the *right* boy. If Silas was wrong—if Andy's decision to return the money was a fluke—he would almost certainly fail, and he could not afford failure. What he really needed was another test to make sure Andy was the "real thing." He knew that he only had one chance, so it needed to be a fair, true test of his character. If it was too obvious, if he thought even for a second that he was being watched, he might act differently.[1] One of Silas's contacts had overheard Andy on the phone with his grandparents (on his mother's side) making plans to visit them on Sunday afternoon. They lived on the Upper West Side, near Riverside Park, so he would spend the night and return home on Monday, which was Labor

---

1. My own mentor reminds me almost daily that *"character* means 'doing the right thing even when no one is looking.'"

Day. Andy liked going there for two reasons. One, his grandparents were fun to be around, and they always took him to a great pizza place, and two, his favorite store in the world, ModelWorld, was not far away, on Amsterdam Avenue. Although ModelWorld sounds like a hangout for fashion models, it's actually a hobby shop that specializes in model airplanes and ships—the perfect spot for the test, because the shop's owner, Melvin Oresko,[2] just happens to be a retired (and entirely trustworthy) colleague of Silas, one who would be happy to play a part in his little scheme.

Everett Newell, Andy's grandfather, was a retired navy man and had introduced him to C. S. Forester's Horatio Hornblower novels the previous summer. Andy sailed through all eleven books in the series in less than three months, thrilled especially by the adventures of the young midshipman Horatio aboard HMS *Indefatigable*, a 64-gun ship built for the British navy in 1784. For more than a year, Andy had been saving his money—nearly a hundred dollars, Silas learned—to buy a wooden model kit of that particular ship. He was finally going to get his wish, because tucked inside the newspaper (*not* the *Daily Torch*, by the way) that was delivered to his grandparents' house on Monday morning was an advertisement for a "huge one-day-only Labor Day blowout sale!" at ModelWorld, featuring

---

2. Not his real name, of course. The names of all current Agents have been changed for their protection.

wooden ship model kits at twenty-five percent off. At the bottom of the page was a coupon, which Andy neatly tore off and stuck in his pocket.

Silas was certain that the offer was too good to resist, and as predicted, Andy was outside the hobby shop at ten minutes to noon, pacing up and down the sidewalk, waiting for the doors to open. From his vantage point in the back room of the store, Silas couldn't help smiling as Andy checked the time on his phone over and over. Finally, at three minutes past, with the door still locked and the store dark, his patience began to wear out and he pressed his face against the glass to peer inside. Silas gave Melvin the okay to hit the light switch and open the front door.

"I'm coming, I'm coming," said Melvin, taking his time crossing the store. "Where's the fire?"

Like a true New Yorker, Andy ignored Melvin's less-than-positive attitude and slipped past him, heading directly for the back aisle where the model of the *Indefatigable* awaited him. He lifted the box from the shelf, admiring the photograph of the finished product on the front, and took a deep breath. "Finally," he whispered.

He set the box on the counter and reached into his pocket for the coupon. He unfolded it and handed it to Melvin.

Melvin made a big show of removing his reading glasses from his shirt pocket, wiping them clean with a handkerchief, and finally putting them on.

"What's this?" he sneered, holding the coupon inches

from his nose. "Wooden ship models. Twenty-five percent off. Labor Day. Well, it all seems to be on the up-and-up." He leaned over to examine the box. "This for you?"

"Yes, sir."

Melvin raised an eyebrow. "Pretty complicated model for a boy. Lot of parts. *Lot* of parts. This kind of model takes *patience,* and I'm not sure that's your strong suit. Young people today just don't have the . . . Look, are you sure you don't want to start with something a little easier? I've got some nice plastic models that might be—"

"I'm sure," said Andy, a momentary look of impatience clouding his face. "I've built *lots* of models. Nothing as hard as this, but my grandpa can help me if I get stuck. He made a model of the *Bonhomme Richard* that's in a museum in Connecticut."

Melvin shrugged. "It's your money." He then took a calculator from the drawer and started pushing buttons. "Let's see. That's $119.95, less twenty-five percent, so $119.95 times $0.25 . . . and then add the tax . . . and that gives us a grand total of $32.64. Cash or credit?"

"Cash, but—"

Melvin snatched two twenties from Andy's hand and started to make change from the cash register drawer. "That makes thirty-three, thirty-four, thirty-five, and forty. There you go, sonny boy. Good luck. You're going to need it." He shoved the box into a large plastic bag and practically threw it across the counter at Andy.

"Um, mister . . ."

"Yeah, what is it, sonny? Spit it out. I don't have all day."

"I think you made a mistake. About the price, I mean."

In the back room, Silas smiled. His instincts about Andy had been right on the money, so to speak.

"What are you talking about?" Melvin snarled. "You got your discount."

"That's just it. You gave me too much of a discount. Instead of giving me twenty-five percent off, you gave me seventy-five percent. Before I left my grandpa's, I did the math, and it should have been about ninety-eight dollars—I wasn't sure exactly how much the tax was, so I might be off by a few cents, but . . . What's so funny?"

Indeed, Melvin had a huge grin on his face as he clapped Andy on the shoulder. "Well done, young man!" Then he shouted back to Silas, "Come on out. I think it's safe to say that he passed the test."

Poor Andy. He stood there, utterly baffled and scratching his head, as Silas approached. "What is going on? What test? Who—who *are* you?"

"If you can spare me a little of your time," said Silas, "I'll do my best to make it all clear for you. Mr. Oresko— Melvin—just played a part today in this little piece of theater. And played it perfectly, I'd say."

"Sorry I gave you such a hard time, son," said Melvin. "And I want you to keep the *Indefatigable* kit. At the original price of $32.64. After the way I treated you, the extra discount is the least I can do. And by the way, you've got great taste. That's one of my favorites."

"I asked Melvin to be rude to you because I wanted you *not* to like him," Silas said. "If he'd have been nice, it would have been easy for you to do the right thing when he charged you the wrong amount. But if you *didn't* like him, well, it would've been a lot harder—at least for most people. But you're not most people, are you, Andover?"

"How do you know my name?" Andy asked, eyeing him suspiciously and taking a single step toward the door.

"I promise to explain everything. Just give me one hour. Your life will never be the same."

Andy looked doubtful and checked the time. "I don't know. I'm supposed to go home. My dad is expecting me. . . ."

"But not until three, right?"

Andy edged even closer to the door. "I . . . How do you . . ."

"It's good that you're suspicious of me," Silas said. "You should be; you don't know me from the man in the moon. But please . . . hear me out. We can talk right here, and you can stay close to the door. Melvin, are you expecting a big crowd anytime soon?"

Melvin looked around at the empty store. "Not very likely, I'm afraid."

"Perfect. We can chat right here, in the middle of the model trains. I love them. Never had any of my own. . . . Look, there's a clear path to the door from where you are, so anytime you want to leave, you're free to go. And I promise that if you leave, you'll never see me again."

NOW THAT YOU'VE SEEN WHAT KIND OF KID ANDY IS, YOU'RE PROBABLY WONDERING WHY I'M STILL INTERESTED IN YOU. HERE'S HOW I WOULD ANSWER THAT: EVERYBODY'S DIFFERENT. THE QUALITIES WE SEE IN YOU ARE NOT THE SAME AS THOSE WE SAW IN ANDY, BUT THEY MIGHT TURN OUT TO BE JUST AS IMPORTANT TO US ONE DAY. IT'S STILL NOT TOO LATE TO TURN BACK, THOUGH. I'LL MAKE YOU THE SAME PROMISE I MADE TO ANDY: JUST SET THE BOOK DOWN AND WALK AWAY, NO QUESTIONS ASKED.

YOU WON'T HEAR FROM ME AGAIN.

4

What Silas had to tell him would take a lot more than an hour, but first he had to see if he was willing to listen. Andy was his youngest recruit in years, and he had to remind himself to be patient, to take it one step at a time.

"How about a soda?" Melvin asked, handing Andy a bottle of GoodTimes root beer.

"That's your favorite, right?" said Silas.

"Um, yeah . . . How did . . . Oh, never mind. You know *everything* about me," Andy said as he twisted off the cap and took a healthy swig. "What are you, some kind of spy or something?"

Silas tugged on his left earlobe and glanced around the room before saying, "Something like that. I'll tell you a little about myself, but first tell me about Friday afternoon." He pointed to the bandage on Andy's forehead. "Tell me about the bank and the backpack and . . . what happened after that."

Andy's eyes narrowed, staring straight into Silas's. "You're not a spy. You're a reporter, aren't you? I'm not supposed to—"

"I'm not a reporter. I'm not recording you. That's a promise. Here, check my phone. It's turned off. In fact, you can hold on to it until we're done. Have you talked to anybody about that day?"

"Just my parents. And the police. And the FBI. They asked me some questions about what I saw before the bomb went off, but I don't remember anything. I was just walking along and then . . ." Beginning to relax, he told Silas about the fateful pickle, the explosion, seeing the homeless man and his cans get blown into the street, and lying under the delivery truck, listening to all those sirens.

"You were very fortunate," Silas said. "Do you really believe that the pickle was fate telling you that it wasn't your time?"

Andy twisted his lips to the side, thinking. "I don't know. It's just . . . when I picture that poor guy in front of me and think that could have been me . . . that maybe it was *supposed* to be me . . ."

"I think I can safely say that it wasn't supposed to be you or the homeless man, either. It just . . . was. Now tell me about the backpack. Did anybody tell you that you should keep the money?"

Andy squirmed. "Well, my dad didn't exactly seem

thrilled when I said I was going to give it back. But that's just the way he is."

"What about your mom?"

"She didn't know until after I gave it to the police. She left for Africa on Saturday morning. I told her about it on the phone last night."

"What did she say?"

Andy blushed and looked away. "I dunno. That she was, you know, proud of me."

"That's nice. I'm sure she is. Your dad is, too. He just has a harder time saying it, I'll bet. Still, weren't you tempted at all to keep the money?" Silas pointed at the *Indefatigable* kit in Andy's hand. "Would have bought a lot of model ships. Almost would have bought a real ship," he added, laughing.

"I thought about it for a second," he admitted. "My dad said it would pay for college, but . . ."

"So what was it that made you want to give it back to the bank?"

He shrugged and twisted his lips again. "It was . . . the right thing to do."

Silas fought back a smile. Andy had said the magic words: *It was the right thing to do.*

"Do you always do the right thing?"

"I try. I mean, I'm not perfect, but—"

"You did it again today, a few minutes ago, with Melvin. You could have taken that great discount and just walked away with your model ship . . . and no one would have blamed you after the way you were treated. You're not like most people, Andy. You're special—a lot like Horatio Hornblower, now that I think of it. And we want you on our side."

"We? Who's *we*?"

"Before I tell you that, I need you to promise me that you won't reveal what we talk about today . . . ever. To anyone. In a little while, you're going to have a decision to make, and if you choose to join us, you'll understand the need for secrecy. If you decide to walk away and forget you ever met me, though, that's exactly what I want you to do—forget everything you hear today and just go on with your life. Do you understand?"

Andy nodded, even though he didn't really understand what he was agreeing to.

"You probably want to know a little about me, starting with who I am, right? I suppose, in a way, I'm a recruiter, but there's more to it than that. Sorry, I don't have a business card to give you, but they're against our rules. My branch is called Special Services, but it's not like that's written down anywhere. My job is to find people like you—*quality* people who can help us—and bring them aboard. Train them, get them comfortable, work alongside them occasionally. With some people, I'm involved for a few months; with others, for years."

"What's your name?"

"For now call me . . . Silas."

"But it's not your real name, is it?"

"No, but that's not important right now. I know this is what everyone says in moments like this, but it's for your safety as much as mine. It would be impossible for me to explain *everything* in an hour, or even a whole day, so I'm going to give you an abridged version, and then, if you join us, we can fill in the blanks as we go along. Sound fair?"

Another nod.

Silas looked long and hard into his young recruit's eyes. "Do you believe in evil, Andy?"

The question caught him off guard, and his eyebrows rose noticeably. "Um, I . . . guess so. At least, I think some *people* are evil."

"Sorry. I know it's a strange question. And it's a hard one to answer. Let me tell you a story: The organization that I work for—let's call it the Agency for now— has been fighting evil for over eight hundred years. The fact is, Andy, that evil—that is, the tendency to want to do evil, the *need* to do it, in some cases—is in certain people's DNA. They're born with it, the same way you were born with brown hair and hazel eyes. Eight hundred years ago, a young monk named Brother Lucian made a startling discovery in the ruins of a church near Newcastle, in the north of England. The east wing of the church had been built a century earlier along the edge of a rocky precipice two hundred feet above the North Sea. Unfortunately, only twenty years after it was built, an earthquake—very rare in northern England—caused part of the church to collapse, sending the entire east wing crashing into the sea.

"Fifty years later, Brother Lucian was walking along that shore when something caught his eye—a circle of blue glass, about two inches across and worn smooth from decades in the sand and rocks. Realizing that it had come from the stained-glass windows of the ruined church, he searched the area for several more hours, wading out into the icy water, and found more than a dozen pieces in several different colors—reds, greens, yellows, and violets—but no more of the original blue. Tired, hungry, and numb from the cold, he climbed the path back to the church, where he would make the discovery of a lifetime—a finding that would change history.

"Inside the church that day was a group of stonemasons, working on the new east wing. Lucian stopped to watch them work, momentarily forgetting how hungry and cold he was. When the late-afternoon sun began to stream through the west windows, he held the disk of blue glass up to the light, marveling at its beauty. He had never seen that particular shade of blue before—the color of cornflowers, he said. While he was admiring the glass, one of the workers, a heartless, despicable man named Leveraux, stepped in front of him. Now, you've seen sea glass before, haven't you?"

Andy nodded. "Uh-huh. I have a few pieces from the beach in North Carolina."

"Can you see through it?"

"Not really. I mean, except for a little bit of light, maybe."

"Exactly. Light and shadow, and that's about it. So, imagine Brother Lucian's surprise when he found himself staring at a crystal-clear image of Mr. Leveraux in the glass.

"In his journal that night, Lucian wrote that he thought his eyes were playing tricks on him. Leveraux's face, he said, could be seen more clearly through the glass. As if the glass was a filter allowing him to see the 'real' Leveraux. And that terrified him."

Andy leaned in closer to Silas, his curiosity getting the better of him. "What was it?"

"He had a distinct aura around his body—almost as if he were *glowing*. When Leveraux walked away, Lucian tried looking at him through the other pieces of glass, but he couldn't see anything. He went back to the blue glass and looked at all the other workers through it, but there was nothing. It was ordinary sea glass, except when he looked at Mr. Leveraux."

Andy looked doubtfully at Silas. "Is this real? Or, like, a legend or something?"

Silas smiled. "Good. I love the fact that you're skeptical. You should be, at least until you see it for yourself."

"What? You mean you have that piece of glass? Can I see it?"

"In time, Andy. In time. Let me finish my story. So, the next Sunday, Lucian secretly observed every member of the parish through the blue glass as they filed down the center aisle for Mass. Three hundred people walked past him, yet he saw only one person clearly through the glass: Mr. Leveraux."

"What did it mean?"

"It took Brother Lucian ten years to answer that question. After observing thousands of people through his circle of blue glass, which hung from a string around his neck, he finally revealed his conclusions to his superiors. The aura, which he called the *lumen lucidus*—that's Latin for 'bright light'—revealed the presence of a truly evil person. One day, if you're one of the fortunate ones, you'll see for yourself why he used those words. People with the *lumen* look like they're on fire when you look at them through the glass. Let me make this clear, Andy. When I talk about evil and the *lumen*, I don't mean someone who does a bad thing here and there. I mean people who are *consumed* with evil, people whose every waking moment is dedicated to the spreading of misery in the world. For the rest of his life, Lucian continued his research, and those afflicted with the *lumen* he called Syngians. It came from an Old English word that meant 'to commit sin.' "

"Are—are there a lot of them?" Andy asked, glancing up as a boy of fifteen or sixteen entered the store and made his way to the fantasy games section, one aisle away but still in sight.

Silas lowered his voice to a whisper. "More than you'd think. And there are more every day."

"I don't get what this has to do with me." He paused,

and then his face fell. "Oh, no. I'm one of them, aren't I? I'm a Synergism."

Silas laughed out loud, catching himself as the boy in the fantasy aisle looked up. "No, no, no. It's Syngian, and you are about as far from one as you can get. And *that's* why you're here. Over the past few hundred years, the battle has changed and escalated. Brother Lucian first organized a society in 1212. At that time, all that the members could do was identify Syngians and try to keep an eye on them, to warn others—secretly—about them. In 1342, a hundred years after Lucian's death, that all changed when a powerful politician, Abeniz Caiotte, who was surrounded by the clearest, most distinct *lumen* seen up to that time, learned of the existence of Lucian's society and of the *lumen lucidus*, including how it was detected. Over the next ten years, he secretly removed thousands of pieces of that very special blue glass from stained-glass windows across Europe. According to legend, he was buried in a coffin made of blue glass, but his grave has never been located. We've been searching for hundreds of years, but the trail has gone cold. It's also rumored that he had discovered the secret formula for manufacturing the glass and that it was buried with him."

"How did he find out . . . about the glass?"

"As you will learn, Syngians can be very persuasive. And once he knew *how* to find them, Caiotte searched all over Europe for others like himself, eventually forming his own secret organization, which to this day has had disorder and perpetual war and chaos as its primary goals. There's a word that scientists use to describe that kind of chaos: *entropy*."

"You mean like the TV company?"

The National Television and Radio Productions building juts sixty-six stories—666 feet, to be precise—into the sky in Midtown Manhattan, where it has stood since ground was first broken on June 6, 1966. Instead of sounding the letters out individually, everyone in New York pronounces NTRP as *Entropy*.

"That name is no accident," said Silas. "They're taunting us, just like they've been doing for centuries."

"But they're, like, a huge company. How can they be . . . evil?"

"Well, not everyone who works there is, obviously. But at its *core*, its leadership, its very reason for existence— that's another story. And as I said, I'm not going to tell you everything today. More about the Agency and NTRP later, I promise. For now, though, let me tell you why *you* are here. Do you want me to continue?"

Andy nodded, eyes wide.

5

Silas powered up his phone for a quick peek at his messages before continuing. "Sorry, need to be sure no one is looking for me. There, it's off again. Now, where was I? Oh, right, I was about to tell you why we're interested in you. Sure you don't want to sit down? All right. The Agency has spent much of the past eight hundred years studying the nature of good and evil. When it comes to how and why some people have little or no resistance to Syngians, we have discovered that there are two distinct factors— the strength of the *lumen* and the resistance level of the person. If the *lumen* is weak, most reasonably intelligent people can resist the temptation to do bad things. But if it is powerful, only someone with a tremendous 'built-in' resistance has a chance against it. We don't understand why some people have more resistance; we only know that they do. And based on what I've seen so far and what I've been able to find out about you, I believe that you are a very special young man . . . with an *extraordinary* ability to resist evil. Of course, to our knowledge, you haven't been up against a strong *lumen* yet, but that doesn't matter . . . yet. All this is a long way of telling you that we need you on our side."

"Really? Me? I'm not . . . special. I'm just . . . a kid."

"So was Anne Frank. So *is* Malala Yousafzai. The only difference is that they were put into situations that required them to *act*. Maybe you just haven't had that opportunity yet."

"What do you want me to do? I won't have to kill anyone, will I?"

"You've seen too many James Bond movies," Silas said, smiling. "There aren't a lot of promises I can make you, but I *can* guarantee you right now that we will *never* ask you to kill anyone. That would violate one of our most basic rules. No, what we want from you is quite simple. There's someone—a girl, about your age—that we need to learn more about, but her circumstances have made it somewhat difficult, because until now we haven't had an operative young enough to get close to her. On Wednesday, she'll be returning to school at Wellbourne Academy, and we want you to keep an eye on her and report back to us. And that's it for now. Later, if you're comfortable, that assignment may change. You won't be asked to do anything illegal, I promise. Remember, we're the *good* guys. There will be more specific instructions later."

"I don't get it. I go to Wagner Middle School. How am I going to—"

Silas handed him a glossy brochure featuring photos of attractive young people in school uniforms, each face plastered with a huge, contented smile. "Congratulations, Andy. You've just been accepted into the first form—that's the seventh grade—at Wellbourne Academy."

"B-but that school is, like, a *million* dollars a year. My parents can't . . . My dad won't—"

Silas waved off Andy's financial concerns. "It's been taken care of. All we need is for you to say yes. Tonight, someone from the school will call your dad and tell him that, based on some test scores from last year, you were selected for a full scholarship to Wellbourne. How can he say no? It's a tremendous opportunity."

"You really think he's going to believe it? That's crazy."

"There are three crazier stories every day on the Internet. Before noon. And believe me, whoever calls will be *very* convincing. Oh, I almost forgot. You're getting a dog."

"What? I can't get a dog. I asked for one last year, and my parents said no way."

"Well, you have about a week to convince them that you really *need* this dog. She'll be done with her basic training by then."

"But . . . why do I need a dog? What kind of training? Is it like a police dog?"

"It will all be explained."

Andy stared out the store window. "A new school. A dog. I don't know. I'm used to things the way they are. I *like* the way they are. And what about . . . you know, fitting in? The kids at Wellbourne are all super brainy. Or rich. Or both. I'm not like that."

"I think you'll be surprised at how well you fit in, Andy. Wellbourne kids are just kids. They're no different from you and your friends at Wagner. Sure, some of them are rich, and there's a handful of truly gifted students, but in the end, you're all more alike than different. You'll be assigned a 'buddy'—someone from a grade above you to help you find your way around. If you have any questions at all, she'll be able to point you in the right direction. . . ."

Silas paused when he realized that he might be losing Andy—that doubt and the fear of the unknown were winning out.

"Look, I understand what you must be going through," Silas continued. "It's been a crazy couple of days, hasn't it? The bomb, the money, my little morality play, and then, to top it off, I tell you a story full of monks and magical glass and Syngians. Preposterous, right? And if I'm being completely honest, the parts I left out are even more outrageous. The truth is, Andy, that I wish I didn't have to ask you to do this. I wish that the world was a safe, wonderful place and that there was no longer any reason for my friends and me to be in business. But it's not, and if NTRP gets its way, it's going to get a lot worse."

◆ ◆ ◆

Andy asked for a few hours to think it over, which was entirely reasonable under the circumstances. Silas sent him on his way with instructions to wait for a call at six o'clock sharp.

"Okay," he said. "My number is—"

Silas held up his phone. "Already have it."

"But I never . . . Do I get your number?"

"Not yet. Remember, six o'clock."

Andy, well trained by his father, stuck out a hand for Silas to shake. It was Silas's turn to be caught off guard; he hesitated, then slowly reached for the offered hand, grimacing and closing his eyes as he shook it, as if he couldn't bear to watch.

"Are you okay?" Andy asked. "Did I do something wrong?"

"No, no, it's nothing like that," said Silas. "I . . . have a little problem. . . ."

"Is it germs? 'Cause I wash my hands a *lot*."

"No, it's not germs. It's hard to explain. Something I'm working on. Go."

Andy nodded, then started for the bus stop. After a few steps, he turned back to face Silas. "What *kind* of dog?"

"What's that? Oh, right, the dog. Don't worry, she's terrific. You'll love her."

"It's just that if I'm going to tell my parents, I should know a little bit about her. Like how big she is and where she's coming from."

"Thirty, maybe thirty-five pounds. She's a mutt—a little spaniel, a little setter, a little . . . well, who knows? Her name is Penny, and she came from a shelter in Trumbull County, Ohio."

"What color is she?"

"White, with lots of spots about the size and color of a penny, which explains how she got her name. Anything else?"

Andy shook his head and smiled. "She sounds nice."

Got him, thought Silas.

NO, YOU SHOULD NOT ASSUME THAT YOU'RE GOING TO GET A DOG, TOO. ANDY'S CASE WAS SPECIAL, AND WITH THE ENEMY HE WAS FACING, HE NEEDED ALL THE HELP WE COULD PROVIDE HIM. AND THAT'S MY FINAL WORD ON THE MATTER.

6

At the Brink with Jensen Huntley

Epic Fail at NTRP

Civilization, as we know it, has taken another direct hit from our old friends at the NTRP Broadcast Center. For a company with a ritzy Park Avenue address like theirs, they are seriously low-class. If their new program, called *How Far Will You Go?,* is any indication, they will stop at nothing to gain control of the airwaves while trying to turn its viewers' brains to mush.

With *How Far Will You Go?,* NTRP has taken bad taste to levels no one has seen since the Roman Empire or, at least, Saddam Hussein's gold-plated toilets. Each week, a group of contestants is given a task and encouraged to "do whatever it takes" to get the job done. The winner gets a hundred grand; the losers get ridiculed by the judges—a panel of three has-been "celebrities."

In the pilot episode, contestants were challenged to borrow as much money as possible from an unsuspecting relative. The winner, a knuckle-dragging plumber named Ben, used a river of crocodile tears to convince his unsuspecting grandmother (retired and living in Florida) that if she didn't loan him $20,000 for a lawyer, she would never see her great-grandson again. His evil ex-wife, he said, was threatening to move to Singapore with her new husband and the child. None of it was true, of course, but poor Granny cashed in some stocks to the jerk. Following the network's tried-and-true formula, they brought her out at the end of the show and told her that it was all "just a game" and that she had "helped" her grandson win $100,000!

When host Wilkie Wonderly asked Ben if he would share the loot with the woman he'd duped on national TV, you might have thought he'd asked him to donate a kidney to a total stranger. Class act.

Then came the parade of losers. The judges took turns mocking their inability to lie, cheat, and/or steal. According to the judges, we can all learn something from Ben the plumber—namely, that the principle that all's fair in love and war is no longer true.

"All's fair, period," remarked sports agent Allen Ullman.

A proud day for humanity.

◆ ◆ ◆

"Hello, my little friends," said Silas as he reached into a cage where two pairs of zebra finches fluttered about, singing happily. One of the birds hopped onto his index finger, joined by its mate a moment later. "Be free." He let them fly about in his studio apartment, and the other pair soon followed. After a few laps around the room, the first pair landed on a bookcase; the second settled on the ledge of a large wooden easel that was set up in a corner.

In the kitchen, Silas turned the knob on an antique Zenith, a gift from Mrs. Cardigan, and waited for the radio to warm up. When it came to life, he fiddled with the tuner dial until he was satisfied that the sound of the Beethoven quartet was as clear as it could be, and then he sat in the only chair he owned, staring at the painting on the easel. The enormous canvas—six feet tall and eight feet wide—dominated the room. Barely visible pencil sketches, drawn and redrawn over and over, covered most of the surface, but here and there were a handful of spots, a few square inches each, that had been completed in such detail that a casual observer might have thought they were photographs glued onto the canvas.

He had been working on the painting for more than three years. Those small finished sections were bits and pieces of his childhood—the only clear memories that he had. A grandfather clock at the end of a long hallway. Nameless men and women in lab coats, hurrying past him, speaking a language he didn't understand. A young girl, her face always turned away from him. Waves crashing onto a rocky seacoast. And a pair of zebra finches. How they were all connected to him he had no idea, and every other memory of the first twelve years of his life was a mere sketch, an outline at best.

Three years ago, however, Silas began to train himself to remember his dreams in vivid detail. He kept a tape recorder on his bedside table and switched it on the moment he opened his eyes every morning (or in the middle of the night, which was not uncommon for him). At first, he was frustrated. The memories were like watching someone else's home movies: fleeting, seemingly unconnected images flickering on for a few seconds, then disappearing. Sometimes they returned the next night, sometimes not. But three months into his experiment, he realized that he was no longer seeing anything new in his dreams; he was watching reruns. Once he knew what he was looking for, the details began to emerge, first on the tape recorder and later on the canvas. His past was coming to life.

His watch alarm buzzed at nine o'clock, snapping him out of his daydream. He went to the kitchen and changed the radio station to the call-in talk program *Tellin' It Like It Is*, hosted by Howard Twopenny.

A deep, authoritative voice filled the apartment, a far cry from the soothing sounds of Beethoven. Howard began with a plea to his listeners: "Folks, I have to tell you about a great new show on NTRP! It's called *How Far Will You Go?* My producer Wally and I were watching it in the control room tonight before we went on the air, and we could . . . not . . . stop . . . laughing. I tell you, watching that enterprising young man finagle twenty grand out of that old bat . . . made me proud to be an American, I tell you. What does she need that kind of money for, anyway?

You saw her. She's got one foot in the grave already. She might as well give it to him now, am I right, listeners? Tell me what *you* think at 212-555-TELL. While we're waiting for your call, let me tell you another story. I have some contacts at the NYPD who tell me another side to the story of Friday's bank bomber—you know, the guy who turned himself into a human jigsaw puzzle? Turns out that while all the king's horses and all the king's men are still trying to put enough pieces together to identify Humpty Dumbbell, the loot itself actually survived the blast. It was all in a backpack picked up by some random bystander. Two hundred grand. And do you know what that . . . moron did? He turned it in to the cops. Let me say that again: He turned it in. Two hundred grand. People kill me. I told my kid that if he ever did anything that dumb, I'd send him off to live with my idiot brother and his seven kids in Alaska. Hey, we've got a caller. . . ."

7

Cutting Howard off mid-sentence, his voice still hanging in the air, Silas returned to the classical station. He turned the volume down low and scrolled through the contacts in his phone, landing on *Mrs. Cardigan* and pressing the call button.

"Have you seen Miss Huntley's story about the new NTRP show?" he asked, filling a kettle for tea.

"I have. Interesting girl. She may turn out to be quite useful. Anything new to report on the Wellbourne situation?"

"Yes, ma'am. I found someone who's perfect for the job. I'm certain of it. There's something about this kid. . . ."

"You have my attention. Tell me about him. Or is it *her?*"

"*Him.* His name is Andover Llewellyn, goes by Andy.

He's the kid who almost got blown up in that bank heist on Friday."

"Oh?"

"There's more to the story. Somehow, he ended up with a bag full of the bank's money, which he turned in the next morning. And then Melvin and I ran him through a little test, which he passed with flying colors. Now, are you ready for the strange part? Ironic, really."

"Is this where you tell me that he's Howard Twopenny's son?"

Silas, who had been reaching for a mug in the cabinet above the sink, fumbled it, catching it inches before it smashed onto the counter. "How on *earth* could you possibly know that?"

"It's my job to know things like that. The important thing is, are you sure about this boy? As in, absolutely certain?"

"Yes, ma'am. He's the real thing, I'm sure of it. The father worries me a little, I'll admit. He's the unknown variable in this little equation."

"Yes, you'll have to be careful. What do you know about him?"

"Not much. His show's been on the air for years, standard talk-show stuff: Congress stinks, the country's not what it used to be, people calling in and blaming all their problems on somebody else. Decent but not spectacular ratings. He did turn up once when I was doing a little surveillance on our friend from NTRP. They were chatting on a park bench. Might have been a coincidence."

"There are no coincidences. See what else you can find out."

"But I should proceed with the boy?"

"Definitely. I look forward to meeting this young man. One more thing: I met again with Karina Jellyby, and the announcement goes up on her website at midnight. I think you're right. We've been on the defensive long enough when it comes to NTRP. It is time to go on the offensive, to find out what they're up to . . . by any means necessary."

◆ ◆ ◆

A few minutes past midnight, after a third cup of strong tea, Silas brought up Karina Jellyby's website on his tablet and clicked on the News tab on her home page.

karina jellyby

| Home | Archive | The Band | Recordings | Stuff4Sale |
| News | Operation THAW |

Big News!

If you're a fan, you know that my bandmates and I believe in doing GOOD, and we don't just talk the talk, we walk the walk! We are proud to say that half of our shows are for charity, and with the help of great fans (like you!), we have raised over three million bucks for organizations like Concern Worldwide, the International Committee of the Red Cross, and WhyHunger. (For a complete list of our partners, click here.)

We want to thank you for doing your part, but we wanted to do it with style, so we came up with a little contest to find our BEST, MOST COMMITTED fans. It's not what you think, though! We're not looking for fans who know the name of Sdix's first dog, or what size shoe Charles C. Charles wears, or the name of the street where I grew up. Nope. We're looking for fans who are helping to make the world a "warmer" place by taking part in Operation THAW.

(If you're a newbie fan, THAW = Two Hours a Week, which is the amount of time we ask all our fans to commit to doing good. Local or global, we don't really care. All we ask is that you GOYB—that's Get Off Your Butt—for two hours a week and do something for somebody! For more information and THAW opportunities in your town, click here.)

And now the contest! Here's all you have to do:

1. Click on the THAW Contest Entry button on the home page.

2. Read all the contest rules, even the legal mumbo jumbo that our lawyer makes us include! Sorry, but the contest is open only to students in grades 7 to 12!

3. Fill in the short form that tells us a little about you and how we can contact you.

4. In 500 words or less, tell us about your THAW experience: what you did, how you did it, who you helped, what's next—that kind of stuff.

Now the Good News: The best entry of each day of the contest wins a T-shirt and free download of our new album!

But wait! As they say on TV . . . there's more! There is GREAT News! The 250 most inspiring, most incredible, most awesome entries will be our special guests at a special concert JUST FOR YOU! You read that right— you, me and the band, and 249 of our closest friends! Oh, and one more thing: We're putting together EPIC goody bags for all 250 winners.

Well? What are you waiting for? GOYB and get those entries in!

8

On Wednesday morning, Andy walked to Wellbourne Academy for his first official day of school. The school was only a few blocks from his apartment. He had passed by it many times but had always kept some distance between himself and those throngs of blazered boys and girls who seemed to exist in a parallel universe—one with nicer clothes, better hair, and straighter teeth. Yet somehow, there he was—uncomfortable in the crested blazer and charcoal-gray trousers that had mysteriously appeared at his door the day before—standing across the street and wondering how on earth he'd arrived at that moment and what lay ahead. The light changed three times while he waited.

"It's going to be okay," Silas said, kneeling behind him and pretending to tie his shoe. "You're ready for this,

Andy. Just be yourself." By the time Andy realized who it was, Silas was already half a block away, watching as his newest recruit took a deep breath and stepped off the curb.

Andy had missed all the usual new-student orientation meetings because of his very late enrollment, so the headmistress, Dr. Everly, had called to welcome him to the school and to answer any questions. Now, standing on the top step at the main entrance, she cut an imposing figure, a stylish, fiftyish woman in a black dress. Her hair, glistening in the morning sun like polished stainless steel, hung past her shoulders as she scanned the sidewalk, awaiting the return of the army of Wellbourne students—*her* army.

She met Andy at the doors at seven-thirty-five. "Mr. Llewellyn, I presume?" she said, shaking his hand. "I'm Dr. Everly. We spoke on the phone yesterday."

"Oh, hi," said Andy, looking around for other students. "I guess I'm a little early."

"A little, but that's all right. I'll show you where the main office is and how to get to your homeroom. Today's an easy day. You'll get your schedule and meet all your teachers, and you'll be assigned an SA—that's a student advisor. Most of your classmates have been here since kindergarten, so they will be able to help you, too, but here at Wellbourne, everyone in the upper school gets a 'buddy'— it's an important part of who we are. Ah, here she is now! Welcome back, Winter. I'd like you to meet a new student, Andover Llewellyn. You're going to be his advisor this year. Andover, this is Winter Neale, one of Wellbourne's star pupils."

Andy's bottom lip fell open—just a crack—when he turned and got his first look at Winter. At first, he thought she was standing on the next step above him. She towered over Andy, who was still awaiting his growth spurt, by nearly six inches. Her uniform was *perfect*, he noticed, looking as if it had been pressed and starched to the crispness of a new dollar bill, and her hair, blue-black and reaching the middle of her back, hung in a flawless, satiny sheet.

"Pleased to meet you, Andover," she said, shaking his hand with a firm grip. Pointing at the bandage on his forehead, she added, "What happened to your head?"

"I, uh, had a little—"

"I'm sorry, it's none of my business," said Winter, her perfect white teeth almost blinding him. "I'm just naturally nosy, I guess."

"It's all right. I fell. A few stitches."

"Ouch." She pointed at the earbuds hanging around his neck. "What were you listening to?"

"Um, Karina Jellyby. Do you know her?"

"Sure. She's okay, I guess. Did you know that she went to school here? Pretty cool, huh? Her name was Karina Carmichael then. Who knows where she got Jellyby.[1] Where were you before . . . Wait, let me guess. Birch Wa-

---

1. Mrs. Jellyby is a character in Charles Dickens's novel *Bleak House*. While she devotes nearly all her time and energy to charitable work for an obscure tribe in Africa, her own family and home suffer from neglect.

then? No, Buckley. That's right, isn't it? You definitely seem like the Buckley type."

"I, uh, actually, Wagner, on Seventy-Sixth."

"Really? Wow, public school. I know some kids who go there. Well, you're going to *love* it here. Wellbourne is the best. The teachers, the other kids, Dr. Everly—all *amazing*."

"Why don't you give Andover a quick tour of the school before homeroom, Winter? He just registered the other day and didn't have a chance to go through the usual orientation process. You can drop him off in his homeroom when you're done."

"Sure thing, Dr. Everly. Come on, Andover," said Winter, leading him through Wellbourne's enormous, freshly polished bronze doors for the first time. "So, does everyone call you Andover? Here, let me see your schedule."

"Andy, usually." As he handed her the paper, he noticed Winter's strange pale eyes, but he quickly looked away so she wouldn't think he was staring.

"Good. You have Ms. Albemarle for English. She *rocks*. I learned so much from her last year. Oh! And I see you signed up for the BC!"

"I did?"

"That's what it says here. The schedule doesn't lie."

"Huh. What is it?"

"The Broadcast Club. It used to be a newspaper, but now it's the school's TV station. Everyone has to be in at least one club, and it's the best. You're going to love it. Ms.

Albemarle is the moderator. The only thing is, the older kids usually take all the good jobs and try to hog all the interesting stories, but there's still lots to do if you're creative, and willing to work. There's a meeting today after school. You can come, right? Actually, you *have* to come," she said, smiling.

"I guess so. Although I'm still not really sure how I . . . Yeah, I'll come."

Ten minutes later, Winter took him up the elevator to his homeroom on the seventh floor. "Remember, you can use the elevator on the right before and after school, but not during the day. Don't worry, most of your classes will be on six and seven. Except PE. And lunch, of course. We have the same lunch period, so look for me when you come down, okay? Any questions so far? I feel like I've been doing all the talking and not giving you a chance."

"Uh . . . no, not yet, anyway. Except . . . um . . . this whole 'buddy' thing. How is it supposed to work?"

"Oh, that's easy. For the first few weeks, we're supposed to meet every day to, you know, make sure that you're fitting in and understanding your assignments and everything. After that, it's totally up to you. Who knows, you may decide that you hate me and don't *ever* want to talk to me," said Winter, her pale eyes flashing as she laughed.

9

Andy's first day at Wellbourne was much like the first day at any school. The classes were smaller, with most having only fifteen or so students, and teachers, he noted, were especially fond of the word *expectations*. A *very* big deal was made about the school's honor code. Before turning in any work, all upper school students were required to write the following statement across the top of the paper, followed by their signature: *On my honor as a Wellbourne student, I have neither given nor received aid on this assignment or examination.*

As he moved from class to class, Andy wrote the pledge across the front of each of his notebooks. He had never really thought about cheating on a test or copying homework, probably because he had never needed to. School had always been easy for him—too easy, at times—but all that was about to change.

When the final period ended (there are no bells at Wellbourne, another difference), he went to his locker to drop off his books before heading down to the Broadcast Club meeting in the basement. Winter was waiting for him at the bottom of the stairs.

"So . . . how did the afternoon go? You just came from Ms. Albemarle's class, right? What did you think? Pretty great, huh?"

"Yeah, I guess. She seems okay. . . . Gave us a lot of homework, though." He pointed to his planner, where he had written down the assignment. "I have to read this story online tonight, from some magazine or newspaper. It's, like, twenty pages, and we have a quiz on it *tomorrow*."

"That sounds like her, all right. She doesn't waste a minute. Don't freak out about the quiz; it won't be hard. She just wants to make sure you're doing the reading." She peered over his shoulder to see what he'd written. "Oh, right. I remember that one from last year. It's about Joshua Bell playing violin in the subway. He's one of the best violinists in the world, and he . . . Well, you'll see. Everything else go okay?" Suddenly, she turned serious, asking, "You didn't forget about the meeting, did you?"

"No, I was on my way there, really."

Winter laughed. "I'm just messing with you. Don't worry, you'll get used to me." Then she did something Andy *really* wasn't expecting. She took him by the hand

and started leading him down the hall, her fast walk quickly turning into an out-and-out run for the staircase. "Come on, we have to hurry. If we're late, we won't get a seat."

When they arrived at the broadcast room in the basement, they found a sign on the door directing them to a classroom on the first floor, so they turned around and ran back up the stairs. Winter laughed as Andy wriggled free of her grip before they entered the room.

"Oops. Sorry, I didn't mean to weird you out. I do that to all my friends. I don't mean anything by it. Sometimes, I don't even realize I'm doing it. My friend Katelyn says I'm a control freak. You're not, are you?"

"A control freak?"

Winter giggled. "No, weirded out."

"I'm all right," said Andy.

"Phew! That was a close call. Not good, Winter," she said, shaking her head. "Make the new kid uncomfortable on his first day at Wellbourne."

Andy grinned at her, his first real smile of the day. She had been really nice, after all, and on top of that, she was pretty. "It's cool, really."

She pointed to two empty desks in the front of the room but let him lead the way.

After welcoming members old and new, Ms. Helen Albemarle got the meeting off to a raucous start with a major announcement about the future of the Wellbourne Broadcast Club.

"I have some very exciting news. Wellbourne is about

to take a giant leap forward into the world of twenty-first-century broadcasting. Over the summer, I approached a number of television stations in town in an attempt to develop a *real* partnership—one that would improve and expand our skills, certainly, but also one that would give us actual exposure on a local and, possibly, a national scale. I met with people from all the big networks, but right from the start, it was clear to me what the best choice for Wellbourne would be. Today, I'm proud to announce our partnership with the news division of NTRP."

A few kids, Winter included, clapped and cheered, but the focus soon switched from Ms. Albemarle to a lone black girl in the back of the room, leaning against the wall, her arms folded in defiance. All of the other kids' uniforms were first-day-of-school creased and crisp, but hers hung limply from her square shoulders. Wrapped around her neck was a decidedly unofficial scarf, its bright green-and-yellow plaid clashing violently with her school blazer. Andy guessed that she was a junior or senior.

"No. No, no, *no!*" she said. "Ms. Albemarle, you can't be serious. *NTRP?* I thought we were supposed to be all about journalism—being *objective* and all that. Does anyone at NTRP even know what that word *means?*"

"Here we go again," said a boy in the front row. "Why don't you just quit, Jensen?"

"Why don't you go—"

"Stop!" cried Ms. Albemarle. "For once, *don't* say what you're thinking, Jensen."

"Perhaps I can answer her question," a woman announced in a clear, authoritative voice. She was sitting in a back corner, where she had gone unnoticed.

As everyone else in the room turned to see who had spoken, Ms. Albemarle said, "Come on up, Deanna. Time to face the enemy. Everyone, say hi to Deanna Decameron. She's the executive producer of the *NewsNight* program at NTRP, and she has *generously* offered a few hours of her valuable time each week to help us out."

Winter leaned over to whisper to Andy as she applauded enthusiastically. "I *love* her. She's the youngest EP—that's executive producer—at NTRP. My dad says that she'll probably be president of the network before she's thirty."

The girl at the back of the room who had objected so loudly to the NTRP announcement was *not* impressed, Andy noticed. Her arms remained folded across her chest, her eyes narrowed, her jaw firmly set. When he turned to look at her, she glared at him, and he quickly turned around.

"I understand that not everyone is thrilled by my presence here at Wellbourne," said Deanna Decameron, "but I want you to know that *I* am quite excited to be here." She looked right at the girl with the crossed arms. "Contrary to what you may have heard, the news division at NTRP *is* committed to objective journalism, Miss—"

"Huntley. Jensen Huntley," said the girl.

Decameron's lips turned upward in the slightest indication of recognition. "Ah, of course. I've read some of your work. Very . . . *creative*. Well, Miss Huntley, I look forward to working with you and, I hope, changing your mind about us."

"I wouldn't count on it," said Jensen. "I've seen what your network calls 'quality programming.' There's nothing you can say to me that could justify the existence of a program like *How Far Will You Go?*"

Ms. Albemarle stepped forward again, hand raised in a peacemaking gesture. "All right, Jensen. You've made your point. We get it. You're not a fan. If you're going to continue in your position in the club, you're going to have to learn to deal with it."

"But, Ms. Albemarle, I—"

"We can talk about it *later*. Now, everyone, I have more exciting news. Ms. Decameron's decision to assist our club is only half the story. Starting tomorrow, Wellbourne is going to be part of something *revolutionary*—a glimpse into the future of education. Deanna, would you like to tell them about it?"

"I'd be happy to," said Decameron, standing confidently in the center of the room, seemingly unfazed by Jensen's hostility. "First, let me back up a bit and reiterate how pleased I am to be joining you for the next ten months. Ms. Albemarle showed me some tapes of your broadcasts from last year, and I have to say that I am *most* impressed. You have done some fantastic work, and I congratulate you all. But now on to new business. Starting soon, you will be watching a new program that is being produced by NTRP especially for *you*. Three times a day, for nine minutes at a time, you will see in-depth reporting of world, national, and local news. We call it NED—that's NTRP Education—and each segment will consist of new material and will be presented in exciting ways. You will have the opportunity to send questions to the reporters, with the best questions to be answered during the next broadcast. So, what do you think? Pretty exciting, isn't it? Anyone have any questions?"

Andy sneaked another look back at Jensen, whose hand was already in the air. "What is her problem?" he whispered to Winter.

"Crazy," said Winter, leaning close to him. "Really intense. Thinks everything is some big conspiracy. Last year, she freaked out because Ms. Albemarle cut two sentences from her review of *Take That,* which is, like, the funniest show on TV."

"Yes? Jensen?" said Decameron. "You have a question. How . . . *surprising.*"

Everyone except Jensen snickered. "Twenty-seven minutes. By my calculation, that's almost *seven* percent of the school day. Is that time really going to help me get into an Ivy League college? Or would I be better off listening to my teachers? And how many commercials will I have to sit through, or promotions for those so-called reality shows on your network?" she asked. "What kinds of products will be advertised? And who makes those decisions? Do students get any say in what—"

"Give her a chance," said Ms. Albemarle.

Still smiling, Decameron nodded at Jensen. "That's a fair question. *Questions,* actually. While a certain amount of time in each segment will be appropriated for sponsored material, the total will be considerably less than you'd see if you were watching at home. As for the types of products, I can assure you that someone from Wellbourne will have a say in those decisions. We have many, many advertisers eager to have you get to know them. Most will be offering incentives—coupons, for example—to both students and teachers, as a kind of trade-off."

Jensen tried to ask more questions, but she finally gave up when Ms. Albemarle reminded her that she was not the only person in the club.

"Maybe not," she said. "But I appear to be the only one with a spine."

"Oh, boy," said Winter, leaning closer to Andy. "Here we go again."

Ms. Albemarle ended the meeting with a reminder that reporters should have story ideas ready for Friday's meeting. "Our first broadcast is coming up fast, and we have lots to do in the meantime. Auditions for the anchor position are in three weeks, if you're interested. You should prepare a short news story to read on camera for us."

Winter bounced up and down in her seat. "I *have* to get that job," she told her friends Natalie and Megan, who ran up to see her as soon as the meeting ended. "You guys, this is Andy. He's new. I'm his SA. Be nice to him."

Winter said it with a smile, but both girls seemed to know that it wasn't said entirely in fun. She meant it. When they got their first good look at the boy-band-cute Andy, however, it was also clear that Winter had nothing to worry about. They immediately began trying to out-charm each other.

"Do you want to be a reporter?" Natalie asked, her eyes sparkling, her voice bubbling.

"Not really," Andy admitted. "Actually, I'm not sure what I want to do."

"Well, whatever you do, don't get stuck working for one of the high school kids. They're *brutal*," said Natalie.

Megan nodded in agreement. "Yeah, they make you do all the work, and they take the credit. Except for that girl Jensen. She's insane. No, really! Last year, I got stuck on her story about the local pizza shops, and she wouldn't let me do *anything*. One place got a B grade from the health inspector, and she was so *mean* to the guy. I'm *still* afraid to go in there. She said I wasn't 'serious enough' to work with her. I think I wasn't *crazy* enough."

Andy looked around to see if Jensen was still in the room as the three girls laughed about her, but she had already gone.

Is she *the girl I'm supposed to be watching?* he wondered.

◆ ◆ ◆

A reasonable guess, I suppose, but, no, it's not Jensen. If you're as clever as I think you are, you've probably already figured out who Andy's target is. If you haven't, keep reading, and pay attention; you only get one chance to read this. When you're done, I'll make every word of it disappear.

10

Two blocks from Wellbourne was a bodega with the unlikely name YouNeedItWeGotIt! spelled out in squished-together orange letters across the awning. Andy went inside, reached into a cooler for a bottle of GoodTimes root beer, and squeezed it to make sure it was nice and cold.

"How was your first week?" Silas asked.

Andy's head jerked to the left, and his eyes widened in surprise when he recognized him. "How did . . . You *scared* me."

"Sorry. Just wanted to check in, make sure you're all right. Any problems?"

"No, it was okay. Everyone was pretty nice, I guess. My student advisor is a girl, Winter, uh . . . Neale. Yeah, that's it. She showed me around. Oh, and I found out I'm going to be in the Broadcast Club, even though I . . . Did you have anything to do with that?"

"Maybe a little," Silas admitted.

"Can I ask a question?"

"You can always ask. I can't always promise an answer."

"The girl I'm supposed to be watching—is her name Jensen, by any chance?"

"Why? What makes you think it's her?"

"Just a guess. She seems like someone who might . . . *need* watching. Based on what you've told me about your job, at least."

"I see. Well then, I suppose you should keep an eye on her."

"But is she *the* girl?"

"Enjoy your root beer, Andy. I'll try to check in with you in a few days, but don't worry if you don't see me or hear from me. I'll be out of the . . . out of town for a while. In the future, if you have any problems, or if you *really* need to talk to me, come in here and buy a soda—any flavor *except* root beer—and I'll be in touch as soon as I can."

Andy turned to look at the woman at the register. "Is she one of—"

Silas didn't let him finish. "When I get back, I'm going to introduce you to some important people, and get you started on your service requirements down at the Twenty-First Street Mission. You're going to be volunteering there occasionally. Don't worry about your dad; he'll get a message from the school reminding him of your community service obligations. Remember . . . not a word about any of *this*—that is, *me*—to anyone. Have you told your parents about the dog yet?"

"Yeah. They're cool. I thought Mom would have a problem with it, but she thinks it'll be good for me to have some responsibility. Dad doesn't care as long as she's quiet during the day. He doesn't get home from the radio station until three in the morning, so he sleeps late."

◆ ◆ ◆

By the middle of his third week at Wellbourne, Andy was already fitting in. He quickly learned that he had no reason to be intimidated by his classmates' brilliance; sure, some of them were pretty darn smart, but nobody was "off the charts," as he put it.

Before classes began on that Wednesday, he opened his locker to find a paper bag from an exclusive French bakery propped up on the top shelf. Across it, written in flowing, perfect cursive, was a message: *Have a great day, Andy! So glad that I get to be your SA this year! See you at lunch, Winter.*

"That's weird," he murmured as he examined his lock and mentally retraced his steps from the previous afternoon. "I guess I forgot to lock it."

He unrolled the top of the bag, and the scent of what was inside rose to his nostrils, triggering a memory that made his mouth water. Once—*once*—a few months earlier, he had been in that same bakery with his mother to buy a baguette, and she treated him to an almond croissant. It was the best thing he had ever tasted. He walked by the bakery almost daily but couldn't bring himself to spend four of his hard-earned dollars on something so . . . so *frivolous*, and French, besides. (His father—well, Radio Dad, anyway—*hated* the French, refusing to eat anything with a French name, and Andy wondered if some of those negative feelings had rubbed off on him.) He tore at the bag, staring in disbelief at the flaky, almondy goodness that lay at the bottom. With a quick glance around to make sure no one was watching, he took the first bite, closing his eyes as he chewed. It was as good as he remembered.

During his lunch period, he found Winter and thanked her.

"*De rien*," she said. "Just a little welcome-to-Hellbourne present. I'm so glad you liked it. I took a chance that you're not on a gluten-free diet like everyone seems to be these days. And the almonds. I mean, chocolate is so last week, right? Almonds are just so much *more*, don't you think?"

"Uh, yeah. They're definitely . . . more. Did I . . . uh, forget to lock my locker?"

"What? Oh . . . yeah. The lock was just hanging there. Did you decide? Are you going to try out for the anchor job?"

Andy blinked, surprised by the sudden change of subject. "Um, yeah. I mean, no. I don't think I'd be very good. I watched the news last night, and I have a *lot* to learn first."

"Well, come and cheer for me, anyway. I'll do better if there are friendly faces in the audience."

◆ ◆ ◆

From the moment she sat behind the desk and stared into the camera, there was no doubt who would be Wellbourne's news anchor. Even the juniors and seniors who were competing with her for the job congratulated Winter after her audition. She was *that* good. ("It didn't even matter what she was saying," Andy told Silas. "It was like you just couldn't . . . *not* watch her.")

Ms. Albemarle invited him into the control room to watch on the monitors, and between auditions, she talked about possible roles for him in the club.

"Something tells me that one day you're going to make a great producer," she said. "I think you'll fit in perfectly. How are you with tech stuff?"

"Pretty good. I'm not, like, a computer genius or anything, but I can usually figure things out. My dad showed me a few things. He works . . . at a radio station." He felt a little guilty about it, but Andy hated telling people that Howard Twopenny was his dad. He had learned at a young age that there was no middle ground when the subject was *Tellin' It Like It Is.* People either loved the show or thought that it—along with Howard Twopenny—was a symbol of everything that was wrong with the world.

"Well, it's best if you learn from the bottom up, anyway. Luckily, we have some older kids who can teach you how to use the equipment. And if it's all right with you, I'm going to pair you up with my best reporter. She can be prickly as a rosebush at times, but if you can get past the thorns . . ."

"Talking about me again, Ms. A.?" said Jensen Huntley, suddenly standing next to Andy, much to his surprise. Neither he nor Ms. Albemarle had heard or seen her come in. "Best reporter. Prickly. Thorny. There's only one person at Wellbourne who fits that description."

"Don't be so sure about that, Jensen," said Ms. Albemarle. "We have a *number* of excellent reporters, and some of them actually wear the proper school uniform."

"Maybe, but only one that you would describe as prickly." She tugged on a frayed end of her scarf.

"Hmm. We'll see. I want you to meet someone. This is Andy Llewellyn. He's new, and he learns fast. I want you to show him the ropes. Andy, this is Jensen Huntley."

He held his hand out, which Jensen shook reluctantly with a mumbled "Heywhat'sup," reminding him instantly of his uncomfortable handshake with Silas, and causing him to wonder if it was something about *him* that made people not want to shake his hand.

"I want you two to work together."

"What? I thought you said I could work alone," Jensen protested, looking with disdain at Andy. "Sorry, nothing against you personally, but I work better alone. I'm an investigative journalist, not some fashion blogger. Don't sweat it, though. You're cute enough. There'll be plenty of girls dying to work with you. I just hope you like stories about how to do your eye makeup."

"Give him a chance, Jensen. Call it a hunch, but I have a feeling you two will work well together. One story. If it doesn't work, I won't push it."

Jensen looked Andy up and down. "I guess it's your lucky day, Sandy."

"Andy."

"That's what I said."

"No, you said Sandy."

"What if I like Sandy better? You look like a Sandy to me."

"At least I'm not named after a *car*," said Andy. "My uncle used to have one. Stupid thing was always breaking down."

"That was a Jensen-*Healey*, you imbecile. I'm Jensen *Huntley*. What's that scar on your forehead from, anyway? Did you bump into a coffee table? You're too short to run into anything else."

Ms. Albemarle grinned broadly. "My work here is done. I can see that you two are going to get along just fine."

11

Andy struggled to keep up with Jensen as she raced through the halls and up the stairs to the library, located on the second floor.

"Are you coming, Sandy? You have to keep up with me if you want to be a reporter. So, what's with you and that Winter chick? You were with her at the first meeting, and today you came to the studio to watch her audition. You have a crush on her?"

"She's my SA!"

"There. You see, you didn't answer my question. In my experience, people who don't answer questions are usually trying to hide something."

"I'm not hiding anything. I don't have a crush on her. For one thing, she's about a foot taller than me. We would look ridiculous."

"Ah, so you *have* thought about what it would be like to be her boyfriend. Interesting."

They arrived at the library—and the end of the interrogation, much to Andy's relief. As Jensen reached for the doorknob, the door swung open. The librarian, Mr. Brookings, with keys in one hand and a worn leather briefcase in the other, was on his way home.

"Sorry, folks, closing up for the day." He closed the door and stuck his key in the lock.

"Just one minute, pleeeaaase?" begged Jensen. "I'm working on a story about the new library."

"Oh?"

"I'm Jensen—"

"I know who you are, Miss Huntley. Everyone knows who you are."

Jensen grinned at him. "Wow. That's good. Means I'm making a difference."

"Yes, aren't we all?" said Mr. Brookings as he opened the door and ushered Jensen and Andy inside. "Welcome to the new library."

"So . . . it's actually happening. Everly is really going to go through with it. I thought she was bluffing."

"What the . . . Where are all the books?" asked Andy, twirling around the room as he took in the miles of empty shelves. "What's going on?"

"Progress," said Mr. Brookings, practically spitting the word out. He pointed at a stack of boxes—hundreds of them—against the back wall. "There are your books."

"Wait . . . back up a second. *Where* are they going? Why?"

Mr. Brookings shook his head. "All I can tell you is what I know. A week before school started, I got a call from Dr. Everly, who very matter-of-factly told me that the library was, to use her words, out of date. All this paper and ink is just taking up valuable space, she said. Without the shelves, she can get more tables in here. Like it or not, we're going all-digital. I tried to argue with her—there are many, many studies showing that people who read traditional paper books and magazines read faster, more accurately, and with better comprehension. She didn't want to listen. The board had already decided, she said. They made a deal with some new Internet company."

"It's a company called 233dotcom," said Jensen. "They're replacing every real book that we pack up and send off with an electronic version. According to Dr. Everly, we're going to be the first school in town to go one hundred percent digital—as if that's a *good* thing. No more shelves to browse, no more library. Instead of a library card, you get a password."

Andy glanced at the mountain of boxed-up books. "What's going to happen to these?"

"Supposedly, they're going to libraries in poor places around the world," said Jensen, "although I don't know what a bunch of kids who speak Swahili are going to do with them."

Mr. Brookings scoffed in agreement and headed for the door. "Lock up when you're done."

Winter Neale stuck her head in the door as the librarian exited. "Hey, Andy—what are you doing in here?"

"He's with me," said Jensen, stepping in front of Andy.

Winter was momentarily surprised to see Jensen but didn't seem at all intimidated by her. "Oh . . . hi. I was just leaving school and saw that the door was open. . . . Wow, this is going to be so cool. A real twenty-first-century library. I can't wait to see it when it's all done."

"It's a travesty," said Jensen. "They're always bragging about the tradition of Wellbourne, how everything here is tried and true. And then they do this, without really even talking about it."

"But it's going to be *better*," said Winter. "You'll be able to download any book you could possibly want."

Jensen glared at her. "I don't want to . . . Oh, never mind. Why am I arguing with you? Your daddy probably *owns* 233dotcom."

Winter smiled at Andy. "Oh, well, I guess I'll see you tomorrow."

"Uh, yeah. See you," he said.

When Winter was gone, Jensen pushed Andy against the empty shelves, holding him by the front of his shirt. "This is a *huge* story, Sandy, but we're going to have to get our hands a little dirty to do it justice. You're not afraid to do that, are you?"

Poor Andy. Starting from the moment he pushed that pickle to the side, his life had been turned upside down and inside out. He looked Jensen right in the eye. "I'm not afraid. And it's *Andy*."

◆ ◆ ◆

Checking to see that no one was watching, Andy reached past the root beer, his hand landing on an icy bottle of cream soda. He hesitated, then released it and picked up his usual root beer.

"Excellent choice," Silas said.

Andy almost jumped out of his sneakers when he saw him less than five feet away. "How did you do that? I *just* looked—there was nobody here."

"I've had a lot of practice. Everything still okay?"

"Yeah, fine, I guess. So, you're back. Does that mean I'm going to find out who I'm—"

"Saturday, I promise. Trust me, at this point, it's best if you don't know—you'll be more natural. Just keep doing what you've been doing. I see you're going to be working on the library story with Jensen Huntley."

"You already know about that?"

"I wouldn't be doing my job if I didn't. Anything else? Classes okay? Making friends?"

"Yeah, I guess. A few. Winter brought me breakfast the other day, from that French bakery over on Third."

"Oh? That was nice. What was it?"

"An almond croissant. My favorite. I had one once before."

Silas's ears pricked when he heard that, remembering his golden rule: *There are no coincidences.*

"Oh, and there was something strange. She left it in my locker for me."

"Why is that strange?"

"I'm positive that I locked my locker. I never leave it unlocked. Winter said it wasn't locked when she got there, but . . . I don't know. I guess it's *possible* that I forgot."

"Hmm. Nothing missing?"

"No, I checked. It's not like I keep anything valuable in there, but it was just weird."

"Listen, if anything strange happens—anything out of the ordinary at *all*—use that email address I gave you. In the meantime, don't do anything crazy, and don't forget about Saturday. And lock your locker."

12

A few minutes before the start of homeroom on Friday, Jensen pulled Andy aside in the seventh-floor hallway. His classmates gave him funny looks as they passed, no doubt wondering what the new kid, a seventh grader, could possibly have to do with Jensen Huntley, a junior—and a notorious one, at that.

After Jensen snarled ("What are *you* looking at?") at Parker Elmsford, a sweet, quiet girl in Andy's homeroom, the others gave her a wide berth.

"I've got something to tell you. Guess who bought 233dotcom last year."

Andy shrugged. "I—I don't know. Who?"

"NTRP. The same company that's suddenly so interested in helping out our Broadcasting Club. Something is going on. It's like they're taking over the school. Dr. Everly must be involved with them. I'm going to get to the bottom of it. In the meantime, don't talk to *anybody* about this story, unless you talk to me first." She stormed off, running directly into Patricia Elmsford, Parker's twin sister, sending books and paper flying in all directions.

As Andy kneeled down to help her, the elevator door opened and Winter stepped out.

"What happened here?" she asked. "Looks like a tornado went through the hall."

"Something like that," said Andy. "Hurricane Jensen."

"Jensen Huntley? What was she doing on the seventh floor? Upper school kids *never* come up this far."

"She wanted to tell me something about the story that she's—I mean, *we're*—working on."

"Oh, you poor thing," Winter said. "She is *such* a bully. What's the story? Is it interesting, at least?"

Remembering Jensen's parting words, Andy played dumb. "About the changes in the library."

"Yeah, she *is* in a tizzy about that, isn't she? Well, she probably won't let you do anything, anyway; she's such a control freak. Do you want me to talk to Ms. Albemarle for you? I can't promise, but I can probably get you assigned to somebody—*anybody*—else."

But Andy was already too intrigued by Jensen and the library story to let it go. "Nah, that's okay. I'll stick it out. She's not that bad." When Winter eyed him skeptically, he added, "Okay, she's a little intense."

"A *little*? That's like saying Einstein was a little bit intelligent. You're sure?"

"I'm sure."

"Well, if I don't see you, have a great weekend. If you have any questions, call me." She handed him a business card that read *Winter Isabella Neale, Wellbourne Academy Broadcast Club,* followed by two phone numbers, an email address, her personal website, and her Twitter handle. The girl was connected.

"Wow, this is *nice*," said Andy. "Does everybody get these?"

"No, I had them made up special."

"Oh, right! I almost forgot—you're the new anchor. Congratulations! I was in the control room for your audition, and as soon as you started, everyone was like, 'Well, we can stop looking for an anchor right now.' Even the janitor stopped working to watch. You looked like a real newsperson, and sounded like one, too. Where did you learn how to do that?"

"I guess I'm just lucky," said Winter. "I was born with it."

13

When the van pulled up in front of the Twenty-First Street Mission, the driver, who had remained silent during the trip, looked in the rearview mirror at Andy.

"This is the place, my man. It doesn't look like much from the outside, does it? It ain't exactly the Ritz. They'll have coffee and bagels inside, if you're hungry. Bagels are a little stale, but they're free, you know what I mean?" He turned around and held out an enormous hand. "I'm Billy, by the way. Billy Newcomb. Pleasure."

Andy gaped as his hand disappeared in Billy's. "Hi, I'm Andy. I guess I'll be seeing you around. Thanks for the ride." He climbed out of the van and stood on the sidewalk for a moment before turning back to look at Billy. "Hey, I know you. You were a football player, right?"

"Guilty as charged. Seven years with the Browns, two

with the Steelers. But I was nobody till I met these folks," said Billy, getting out of the van. "But I hear you've had quite a couple of weeks yourself."

Andy touched the remains of the scab on his forehead. "Yeah, I guess it's been a little crazy."

"Right on time," said Silas, appearing, it seemed to Andy, from a crack in the sidewalk.

"Man! Where did you come from? Seriously, you have to stop doing that. You're going to give me a heart attack."

"I was standing here the whole time," Silas teased. "Wasn't I, Billy? Come on inside. We have a busy day ahead of us. I hope you got a good night's sleep, Andy."

"It was okay," said Andy, still recovering from the shock.

Billy moved toward Silas as if to hug him but changed his mind when he saw the look on Silas's face. "Oh, right. Sorry, my man."

Silas motioned for Andy to follow him. "It's time you learned a little about who you're working for. The others are already here, so we can get started right away. Follow me." He led Andy and Billy into a small room in the back, where he lifted the cover of a fake thermostat on the wall and punched a code into the keypad hidden inside. As Andy watched in wide-eyed wonder, Silas then tugged firmly on a bookcase, which swung open like a door to reveal a flight of stairs.

"Just like in those spy movies, huh?" said Billy, nudging Andy.

Without another word, they followed Silas down the eighteen stairs to a simply decorated room with a round table with nine chairs around it. There was nothing special about the table or chairs; it's all simple wooden furniture, the kind you can buy anywhere. It took Andy about five seconds, which is faster than most people, to realize that the room itself was round.

Two of the chairs were occupied, one by a stern-looking man of thirty-one in jeans and a well-worn crew-neck sweater, the other by a seventy-six-year-old Japanese gentleman in a hand-tailored three-piece suit. They both nodded greetings at Billy and Silas while eyeing Andy with a mixture of surprise and, in the case of the younger man, suspicion.

"Was it necessary, or wise, to bring him here so soon?" he asked in a posh British accent.

"It was my decision," Silas responded. "And Mrs. Cardigan has given it her blessing." He guided Andy to one of the empty chairs and stood behind him. "I understand your concerns, but in no time at all, I am certain, you will share my confidence in Andy. Some introductions are necessary. The distinguished-looking gentleman in the suit is Mr. Nakahara, and this is Martin Gardner."

Mr. Nakahara bowed his head at Andy. "It's a pleasure to finally meet you, young man."

Andy smiled back at him, wondering whether he should bow in return and why Mr. Nakahara had said *finally*. His first meeting with Silas, at ModelWorld, had been just a few weeks earlier. Since buying the model of *Indefatigable*, he had barely had a chance to admire its thousands of parts, let alone actually begin construction. "Thanks. I . . . Um, it's nice to meet you, too," he said, adding an awkward bow at the end.

"Sorry I'm late, everyone," said a woman, rushing into the room in a traditional hijab that covered her head and neck but not her face. "Traffic was—Oh, hello there. You must be Andy. My, you really do look—" She stopped mid-sentence and smiled broadly at him. "Hi, I'm Reza Benali." She shook his hand enthusiastically, then turned to the others. "Mr. Nakahara, it's been too long. You gave us quite a scare in Moscow. Wasn't sure you'd be back on your feet so quickly."

"There's still a lot of life left in this old body," he said. "I'm like a fine old automobile—the older I get, the more time I spend in the shop."

"Well, next time, wait for help before you take on three of them at once. Martin, how are you? You look pale. And you've lost weight. Everything okay?"

"I'm fine. Can we please get started? You have a long way to go to convince me that this isn't a waste of my time."

"Ah, there's that cheerful, positive attitude I know and love," said Reza.

"It's not my job to be cheerful. We're dealing with a serious threat, and Silas brings us a *kid*. An *untested* kid."

"Enough, Martin," said Mr. Nakahara. "Let us not forget that the threat of whom you speak is also quite young."

Andy turned to Silas, his eyes pleading for support.

"Sorry about all this, Andy," said Mr. Nakahara. "Martin, you've made your point. Now let Silas do his job."

"I agree," declared the voice of a woman.

Andy spun around in his seat and found himself facing a tiny woman with bones as fine as a sparrow's, standing at the bottom of the stairs. Well into her seventies, she had the face of a much younger woman, with dark, piercing eyes that sparkled when she saw him. In her hands, she carried a canvas tote filled with balls of yarn, a pair of knitting needles sticking out of one the color of rust.

"I didn't think you were coming today," said Silas. "You should have let me know. I would have—"

She held up a hand to stop him. "Last-minute change of plans. I'm fully capable of finding my way here on my own. Besides, it's time I met our new friend. Hello, Andover. I'm Mrs. Cardigan . . . like the sweater. I'm so pleased to meet you."

Andy stood to greet her. "Hi . . . I, uh . . . It's nice to meet you."

"Mrs. Cardigan is our . . . Well, if it's okay with her, I'll just start the presentation, and we can get better acquainted later."

"A capital idea. Andover, do you mind if I sit next to you?"

"N-no. That's fine."

"I think he prefers Andy," said Reza. "Don't you?"

"Yes, ma'am," said Andy.

"Andy it is, then," said Mrs. Cardigan. "Can't say as I blame you. Andover is a little stiff-sounding, a bit like the butler on a PBS series."

She took her knitting from the tote and quickly counted the rows that she had already done. Andy watched with amazement as her fingers began to fly, wrapping the yarn this way and that—without her so much as glancing at the sock that was rapidly taking shape.

"Great. Let's move on, then," said Silas. Using a remote control, he turned on the projector mounted above the table. While it warmed up, he inserted a flash drive into a notebook computer, tapped a few keys, and then motioned to Billy to dim the lights. "We have a little slide show for these occasions. Don't worry if you can't remember everything we tell you today. If it's really critical, we'll let you know."

The first slide appeared on the screen:

AGENTS OF THE GLASS

COMPASSION · HUMILITY
INTELLIGENCE · DISCIPLINE
INTEGRITY · DIGNITY
LOYALTY · COURAGE

Silas began: "If you remember from our very first conversation, I told you that I worked for a group that I called the Agency. Well, it's actually a bit more complex than that.

The full name is the Agents of the Glass. The symbol that you see there was first drawn by Brother Lucian more than eight hundred years ago."

"There are eight Level 3 Agents," added Mr. Nakahara, "each representing one of our core ideals: Compassion, Intelligence, Integrity, Loyalty, Courage, Dignity, Discipline, and Humility."

"Today, we have Dignity, Loyalty, and Integrity— we'll leave who's who for later," said Silas. "Billy and I are Level 2 Agents; we're both in what we call Special Services. You'll be meeting the others soon. Except for Discipline. That spot is unoccupied at the moment; the previous occupant . . ." He glanced at Mr. Nakahara, who shook his head ever so slightly.

"Perhaps it's best if we leave that for another time, too," said Martin. "Until any doubts we have about Mr. Llewellyn have been erased."

"Play nice, Martin," said Reza.

"How do you get to Level 3?" Andy asked, hurt but trying to ignore Martin's insults.

"Excellent question," said Reza. "Finding the right person has always been difficult, and in today's world, I'm afraid, it's become nearly impossible. The people you see around this table have been chosen by the other members, based on their words and their deeds—their *character*. We have all known each other a long time, and we trust each other completely—or we're supposed to. That's why Martin is so testy. You see, we were betrayed by one of our members. *That's* the reason the Discipline chair is empty. We're still deciding what to do about it."

"And in a tradition that goes all the way back to Lucian," said Silas, "there is always a ninth chair reserved for a very special person, someone who is, in a sense, at the center of the circle, someone who is at the intersection of all eight qualities." He turned and looked straight at Mrs. Cardigan. "Someone like her."

Andy sat up a bit straighter in his seat, and Mrs. Cardigan put her hand on his arm to put him at ease. Silas clicked to the second slide, which had the heading *Lucian's Army*.

"Here's where the rest of us come in, Andy," Silas said. "You and me, along with hundreds of others in the city and around the world, are the foot soldiers in the battle against chaos and hatred and greed, all the things that our enemies hold dear. Billy, Melvin at the hobby shop, the woman at the bodega, all the Level 1 and Level 2 Agents—we're all soldiers in Lucian's Army."

"Everyone at this table started out at Level 1," said Martin, breaking his long silence. "But obviously only a very few foot soldiers end up here, seated at this table with Mrs. Cardigan, so don't get your hopes up."

"Please, Martin. Let us remain civil," said Mr. Nakahara. "Mr. Llewellyn is on our side, remember?"

"We'll see."

"Let's continue, shall we?" Mrs. Cardigan said calmly.

Silas gritted his teeth. Andy had done everything he'd been asked, with an absolute minimum of questions in return. Martin's questioning of the boy's loyalty without any reason didn't sit well with him.

"Right. Moving on," he said, clicking to the next slide, a photograph of the NTRP tower, the letters brightly illuminated against an ominous, dark sky.

"This is why you're here today, Andy," Silas continued. "For years, NTRP's programs have encouraged, even rewarded, viewers for abandoning any sense of right and wrong. All in the name of entertainment."

"And the almighty advertising dollar," added Reza.

"All the values and qualities that we stand for have been swept into the gutter," said Mr. Nakahara, "replaced by greed and selfishness, dishonesty and corruption, pride and vanity. I can only guess at the damage they are doing to impressionable young people, especially those who don't have anyone in their lives to provide some direction."

"They're going to be broadcasting inside Wellbourne," said Andy. "I bet you already knew that."

"We've known about it for several months, from the moment your teacher approached Deanna Decameron," said Silas. "Tragic, really. Wellbourne is a fine school, and it's just unconscionable that they should allow this to happen."

"You can't really blame the school," said Reza. "They don't know what they're getting themselves into. They think it's going to be educational programming. That's what they were promised."

Martin scoffed. "You're all assuming that Dr. Everly,

the head of the school, has no connection to NTRP. I'm not so sure."

Confused, Andy turned to Silas. "What kind of programming is it going to be?"

"*That* is the million-dollar question. I'm sure there will be some educational content—enough to please the skeptics—but after that, who knows?"

"We know that they're up to something new," said Reza. "Something more dangerous than ever. We don't have much information, but we do know that *she* is a big part of their plan."

Andy's jaw almost hit the table as the next slide appeared. Staring back at him from the screen were the strange pale eyes of Winter Neale.

IF YOU ALREADY GUESSED IT WOULD BE WINTER, GIVE YOURSELF A PAT ON THE BACK. SO, YOU ASK, IF ANDY IS SO SMART, WHY WAS IT SUCH A SURPRISE? THE ANSWER IS SIMPLE: ANDY HAS LOOKED DIRECTLY INTO THOSE STRANGE, AND STRANGELY HYPNOTIC, EYES, AND YOU HAVEN'T. WINTER HAS A WAY OF MAKING PEOPLE BELIEVE EXACTLY WHAT SHE WANTS THEM TO BELIEVE—AND THAT, IN A NUTSHELL, IS WHAT MAKES HER SO DANGEROUS.

14

"Winter? Are you sure?"

"Andy, do you remember the story I told you about Brother Lucian and his disk of blue glass?"

"Sure. When he looked at people through it, some of them had this kind of . . . like they were glowing or something. You told me what it was called but I forget."

"The *lumen lucidus*."

"But it only worked on people who . . . Syngians, right?"

Silas nodded. "Exactly."

Mrs. Cardigan set her knitting on the table and then removed a velvet pouch from her sweater pocket.

"Wait!" said Martin. "I thought we had decided—"

Frowning at him, Mrs. Cardigan untied the string at the top of the pouch. "Martin, sometimes you have to trust your instincts. Maybe he'll prove me wrong, but I doubt it. I have faith in this young man."

From the pouch, she removed a not-quite-round piece of blue sea glass, slightly larger than a quarter and worn smooth on all sides. It was nearly a quarter of an inch thick, and around the circumference were engraved the first letter of each of the eight qualities. Mrs. Cardigan pushed a loop of simple black cord through a hole in the glass, pushed the other end through the loop, and pulled it tight.

"Yes, it's what you think it is," said Silas. "We call it Lucian Glass. That is one of the original pieces, found by him in the church ruins."

"I want you to have it, Andy," said Mrs. Cardigan.

Andy stared at it for a few seconds, mesmerized, before gently reaching for it. He held it in the palm of his hand as if it were as fragile as a robin's egg.

"Don't be afraid of it," said Silas. "It's already survived an earthquake, fifty years of bouncing around on the rocks in the North Sea, and more than eight centuries in the service of the Agency. You're not going to break it."

"But you must take great care with it," said Mr. Nakahara. "There is a . . . limited supply. You see, this particular shade of blue has never been duplicated. It was made by an unknown glassmaker, using a method, or a formula, that has been lost to time. Have you told him about Abeniz Caiotte? The legend?"

"Is that the guy in the glass coffin?" Andy asked. "The one who stole all the glass from the churches?"

"That's the one," said Silas. "You have a good memory."

"So, w-why are you giving this to me?" He held it up to the light, rubbing the worn surfaces between his fingers.

"You asked how we came to these positions," said Mrs. Cardigan, tugging on the cord around her neck to reveal a slightly larger version of the glass in Andy's hand—the same slightly irregular shape, the same strange blue color. "There's something we left out. You see, not everyone has Brother Lucian's gift. Only one person in a hundred thousand or so is able to use the Lucian Glass to identify people with the *lumen*. All of us—the Level 3 Agents, that is— have that ability. All these years later, we still don't really know how it works, only that it does. And we don't know for sure, but we . . . well, some of us, at least . . . believe that you may have the gift, Andy."

"Me? What . . . why do you think I can . . ." He held the sea glass up to the light and shook his head. "I don't see anything. It just looks like ordinary glass to me."

Reza glanced across the table in Mr. Nakahara's direction and then at Martin before speaking. "There are some things that we can't tell you . . . not until we've had a chance to discuss them with the rest of the Level 3s. I hope you can trust us."

"If it makes you feel any better, I don't know the answer to your question, either," said Silas. "It has to be that way, sometimes."

"There are some rules about the glass," said Martin.

"Don't go showing that thing around. You should wear it, but keep it secret. If anyone asks, it's just a piece of beach glass that you picked up last summer in North Carolina."

"W-wouldn't it be better if I just left it in its bag . . . at home?" Andy asked.

"No doubt it would be safer there," said Martin, "but you never know when you'll need it—assuming that you actually are able to use it. Which I, for one, have my doubts about."

"Yes, we're well aware of your concerns, Martin," said Reza. "Now let's get back to the business of Winter Neale. Silas, the next slide, please."

"I took this photograph six years ago at a friend's wedding," said Martin. "The bride is related to the Neales, and Winter was the flower girl; that's her in the center of the picture. She was seven at the time and looked like a perfect angel, but something about her seemed . . . Well, I can't explain it. And then I sneaked a peek at her through the glass. It was unlike anything I'd ever seen. And I've seen plenty."

"What was it?" Andy asked.

"A textbook example of the *lumen lucidus*. I had to look a second time, because I couldn't believe what I was seeing. It was the clearest, brightest, most perfectly defined *lumen* that anyone has observed since Abeniz Caiotte in the fourteenth century."

"But . . . is that . . . Does that really prove that she's, you know, evil? Maybe it was—"

Martin cut him off. "No offense, kid, but this is eight

hundred years of experience talking. I know a *lumen* when I see one, and I know what it means."

"There is other evidence," added Mr. Nakahara softly.

"That's right," added Reza. "The dogs."

Bewildered, Andy could only shake his head and ask, "Dogs?"

"I'll bring her in," said Billy, opening the door to another room. "Penny! Come on, girl."

Penny, white with copper-colored speckles and spots, ambled into the room, her tail wagging wildly.

"Andy, meet Penny, your new best friend," said Silas. "As promised."

Andy kneeled, laughing as she licked his face. "She's beautiful. She's really . . . mine?"

"Absolutely. She's no ordinary dog," said Mrs. Cardigan. "She may be a mutt, but she has a pedigree of a different and more important kind, one that goes back to the days of Brother Lucian himself."

"There were always stray dogs hanging around the church," Silas explained, "hoping for scraps of food. One day, Lucian noticed that whenever the first Syngian, Leveraux, was around, all the dogs would scatter—all but one, that is. That dog, named Argos, got very agitated every time he saw Leveraux, but he wouldn't leave. The hair on his back went up, and he bared his teeth, snarling viciously."

"Lucian was fascinated by the coincidence," said Mrs. Cardigan. "Over the years, he learned that Argos acted the same way around *anyone* with the *lumen*. Argos became an important tool in identifying Syngians, but the problem was—and *is*—that only a few dogs in a million have this gift. They are even rarer than people who can see the *lumen* with the glass. Adding to the problem, they're *always* mutts, which makes them even harder to locate. We have people constantly checking shelters for spaniel-setter mixes, because many of their bloodlines go back to England and France, and the dogs with the gift tend to look a lot like Penny. For all we know, she may be a direct descendant of Argos."

"But . . . if she's so valuable, why are you . . ." Andy's bewilderment seemed to have multiplied. "What am I . . ."

"For the moment, you are going to take excellent care of her. Get to know each other. In a few days, Silas will instruct you to take her for a walk in Central Park; someone will meet you there and go over the training with you. Penny isn't fully trained yet, but she's ready to start work out in the field. There will be times when you can't use the glass—that's where Penny comes in. She can pick Syngians out of a crowd, and there will be times when that is going to be extremely helpful. For now, though, the most important thing is for you two to get to know each other."

With a sigh, Mrs. Cardigan stuffed her knitting back into the tote. "I think that's enough for today. It's a lot to digest in one morning."

Andy pushed his chair back from the table. "What about Winter? What am I supposed to do about her?"

"Pretty much the same thing you're doing with Penny," said Reza. "Get to know her. Get her to trust you. Hang around as much as you can, without being obvious."

"Just don't trust her," said Martin. "And for God's sake, don't fall in love with her."

"I'm not going to . . . Jeez! It's like I'm on trial or something."

Martin's dark eyes bored into poor Andy. "There's no something about it. You *are* on trial."

"To be honest, we don't know what NTRP has in store for Winter," said Reza. "We've had our eyes on her for a long time, and we know there's been contact with NTRP. They're being very careful, but they must think that she's ready to . . . Well, that's what we need to find out."

"For now your job is simply to observe, to listen, and to report *everything* back to me," said Silas. "When in doubt, tell me. I'll decide if it's unimportant."

"If you're right about Winter, and she does have the . . . *lumen*-whatever-you-call-it . . . I still don't get how that makes her so dangerous. Or what you can do about it. You told me that the Agency doesn't kill people. That wasn't a lie, was it?"

"We won't lie to you, Andy," said Mrs. Cardigan. "But you also have to understand that we can't always tell you *everything*. At least not yet. You're safer . . . you're better off not knowing for the moment."

"Before you go, please allow me to try to explain why

Winter Neale is so dangerous," said Mr. Nakahara. "I think it's crucial that you understand what is at stake. Winter isn't like anyone you've ever met. In addition to her . . . gift, she comes from one of the wealthiest, most politically and socially and financially and just-about-any-other-way-you-can-imagine connected families in the country. One way or another, with her talent and looks and all those connections, she's going to end up in the public eye. And when you combine that with the bottomless resources of NTRP . . ."

Reza finished for him: "Frankly, it scares us all half to death."

"B-but why?" Andy asked. "What do . . . Syngians *do*? You make it sound like they have superpowers or something."

Mrs. Cardigan placed a hand on his shoulder. "They *do* have superpowers—not like Superman or the X-Men. But believe me, their power is all too real. They have a kind of personal magnetism that blinds ordinary people to their words and actions. People want to be—no, it's more than that, they are *desperate* to be—friends with them."

"Actually, magnets are a good way to illustrate the point," said Martin. "I've been tough on you, but I'm sure you're a nice, personable kid who has no trouble making friends. So, imagine for a moment that you're a magnet, maybe something stuck on your parents' fridge, holding up that Valentine's Day card you made for your mum in the second grade—you know, the one you finger-painted.

Compared to you, Winter Neale is one of those huge electromagnets they use in scrapyards to pick up cars."

"He's right," said Reza. "The difference is that dramatic. You'll see. People who should know better will fall under Winter's spell, and she will manipulate them in ways that will shock you. You're here because you've demonstrated many of the qualities that we hold dear, and an unusual ability to resist the ones that we have been fighting against—at least, so far. The real tests lie ahead, I'm afraid."

Mr. Nakahara rose from his chair and walked around the table to shake Andy's hand. "We're asking a great deal from you, we know. It may sound like something from a bad movie, but the very future of humanity—at least the way we know it—may be in your hands. This girl, Winter, in the hands of NTRP . . . is the stuff of nightmares for an old man like myself. Good luck, Mr. Llewellyn."

Reza gave him a quick hug; Martin stared aggressively, then nodded once and turned away without a word. Mrs. Cardigan reached toward him, her bony fingers landing so lightly on his arm that he barely felt them. The skin on the backs of her hands was waxed-paper thin and translucent; veins and tendons stood out when she gently squeezed his forearm.

"You're going to do just fine, Andover," she said. "Trust your instincts—they have served you well so far. I hope to see you again very soon."

"I . . . uh, hope so, too," said Andy.

Silas opened the door and called for Penny. "Let's get you two home, shall we?"

"After you've seen Andy and Penny off, come back down for a moment, won't you?" Mrs. Cardigan said to Silas.

"Yes, ma'am," he said, following Billy up the stairs.

"Man, why does that guy hate me so much?" Andy asked at the top step.

"Martin? Don't worry about him; he's like that with everyone. He spent five years in MI5, looking for spies."

"What's MI5?"

"Sort of the British version of the FBI. Only tougher. He's absolutely obsessed with loyalty. The first person he arrested was his wife. The second was his own father."

"Seriously?"

"That's what I heard."

"I still can't believe it's Winter. I was so sure it was Jensen. Are you positive *she* isn't a Syngian, too? She's awfully pushy, and she always seems to get her way."

"Quite sure. I've had her checked out. No *lumen*. You don't have to worry about Jensen Huntley."

◆ ◆ ◆

When Silas returned, the others were back in their seats around the circular table.

"Please, join us," said Mr. Nakahara. "There's something you should know . . . about Andy."

"Oh?" Silas felt his heart lurch. "Did I miss something?" He wondered how serious his mistake could possibly have been. After all, whatever it was, they knew it an hour ago—before they opened up to Andy, revealing themselves and a number of secrets critical to the Agency.

"Not at all. Your background work on Mr. Llewellyn was top-notch, as usual," said Reza. She slid an unmarked file across the table to him. "There's no way you could have known this. You're aware, of course, that we go to great lengths to keep secret the names of at least two of our group and that we are never all in the same place at the same time, for the obvious reason that we want to ensure the survival of the Agents of the Glass in the case of a catastrophe. However, under the circumstances, we feel that this information must be revealed to you. Go ahead, open it."

Silas lifted the cover of the folder and began to read the single sheet of paper inside. His heart was racing, but he somehow managed not to reveal his utter astonishment at the bombshell he held in his hands. Pointing at the file, he asked, "Does she know? About Andy?"

Mrs. Cardigan shook her head. "I had to wait until we could arrange a secure phone line. I'll be telling her tonight."

"Are you okay with this?" Martin asked. "Your mission hasn't changed. The Llewellyn kid is your responsibility, and you need to get him moving. The Loom is reporting increased activity in the NTRP building lately. They're cooking up something big."

Silas pushed the file across the table to Mrs. Cardigan. "This makes no difference to me. My only concern is getting the job done. You can count on me."

"We never doubted it," said Reza.

"Interesting choice of words," said Martin. "That's exactly what my wife told me ten minutes before she betrayed her country. I reminded her of what she'd said when I arrested her."

So that part of the story really is true, thought Silas.

ON ANDY'S WAY HOME FROM THE MEETING, HIS MIND WAS A WHIRLPOOL OF UNCERTAINTY. IT'S THE SAME WITH ALL NEW RECRUITS—A DANGEROUS TIME. ONE DAY SOON, PERHAPS, YOU WILL UNDERSTAND WHAT HE WAS GOING THROUGH. THE NEED TO TALK TO SOMEONE—ANYONE—ABOUT WHAT YOU'RE GOING THROUGH WILL BE OVERWHELMING. BUT YOU WILL HAVE TO RESIST, JUST AS ANDY DID. BELIEVE ME, IF I DIDN'T THINK YOU COULD DO IT, YOU WOULDN'T BE READING THIS.

15

"You're sure you want to do this?" Billy asked. "I don't know—they told me to take you straight home."

"She needs to go for a walk," said Andy, pointing at Penny. "And I have to get to know her at least a *little* before I take her home."

"I guess that's okay. Just don't get lost in the park, all right? Wait a second, that reminds me. Silas wanted me to fill you in about the taxis."

"What about them?"

"Give me your phone." Andy handed it over and watched as Billy added a contact to his list. "It's really simple," Billy said after he returned the phone to Andy. "One of the perks of the job. Whenever you need a ride or you're scared or late getting someplace you need to go, just pull up this number and text the word *glass* to it. That's it. A cab will find you, usually in less than a minute. The number on the roof will always have the letter *C* in it. That's how you'll know for sure."

"What if I don't have any money?"

"That's the whole point. You don't need money. Just the magic word."

"*Glass*, and a cab will just show up? And I don't have to pay?"

"You got it."

"That's crazy."

"Welcome to the team. Have fun, kid, and take good care of Penny. She's a good dog."

Penny, wagging her tail enthusiastically, hopped out of the van and pulled Andy down the sidewalk toward Central Park.

"Thanks for the ride!" Andy called, laughing as Penny pulled him faster and faster. When they got to the park, she headed north, past the zoo and the small boat pond, then on to Cedar Hill, where Andy dropped onto the lawn and stared up at the wispy white clouds rushing by. The disk of sea glass had bounced out of his shirt, and the sight of it caught him by surprise. In the excitement of meeting Penny, he had momentarily forgotten about it.

He tucked it back into his shirt, remembering what he had been told: *Keep it secret.* Quickly checking that no one was nearby, he took it out again and held it up to his eye. It was a picture-perfect fall day, and streams of tourists and locals poured past him on the narrow walkways. A hundred or more people passed, then another hundred, about half of them walking dogs or pushing strollers. But no matter how hard he tried, he couldn't see anything through the glass disk, let alone the mysterious-sounding *lumen lucidus* that the Agents spoke about in hushed tones. The more Andy looked, the more it looked like ordinary sea glass to him, and he wondered how much of the story about the glass was even true. After all, if it was (which he seriously doubted), why would they give him a piece of it?

But then, as he was about to slip it back under his shirt, something completely unexpected happened: Penny suddenly sat straight up and growled, a low, deep growl that came from the back of her throat. She was staring intently at a spot in the distance, where a man and woman in matching spandex outfits had stopped at a drinking fountain.

"What is it, girl?" Andy asked. He was reaching over to stroke the top of her head when he realized that the sea glass was still in his hand. By the time he got it up to his eye, the couple was on the move, but the view was different. He had seen something through the glass. It was, as he described it in his journal later, a sudden flash of light, as if a curtain of heavy fog lifted for an instant and then, just as quickly, dropped back down. Andy looked with newfound respect at the sea glass and then at Penny. For some unknown reason, his grandfather's favorite expression found its way into his brain.

"Hell's bells."

The couple jogged away, disappearing into the crowd,

so Penny tugged on her leash, following them back toward the small boat pond.

"Easy, Penny. I don't know if I want . . . Hey!" But she pulled even harder, and Andy found himself running at full speed behind her. The joggers, he saw, were standing on the east side of the pond talking to another couple, so Andy guided Penny right past them, continuing around the pond to the west side and stopping at a bench near the statue of Hans Christian Andersen. From that vantage point, he had an unobstructed view of the couple, and he once again took out the circle of glass and held it up to his eye.

"Amazing," he said as he got his first extended look at an actual *lumen lucidus*—two, actually, although he noted right away that the man's *lumen* was much brighter and more sharply defined than the woman's. He was so caught up in looking and comparing that for a critical few seconds, he didn't even notice that the man was staring back at him.

"Uh-oh," he said, sliding the glass under his shirt. "Come on, Penny. We need to go. Now." Andy led her over the short wall behind them and looked for an escape route, his heart jumping into his throat when he saw that, across the pond, the man had started to come after him, his eyes bugged out in fury.

Andy needed a plan, and in a hurry. As he urged Penny on faster and faster, they sprinted through the Trefoil Arch and up the stairs. He was hoping to make it to the plaza around Bethesda Fountain, where he was sure that there would be a crowd to disappear into. But when he came to a sharp bend in the path and knew he would be (at least momentarily) out of sight of his pursuer, he took a hard left turn, off the path and into the trees, where he ducked behind the biggest one he could find.

Breathing hard, he waited a few moments, praying silently that his plan would work, and then peeked out just in time to see the woman with the less visible *lumen* jogging along the path, looking for the man, who had already passed by. Penny growled again when she saw her, and Andy quickly shushed her. "Good girl. Nice and quiet. That was close. We're going to stay right here for a while." He wanted to be absolutely certain that the couple had given up the search before he showed himself again. Under his shirt, he felt the cool glass touching his sweating chest, and in spite of his predicament, he rubbed Penny's head and smiled. "I guess I need to be more careful with this thing. And we're not going to tell Silas about this, if that's okay with you."

Penny licked his face in agreement.

◆ ◆ ◆

By the time he arrived home, however, he had convinced himself that the incident in the park was simply his overactive imagination playing tricks on him. There was no *lumen lucidus*. It was a trick of the light. The medallion around his neck was ordinary sea glass, and Penny was an ordinary dog, probably growling at another ordinary dog in the park—nothing unusual about that. He was angry with himself for believing any of it, and he began to think of a way to tell Silas that he and his friends were wrong about him: He was just an ordinary kid. And that whole fairy tale about Winter being dangerous? Ridiculous.

Howard Llewellyn was napping on the couch when Andy and Penny tried to sneak past without waking him. It might have worked . . . if Penny hadn't stopped to lick Howard's face.

"Hey! What the—" He sat up with a start, wiping his face with his sleeve when he realized what had happened. He pointed at Penny. "What is *that*?"

"It's a dog, Dad."

Howard paused, closing his eyes. "One. Two. Thr— I know *what* it is! What I want to know is *why* it is in my house."

"You're serious? You don't remember? Dad, we *talked* about this."

Howard squinted at his watch. "How long was I asleep? When did this alleged conversation take place? Was your mother involved?"

"Of course. Phone call? Tanzania? Ringing any bells?"

Snippets of an early-morning Skype call were coming back to Howard. "Right. Remind me—why are we getting a dog?"

Andy repeated the speech that had worked so well on his mom: "Do you know how many dogs get put to sleep in shelters every year? Millions. It's not fair. On top of that, studies have shown that kids with dogs do better in school. *And* are more responsible around the house."

"Uh-huh," Howard grunted, too tired to argue. "So, is that where you've been all morning? Getting him?"

"*Her*. Penny. That was only part of it. I'm volunteering down at the Twenty-First Street Mission."

"You are? Why?"

Andy buried his face in his hands. "Dad! We talked about this! School. Service requirements. Volunteering. Saturday mornings. Any of that sound familiar?"

"Oh. Yeah. Right. Good. Good for you."

16

An afternoon rainstorm gave him an excuse to stay in his room, bonding with Penny, attempting to decipher the sixty-page instruction manual (written in Italian!) for his *Indefatigable* model, and doing his assigned reading for English class. He would read a few pages of George Orwell's *1984*, maybe even an entire chapter, and then set it down with a sigh and return to the dog or the ship.

But try as he might, he couldn't get the story he'd heard at the Mission out of his mind. Finally, he did what every new recruit does: an online search. He was looking for information on the mysterious Agents of the Glass, NTRP, Brother Lucian, Winter Neale's family, and just about everything else that had been discussed at the Mission. He wanted evidence that what he'd been told was *real*, but the results of his search were disappointing. Both the Agents and NTRP are *very* good at maintaining secrecy, and information—the kind Andy was looking for, anyway—has a way of disappearing before it has a chance to spread. The public face of National Television and Radio Productions is quite different from the organization that had been described to Andy. According to its website, NTRP was "dedicated to the return to a better world through quality programming," which made Andy wonder what kind of world they wanted to go back to. Not surprisingly, the site was strangely silent about the activities that Silas insisted were their favorites: celebrating and rewarding the very *worst* in human behavior.

He was about to give up when his phone buzzed. Seeing that it was Jensen, he felt himself tense up, and he wondered if she did that to everyone.

"Why didn't you call me back? I left you a message earlier."

"What? Oh. Hi, Jensen. Sorry. I got it. I just forgot. You didn't say what it was about, so I figured it wasn't important."

"Do me a favor, okay, Sandy? Don't think. Don't 'figure.' If I tell you to call me, call me."

Andy rolled his eyes, happy that she couldn't see his face. "Okay, okay."

"I've been doing some research about 233dotcom, the company that wrecked our perfectly good library. They call themselves 'a portal to the digital future'—what a joke. They want to eliminate paper books completely by 2020."

"That doesn't sound so bad," said Andy. "Especially if you're a tree."

"I don't trust them," said Jensen. "All the books being controlled by one company and a computer? I mean, gee, what could possibly go wrong? It's all just a little too Big Brother-y for me."

"Hey, that's from *1984*, right? I'm reading that book right now."

"My, my. Quite the little intellectual, aren't you? I didn't read that book until I was a freshman. And I hated it the first time. You know what, Sandy? I'm going to go out on a skinny branch here and give you a little present. I don't know why I trust you. I shouldn't; I just met you, and you're, like, ten, besides."

"First of all, it's *Andy*. Second, I'm almost thirteen. *And* for your information, a lot of people trust me." He felt the sea glass pressing against his skin.

"Like who?"

"People. A lot of them."

"Yeah, you said that. Like I was saying, you're a kid. Look, not many people know about this, but I have a private website. Normally, I'm pretty picky about who I give the password to, but you'd probably hack your way in, anyway. You'd better not give it to your little girlfriend, Winter, either."

"I'm not a hacker. And she's not my girlfriend. What kind of website?"

"It's all about information. *Serious* information. There's no pictures of cute boys or stories about your favorite bands. Real news. What's really going on in the world. Stuff that they don't want you to know."

"Who's *they*?"

"Read it and figure it out for yourself."

◆ ◆ ◆

Andy went back to his computer and logged on to Jensen's website. When he got to the bottom of her latest review of one of NTRP's reality programs, he followed a link to other stories that she had written about NTRP. There were more than twenty, and not one had a single positive word about anything that the network produced. He skimmed through them, laughing aloud occasionally as her stories became more and more critical.

Then he clicked his way into the picture files, and things got really interesting.

For the past three months, Jensen had staked out the NTRP headquarters at Park and Forty-Fifth and followed the network executives all over the city, snapping pictures by the hundreds wherever they went—office buildings, restaurants, parks, you name it. Most of the photo files were organized by subjects' names, but there was also a large file labeled *UNKNOWNS*. Andy skimmed through the list of names and clicked on the only one he recognized: Deanna Decameron. There she was on the steps in front of the New York Public Library, and then at a coffee shop, sitting across from Carl Quimby, host of NTRP's *The Family in Penthouse A*, a reality show about a dysfunctional but fabulously wealthy Park Avenue family. In a third, she was standing outside an office building with an unidentified, strikingly handsome man somewhere in his forties, impeccably dressed in a shark-gray suit and wearing dark sunglasses. His hair—the same color as his suit—was pulled back from his face in a ponytail that hung down the middle of his back.

Andy opened the UNKNOWNS file next and began to scroll through the contents. The man with the ponytail from the picture with Deanna Decameron appeared with a number of on-air personalities from NTRP and in a dozen or more photos with others, some of whose names and faces were vaguely familiar to Andy, from the worlds of politics, business, and entertainment.

It was getting late, and Andy was about to shut his computer down for the night when he aimed the cursor and clicked on one last photo in the UNKNOWNS file.

"What?" he said out loud, immediately zooming in on the two men in the center of the picture, who were sitting on a park bench and engaged in what appeared to be a serious discussion. On the left was the man with the ponytail, on the right was Howard Llewellyn.

But that wasn't all. Partially cut off on the far left side of the photograph, a few benches away, sat another man, his face partially obscured by the newspaper he held.

Silas's newspaper. *Silas's* face.

There was more—a second photo of the same two men standing outside the entrance to the NTRP building. And in the background, pretending to be in the midst of an important conversation on his phone—guess who. Silas again.

WHEN THE TIME COMES, YOU AND I WILL MEET FACE TO FACE, BUT UNTIL THEN DON'T EXPECT TO FIND ANY MORE PICTURES OF ME. AND DON'T BOTHER LOOKING FOR THE ONES THAT ANDY FOUND—THEY'RE LONG GONE.

17

Silas had, of course, heard about the incident in the park. What Andy didn't know was that Penny's collar had a GPS tracking device on it, and the second they were out of sight, Billy Newcomb hopped out of the van and set off after them. While Andy was spying on the joggers, Billy was spying on him, and when the chase began, he was ready to step in if necessary. He had smiled when Andy turned off the path just after the bend—it was a classic method for "shaking a tail," and Andy seemed to know it instinctively.

"The kid is a natural. He's going to be just fine," he told Silas after making sure Andy and Penny made it home without any further trouble.

"Maybe. Or maybe he got lucky. Do we know who the guy was?"

"I ran his picture through the database, and he didn't turn up. We're looking into it."

"Keep me posted. And keep a close eye on Mr. Llewellyn. He appears to have a rebellious streak. Let's hope there's no more surprises."

Later that afternoon, Silas checked in with Andy by phone.

"How's everything going so far? How's Penny?"

"Great. Great."

"You okay? That was a lot to absorb in one day. You have any questions?"

"Uh . . . no. Not right now. I'll let you know."

"I just want to say . . . everybody was *really* impressed with you, Andy. They—we, that is—have a tremendous amount of confidence in you. But I need you to promise me something. You're important to the Agency; you're a valuable resource, and we want to take care of you, make sure you're happy and safe. So, if you need anything, or have any questions, don't hesitate to call me. Enter this number in your contacts, but don't use my name. Make something up. And, Andy, it doesn't matter what time you call or where you are. I'll be there. Okay?"

"Okay."

"Good night, Andy. If I don't hear from you, I'll give you a call in a couple of days."

When Andy hung up, he was ninety percent sure that Silas knew about the guy in the park, and he couldn't decide if he was pleased or annoyed that he hadn't mentioned it.

◆ ◆ ◆

Silas spent two hours that evening staring at the canvas that stretched across his living room. Once, he picked up a charcoal pencil and leaned toward the surface, his eyes narrowed and focused on a blank space. But as the point of the pencil touched it, the moment was lost. Sighing loudly, he sat back in his seat and closed his eyes in an unsuccessful attempt to recapture what had been so close, but after a few seconds, he shook his head. It was gone. He consulted the notebook he kept near his bed for jotting down the events and images of his dreams, hoping it might trigger a memory, but it was no use: Whatever he had been close to realizing had slipped away.

For Silas, the one night's failure was nothing new. Three years of waiting had taught him patience. He thought of Andy and his model of the *Indefatigable*, with its thousands of pieces and instructions written in Italian. It was a difficult model—a challenge, for sure—but no one would call it impossible. Silas's task, trying to piece together his past from brief flashes of memories and dreams filled with faces and places he didn't recognize, had less certainty. He believed it to be possible, though he had his doubts. He was building a ship model without instructions—no, it was worse than that: He didn't even know what the ship looked like.

He pushed his chair back and went to the kitchen, where he filled his mug with tea and turned on the radio to catch Howard Twopenny in mid-rant:

". . . and that's not the half of it. If you just joined us, you're listening to Howard Twopenny tellin' it like it is, and, folks, I've got another crazy story for you. As if you needed any more proof that this country is in trouble. Some genius, no doubt from the People's Republic of Massachusetts, has decided that readin', writin', and 'rithmetic ain't enough for kids today—they now need to take part in this Commie plot they like to call community service. Before the kids can graduate, they have to help people, whether they want to or not. And they have to do it for nothing. You heard me right. Nothing. Nada. Zip. Some of these kids are working ten or twelve hours a week for these do-gooder organizations and not taking home a cent. It's not only unpaid, it's downright un-American.

"*Hakuna matata*, slackers. We've got your back. No matter how big a mess you make of your life, there's always going to be a bunch of *unpaid* goody-goody high school kids to bail you out. I'm Howard Twopenny, and that's my two cents' worth. What do you think? Call me."

18

Part of the Sunday afternoon ritual at the Llewellyn apartment included a video call from Andy's mom, Abbey, who was still in the Mtwara region of Tanzania.

"Hey, Mom."

"Move closer to the screen so I can see your forehead. That's looking good. Almost healed. You're going to have a scar, but it won't be bad. Very Harry Potter."

"Great. Just what I always wanted."

"You could do worse. Harry's a hero in the end. So, how's school? Still like it? Making friends? Oh my gosh! I almost forgot—the dog! Where is she? It's a she, right?"

"Penny! Come here, girl. Yeah, she's a girl. She's amazing. Say hi, Penny."

"She's beautiful! Oh, I can't wait to meet her in person. I'm still a little confused about where she came from. I thought you were doing your community service at a shelter for people. Why did they have a dog?"

"I don't know the whole story. . . . She was left at the Mission one night. If they didn't find a home for her, they were going to have to take her to a dog shelter." It was a white lie, but it seemed as if it *could* be true, which was more than he could say about the truth—that Penny was a super-secret spy dog with special powers!

"Hmm. Well, take good care of her. How's your father dealing with it?"

"He acts like he doesn't like her, but just now she was curled up on the couch next to him and he was petting her. I did get a little bit of the Howard Twopenny routine when I first brought her home yesterday."

Abbey laughed. "I'd say you have your dad pretty much figured out. What else is new? C'mon, I feel so bad that I'm missing all this. You starting a new school—and not just any school, but Wellbourne Academy! I'm so proud of you, and I want to see you in khakis and that blazer. And your dad tells me that you're in the Broadcast Club. Is that something you're interested in?"

"Uh, yeah, sort of. I didn't really *choose* it. They kind of chose for me. I think they thought I'd be good at it."

"I'm sure they're right. How are things going with your student helper? What was her name? Winnie?"

"Winter."

"Right. Winter. That's a very *cool* name."

"Ha. Very funny, Mom."

"You still like her?"

"Uh, I never said—"

"I don't mean *like* like. You said she was helping you with all the new-school stuff, that's all. Just wondering if you're still . . . *happy* with her. Is that better?"

"She's . . . fine. I guess." What else could he say? That Winter Neale, age thirteen, was one of the most dangerous people on earth, according to the secret organization that he was now a member of? It sounded crazy *inside* his head; he could only imagine how completely insane it would sound if he said the words aloud.

"Okay, I'll take your word for it. I just want to make sure you're fitting in. I know you were worried about that because of how smart and how rich some of the kids are. And it sounds like this Winter is both of those things."

"Oh, yeah—she's *really* rich. I hear she lives in some penthouse on Fifth Avenue. But she's not, like, a genius or anything." He smiled, adding, "I think I'm smarter."

◆ ◆ ◆

At school on Monday, Andy searched for Winter before first period, spotting her in a deserted corner of the cafeteria, behind a large column and a stack of chairs. A boy from Andy's homeroom, Craig Lessing, was backed up against the wall, cowering as Winter, a full head taller than him, snapped and snarled at him like a junkyard dog. Andy hurried out of sight and found a table where he could just see her out of the corner of his eye. Pretending to be very interested in *1984*, he watched and listened, trying to figure out what the connection between them could possibly be. Although she was obviously angry, she kept her voice down to a low hiss, so Andy was able to pick up only a few snippets of the one-sided conversation:

"*. . . promised that I would have it by today . . . tired of . . . lame excuses . . . do you have any idea . . . cost me? . . . twenty-four hours to . . . or else . . .*"

As she went on, Andy glanced around the room, making certain that no one else was close by, and he fished out the circle of sea glass from beneath his shirt. Keeping it mostly covered with his hand, he raised it to his eye, but as he did, Winter moved a foot to her right, where she was completely blocked by another stack of chairs.

A moment later, Andy heard Winter give Craig one final order: "Go! Now!" Craig slunk out of the corner, head down, and then ran as fast as he could through the cafeteria—as if he wanted to get away from Winter before she changed her mind. Andy quickly tucked the glass back into his shirt and turned away from the corner, burying his nose in his book. Winter, meanwhile, walked off in the other direction without ever noticing that Andy was there.

At his locker in the hallway outside his homeroom, Andy was organizing his books and notebooks for his morning classes while still trying to piece together what he'd seen. He closed his locker, then spun around and ran directly into Winter, who was standing less than a foot behind him.

Caught completely off guard, he gasped, slamming himself backward into his own locker.

Winter laughed out loud, then covered her mouth. "I'm so sorry. I didn't mean to scare you. I was just having some fun."

"I wasn't scared. You just . . . surprised me. How long were you there?"

"Only a second or two. I looked for you downstairs," she lied. "I thought we were going to meet. Don't tell me—you heard all the bad stuff about me and now you want a new SA."

Andy forced a smile. "Yeah. I mean, no."

"You seem a little . . . preoccupied. Are you sure everything's okay? I'm sorry, it's just that it's my job, you see. If you quit Wellbourne and go back to your old school, they'll kick me out, too."

"Really?"

Winter's head tilted back and her shoulders shook as she laughed. *A friendly,* real *laugh,* thought Andy. "No, silly. But I still don't want you to quit. You have to promise to tell me if anyone gives you a hard time. Promise?"

"Promise."

Behind Winter, the kids from Andy's homeroom began to file into the room. Craig Lessing hurried around the corner, his penny loafers skidding to a halt when he spotted Winter. He glanced over at Andy, who nodded a hello.

"Oh, *hi,* Craig," said Winter in a syrupy voice. "How *are* you?"

Craig looked down at his shoes. "Fine."

It was an uncomfortable moment, and one that made Andy even more curious about what had happened in the cafeteria. "Hey, wait up, Craig. I'd better get going, too," he told Winter. "I'll see you after school."

"Okay. Have a great day. You too, Craig."

As she walked away, Andy remembered the glass hanging around his neck. *Something is not quite right about Winter,* he thought, but he still wasn't convinced that she was the devil that Silas and the others had made her out to be. There was only one answer: He had to see this *lumen* for himself.

◆ ◆ ◆

His mind still fogged from his last-period math class, Andy was standing in front of his locker, trying to remember his combination, when he sensed that, for the second time that day, someone was right behind him.

"Well?" It was Jensen, her arms folded, waiting for his answer. As usual, her plaid scarf was loosely draped over her shoulders.

"Well . . . what?"

"My website. Did you check it out?"

"Oh, that. Yeah. Pretty interesting. I didn't realize that you were a conspiracy nut—"

Jensen shoved him hard against his locker. "I am *not* a conspiracy nut. I'm a *journalist*. A real one. Not like those bloggers who just rip stuff off from other sites. I'm digging, getting my hands dirty. Got it?"

"Okay, okay. Sorry. Can you let me go now? Geez, you're so *sensitive*. Come on, you have to admit that you do seem a little obsessed with NTRP."

Jensen released her grip. "Sorry. I get a little carried away sometimes. But, you know, somebody needs to be a little obsessed—no, a *lot* obsessed—with them. You wouldn't believe what they're involved in, or the people they're mixed up with. Did you watch that nonsense they broadcast today in homeroom?"

"It was kind of hard not to. They had the volume up all the way. Especially during the commercials. It didn't seem that bad, though. The news part was kind of interesting, actually."

"Just wait," said Jensen. "Sure, they start off with that pretty speech about the twenty-first century and the future of education and how Wellbourne is on the cutting edge of it all, but what they really want is to take us back to the Middle Ages."

"What do you mean?"

"Have you ever actually *watched* any of the fluff-and-stuff that NTRP puts on the air? There are no writers, no stories, no one with anything approaching *talent*. Hardly any money and absolutely *nothing* creative goes into it. Not that watching it requires any deep thinking. We're turning into a bunch of mouth-breathing zombies. Back in the Middle Ages, when the Catholic Church was in control of just about every part of your life, the church was at least trying to get people to behave. If anything, the junk on NTRP is making people *worse*. It's like they want the country to fall apart."

"Why would they want that?"

"Same reason anyone wants anarchy—so *they* can take over. God knows what they have planned, but I guarantee you it's not good. I mean, just look at their name: *N-T-R-P. Entropy*."

Seeing the confused look on Andy's face, she spelled it out on the cover of her notebook: *E-N-T-R-O-P-Y*. "*Entropy*. Is that a coincidence? I think not."

"What does that mean, anyway?" Andy already knew the answer from his meetings with Silas, but he was curious to hear what Jensen had to say.

"It has a bunch of meanings. Something to do with thermodynamics, serious scientific stuff. But it also has something to do with disintegration of society—you know, like in *1984*. Big Brother. Dystopia. You know how people are always talking about how the world is going crazy? How everything is turning into chaos? Chaos, entropy—same basic idea."

"Wow. I guess you've thought about this, huh? Can I . . . um . . . talk to you about a couple of pictures on your website?"

"Yeah, after the meeting. Ms. Albemarle said she had some big news."

Inside the studio, Winter was talking to a boy who Andy hadn't seen before. She waved him over.

"Your *girlfriend* needs you," said Jensen. "You'd better go."

"Who's that with her?" he whispered.

"Jealous?"

"I'm just *wondering*. Geez. I haven't seem him around, and he looks older, so I thought you might know him."

"And to think you called *me* sensitive," said Jensen, tugging on his sleeve. "Come on, I'll introduce you."

They started across the room at the same time that Winter and the boy did, and they all met near the center.

The boy grinned as Jensen approached him—a confident, smirky smile. "How are you, Huntley? Did you miss me?"

"Oh, were you gone, Butler? I hadn't noticed."

"Who's your friend?" he snorted, shooting a quick glance down his perfectly formed nose at Andy, who was shorter by the better part of a foot.

"This is Andy, the boy I was telling you about," said Winter. As Andy and Robbie Butler shook hands, she held hers out to Jensen. "You know, I don't think we've ever formally met. I'm Winter Neale."

"Hi. Jensen Huntley. How do you know this loser?" she asked, pointing at Robbie. "Nice of you to finally show up, by the way."

"Robbie? Our families have known each other for *forever*. They just got back from Switzerland yesterday. They were staying in our house on Lac Léman."

Jensen elbowed Andy. "They have a house in Switzerland."

Robbie put his arm around Andy's shoulders as if they were old friends. "So, Andy, Winter tells me you were in public school. What was *that* like?" He didn't wait for an answer before continuing. "You play lacrosse?"

Andy shook his head. "I—I've never even seen a game."

"Robbie is captain of the lacrosse team," said Winter. "If you want, he'll teach you. Especially if I ask him to. He owes me, big-time. Don't you, Robbie?" Then, noticing that Ms. Albemarle had joined their circle, she added, "Hi, Ms. Albemarle. Did you have a nice weekend?"

"Yes, thank you for asking, Winter. Hello, everyone. You're just the three I'm looking for. I may have an assignment for you, if you're interested. Sorry, Robbie, but there's only room for three this time."

"Hey, no *problem*, Ms. A. I'm just, you know, checking things out. I don't really have time for Broadcast this year, but my parents are making me do it for college." He shrugged and started for the door.

"Ah, so your heart is really in it," Ms. Albemarle said. "It's so sweet of you to give something back like that."

"Well done, Ms. A.," said Jensen, clapping her hands. "You know, that's the first time I've ever heard you be sarcastic. You should definitely do it more often. You're good."

"Thank you, Jensen. Coming from you, that's high praise."

"There! See! You did it again!"

Ms. Albemarle held up her hand. "Stop. I shouldn't have done it. What if I hurt his feelings?"

Jensen almost fell over laughing. "Robbie Butler? Feelings? That's a good one."

"She's right, Ms. A.," said Winter. "You don't have to worry about Robbie. I'm pretty sure he was born without a heart. So, what's this assignment you were talking about?"

Ms. Albemarle held up plastic badges hanging from red lanyards. "It's very exciting. Deanna Decameron managed to snag press credentials for a conference about technology in education, and I immediately thought of you three. It'll be good experience for Andy, and I think Winter, as our new anchor, deserves the opportunity, too. There will be a lot of important people there, maybe even a former president, I'm told. It's a week from Wednesday, and it starts at nine o'clock, so you'll be excused from your classes after first period. Jensen, you'll be in charge. These give you access to all the programs—*and* you'll get some great stuff. All you have to do is shoot a little video and write a story for the following week's broadcast. So, what do you think?"

"Woo-hoo," said Jensen without breaking a smile. "An education conference."

"Oh, come on. It could be interesting."

"Yeah, if your idea of fun is watching a bunch of people who don't know anything about kids talking about the best way to teach them. *Fascinating*."

Ms. Albemarle appealed to the newest member of the team. "How about it, Andy? Your first out-of-school assignment, and you get to go with my star reporter and our new anchor. Aren't you excited?"

"Uh, yeah. Sure, I'll do it."

"What about the library story?" Jensen asked. "That's still ours, right? Because it's . . . bigger than we thought. We have some investigative work to do, and it might take a little longer than we thought."

"That's still all yours," said Ms. Albemarle.

Jensen took one of the lanyards from her. "So where is this thing?"

"Oh, that's the best part. It's in Midtown, at the NTRP Broadcast Center. They—"

"What?!" cried out Jensen, Winter, and Andy simultaneously.

"Are you serious?" Jensen asked.

"That is so cool," said Winter.

Andy was too surprised to say anything else.

"My, I had no idea that the location would make such a difference in your attitude," said Ms. Albemarle. "Well, I guess I'll call Deanna and tell her to expect all three of you."

19

Jensen couldn't stop smiling as she led Andy to the row of computers in the far corner of the studio. After making sure no one was looking over her shoulder, she logged on to her website.

"This is *awesome*. I have been trying to get inside that building for months."

Then she pushed her chair back abruptly, crossed her arms over her chest, and scowled at Andy. "Wait a second. Why are *you* so excited about getting into NTRP? We've never talked about it; I would remember that. Who are you, really? Did they send you to spy on me? I thought it was kind of suspicious—new kid at school assigned to work with me. Is Ms. Albemarle in on it, too? It's because of my website, isn't it? So they *do* know about me. I had a feeling I was being watched. Somebody was following me this morning."

"What are you talking about? Did *who* send me? And who is watching you?"

"NTRP. As if you didn't know. Tell me the truth: Are they CIA? They are, aren't they! I knew it. And your little girlfriend, Winter, I suppose she's a spy, too. She had exactly the same reaction."

"You're . . . absolutely . . . *crazy*. Nobody sent me. I don't know anything about them. I just think it's a cool building. I like architecture, okay? Why are *you* so excited? How do I know they didn't send *you*? And if I was working for them, why would I be so excited to go there? It doesn't even make sense. And she's not my girlfriend."

Jensen considered all that for a moment, then nodded. "You've got a point. Who's your favorite architect?"

"What?"

"You said you like architecture. You must have a favorite."

"Buckminster Fuller," Andy answered. He had read something about Fuller once in school, and the name stuck.

"Oh. Yeah, he's all right," said Jensen. "I have an uncle who lives in one of those dome things he designed. He's in California. He's an idiot. Raises lambs for some big restaurant in Napa. My parents sent me out there once. God, I hated it. It's all so phony." She pulled up a picture of the NTRP tower. "I can't prove anything yet, but I know there's something big going on. Ever since I wrote that article, I've been trying to figure out what it is, and I'm getting nowhere. I waited outside the building and even talked to a few people who work there. They're like robots. They all say the same thing: this stupid memorized speech about the quality of their programming and some nonsense about being dedicated to building a better world—all *super* vague, you know."

"Do you really think they're like that—spies, that kind of stuff? Aren't they just another network like CBS and NBC?"

"I guess we're going to have to find the answer to that next Wednesday."

"Did you really think *I* was a spy?"

"Hey, nothing would surprise me." Jensen gazed across the room at Winter, who was watching video for a story about the lacrosse team. "What about her?"

Andy looked up at Winter, and their eyes met. Then they both quickly turned away. "She doesn't really seem like the spying type."

"God, you're naïve. She's *exactly* the spying type. That girl could sell a pit bull to the lady in my building who has thirteen cats. You just have a crush on her." She turned back to the computer before he had a chance to protest. "Now let me show you some pictures."

Jensen first clicked on a picture of two men sitting on a park bench. "The one on the right looks kind of familiar, doesn't he? I don't think he's important . . . but *this* guy," she said, pointing to the man with the ponytail, "is definitely *somebody*. I have a bunch of shots of him, but I can't find out who he is. I've tried following him, but it's like he knows. One minute he's there and then—poof—he's gone."

"He is a little creep—" Andy stopped, not believing his eyes as Jensen clicked on the next picture. There they were, ponytail guy and Howard Llewellyn, having a friendly chat on a park bench. But the third person—Silas, on a bench in the background, reading his newspaper—was gone. The bench was empty.

"What the . . . That's impossible."

"What?"

Andy bit his lip. He couldn't tell Jensen about Silas; he knew her well enough to know that she would have a million questions—questions that he either couldn't or *shouldn't* answer.

"You're not going to believe this," he said, shaking his head as if *he* were having a hard time of it. He pointed at Howard. "*That* . . . is my father."

"Get out." She returned to the first photo and zoomed in on the face. "Are you sure? You can't really see—"

"It's him. I'm positive. The way he's sitting, his hand . . ."

"Who is he? Why is he . . . What does he *do?*"

"You really want to know?" Andy cringed. He had been dreading this moment. "You can't tell anyone. Promise?"

Jensen made an *X* over her heart. "Hope to die."

"My dad is . . . Howard Twopenny. You know, on the radio. WUUU."

"No. Way. That crazy *Tellin' It Like It Is* guy? That's your *dad*?"

"Shhh! People can hear you! You promised."

"I'm . . . sorry. I just can't believe it. I never would have made that connection. He's . . . and you're . . . just so . . . *different*. You are, aren't you? It's not like I listen to him, but I know who he is. He's always going on and on about all those stupid reality shows on NTRP, about how great they are."

Andy nodded, his eyes closed. "That's him. Although, to be honest, I don't think he actually watches any of those shows. He's never home when they're on."

"He probably pays some peon to watch and then tell him what happens. So, what do you think this is all about?" Jensen asked, pointing at the picture of Howard on the park bench. "Do you recognize this guy with the ponytail? Maybe he's from the radio station?"

"If he is, I've never seen him, and I used to go there a lot."

Jensen logged out of the computer and turned to Andy. "Is this going to be weird, you working with me? I understand that he's your dad and all, but to me, he's one of *them*. He's the enemy."

"I can handle it. For now."

"One more question. Your real name isn't Sandy, is it? You're, like, Howard Junior, aren't you?"

Andy banged his head on the desk.

♦ ♦ ♦

"Are you sure? You usually have root beer." The woman behind the cash register at YouNeedItWeGotIt! held up the bottle of ginger ale and looked long and hard into Andy's eyes.

"It's okay, Nora," Silas said, fully expecting Andy to jump out of his skin. It was Silas's turn to be surprised, though, as Andy didn't even flinch. "Ah, you're getting used to me."

"I heard you," he admitted. "I thought spies always wore sneakers."

"I'm not a spy. Remember? I'm here to help people like you. Now trade that ginger ale in for a root beer and come to the back room for a minute. Go to the cooler where the beer is and take a right."

The back room wasn't much to look at, but it did have a card table and two folding chairs pushed up against the far wall. A neon advertising sign buzzed annoyingly, so Silas unplugged it, and then he motioned to Andy to sit.

"Before you start, how's everything going with Penny?" Silas asked. "Has she won over your dad yet?"

"She's starting to. He even took her for a walk this morning. That's okay, isn't it?"

"Absolutely. The best thing is to get comfortable with her, and for her to get used to you and the neighborhood. Has she . . . acted strangely around anyone?"

"Only once. The day I got her. We were in the park,

and I think she saw something. There were two people in running clothes. They stopped to get a drink, and she growled. I tried to use the glass, but . . ."

"Oh? And?"

Andy smiled to himself. Maybe Silas didn't know about the incident in the park after all. "I'm not sure. I thought I saw something in it, but it happened too fast."

"Something . . . like what?"

"It was weird. I couldn't see anything through it, but then I could, just for a second. I'm not even sure if it was the guy or the girl."

Silas nodded. "And no one saw you? And you didn't tell anyone?"

"No, I swear. I've been careful."

Even though he knew that Andy hadn't told the whole story, Silas didn't press the matter. He was gaining Andy's trust, and there was no reason to jeopardize that. "Okay, good. Everything else all right? What do you hear from your mom?"

"She's coming home next week. Well, unless . . . you know, she doesn't. That's the way her job is, sometimes. Hey, I have another question for you."

"Shoot."

"Remember that girl Jensen? There are these two pictures on her website. She's . . . well, she's obsessed with NTRP, so she followed—"

"Yes."

"Yes, what? I haven't said anything."

"Yes, I changed the pictures. That's what you were going to ask, isn't it? I had to. I couldn't take that chance. Look, Jensen might be helpful, but we have to be very careful. She's not like you, Andy."

"So you know basically everything I do on my computer? You're spying on me?"

"It's for your . . . Look, I know it sounds bad. As far as the Agency is concerned, though, you're still new, untested. It won't always be like this, but we're at a critical stage. Things are happening fast, and I need to prove to everyone that you are the real deal. For now it's best if we keep some information on a need-to-know basis."

"Why were you spying on my dad? Is he . . . involved? Is he . . . one of *them*? I never even thought to use the glass on him. And who is the guy he's talking to?"

"Here's what I *can* tell you. Your father is not a Syngian. The fact that Penny is able to sleep in the same apartment with him proves that. But he is involved, somehow, with the man with the ponytail, who is from NTRP. We're not entirely sure what it was about, but their meeting had something to do with his program. As for the ponytail guy, the short answer is, he's a mystery to us. One possibility is that he's NTRP's version of me. A messenger, a negotiator. We don't know his name."

"So he was *recruiting* my dad? Like you did to me?"

"Something like that, yes. But don't worry about it. Not yet, at least."

"This is getting really weird."

"You ain't seen nothin' yet."

"Is that supposed to make me feel better?"

"No, it's supposed to make you stay on your toes. If you let down your guard, even for a moment, they will take advantage. Now, I understand that you have some good news for me."

"I do?" Andy was genuinely puzzled.

"Next Wednesday? The NTRP tower? With Winter?"

"Oh, right. And Jensen. What am I going to have to do?"

"No one knows who you are, and we don't want to risk anything too soon. Think of it as a little information-gathering mission. Stay close to Winter—we'd like to see who she talks to, what they talk about. Since you're new to the club, I'm assuming that Jensen will run the video camera herself. That's fine, but they will be very strict about where that camera goes, so I'm going to set you up with a miniature camera and an earpiece so you'll be able to hear me."

"Cool."

"It's just like the movies. The camera will be in the cap of a pen, so make sure you wear a shirt with a pocket. A dark shirt is better—it won't be as obvious."

"I'll have my school blazer on—is that okay?"

"Even better. On Wednesday morning, stop in here at seven-forty-five. The same woman, Nora, will be at the register. If anyone else is here, wait for them to leave. Any questions? Oh, one more thing. Sorry to do this to you, but

I have to ask you to delete the journal you started. It's too dangerous to put anything in writing. Remember, if I can access your files, so can NTRP."

◆ ◆ ◆

"Mom?" said Andy. "It's me, Andy. I know that I'm not supposed—"

"What's wrong?" Abbey asked, feeling her face go pale with panic. "Where are you?"

"I'm home, and I'm fine. There's nothing . . . wrong. I'm sorry for calling. . . . I just need . . . to talk . . . to somebody."

"It's okay, you caught me at a good time. I'm in my room catching up on paperwork. Where's your dad?"

"At the station, I guess. He said he had a meeting or something—said it would only be an hour. That was about three hours ago."

"Have you tried talking to him about . . . whatever it is that's bothering you?"

"No. I mean, I thought about it, but it's too . . . complicated."

Abbey laughed. "Too complicated for your dad?"

"You know what I mean. He's not always the easiest person to . . . you know. And I get the feeling that he's kind of stressed out, too. I think something's going on at the station."

"Oh? What makes you say that?"

"He's just acting weird." The photos of his dad and the man with the ponytail flashed before Andy's eyes. "He goes to these meetings, like today, and then he comes home and doesn't say anything about them."

"Well, he's under a lot of pressure. The station is concerned about ratings. He might have some news very soon, but I don't want to spoil his surprise, so you're going to have to wait. Now tell me what's going on. You sound so serious. Is it school?"

"No, it's not that. It's . . . this is going to sound strange, but . . . how do you know if you can trust someone? Like, *really* trust them."

Abbey was silent for a long moment, considering her answer. "Wow. That is a *really* difficult question. I think I wish your problem was school. At least I would know how to answer. Can you give me a little more to go on? Like, what are we talking about here? A friend? A girl?"

"All I can tell you is this: It's not about a girl. Not in that way, at least."

"Okay, so it's not a girl. I should be grateful for that, I suppose. I have to ask one more question: Has this person done something in particular to make you *question* his trustworthiness?"

Andy twisted his lips, thinking. "I don't think so. It's more of a feeling. I'm not saying I *don't* trust him—er, them—it's more like I *do*, but I'm not sure if I *should*. Does that make sense?"

"Mm-hmm. Absolutely. When I'm in the field in these

countries, I have to give people the benefit of the doubt, but that doesn't mean I don't have any. I keep my eyes and ears open, on the lookout for signs. I'm looking for good qualities, like integrity and loyalty and . . . compassion. There are exceptions, of course, but generally speaking, someone with at least a few of those positive qualities is probably someone you can trust."

After Andy hung up, he pulled out the glass circle and stared at the letters carved into it—letters that stood for, among other things, integrity and loyalty and compassion.

20

The night before the NTRP event, Silas was on his way to meet Andy, whom he had asked to take Penny for a walk at precisely ten minutes to nine. Silas's normal procedure after he exited the subway was to double back, buy a pack of gum or some mints from a newsstand, and then stop in a dark spot on the street to make a call. That gave him a chance to make sure no one was following him. It was no secret that NTRP regularly followed Silas, but as far as he was able to tell, they knew nothing about Andy. He wanted to keep it that way as long as possible.

Maybe it was instinct, or maybe it was just his gut telling him to mix it up a little, but instead of stopping at the newsstand, he stepped inside Gracious Home on Third Avenue. Near the back was a display of bathroom medicine cabinets, and he opened a mirrored door, angling it so that he had a view of the front of the store.

His instincts were spot-on. Stopped on the sidewalk just outside the glass door was Fallon Mishra. The brim of a Mets cap was pulled down low over her face, and she was wearing a several-sizes-too-big jacket, but there was no mistaking her profile, thanks to a nose that had been broken multiple times. Next to her was another familiar NTRP operative, a bearded guy trying a little too hard to look like a hipster in a vintage varsity jacket, bow tie, and straw fedora. Silas's heart pounded as he realized how close he had come to leading one of the worst traitors in the eight-hundred-year history of the Agents of the Glass to Andy's front door. Young, beautiful, and brilliant, Fallon had been a Level 3 Agent, occupying the Discipline seat for more than six years. But somewhere along the line, she began to sell information to NTRP. When her loyalty was questioned by Martin Gardner, she vanished among the eight million souls who call New York City home.

Martin, whose job it was to question *everyone's* loyalty, believed that she had been an impostor all along, planted in the Agency by NTRP. Silas never believed that. To him, she was simply too good at her job to be faking it. He had liked and respected and, to some degree, feared her. The Fallon he'd known was a "true believer" in the cause, and he had a hard time understanding the reasons for her betrayal; it just didn't make sense to him. Yet here she was, she and her cohort, following him, undoubtedly hoping that he would lead her to something or someone of interest to NTRP.

Silas pushed the cabinet door shut, debating his options. If he sneaked out the back of the store, she would know that he had spotted her. It was better to let her think that he was unaware of her and was just making a quick stop to buy lightbulbs, so that's exactly what he did.

When he went back outside, she was standing at the corner, pretending to be waiting for the light to change. As he walked past her, he spoke into his phone: "Hi! Sorry, I'm going to be a few minutes late. Had to run an errand, and the store closes at nine. Okay, see you in five minutes." What he knew, but Fallon did not, was that the words *five minutes* let Andy know that he wasn't coming at all—that there was a problem.

Silas picked up his pace, running to cross the street and catching a glimpse of his two shadows' reflections in a store window. They were still behind him, but at a safe tailing distance.

"Attagirl," said Silas under his breath. He couldn't help admiring her skill; he had trained her, after all.

To complete the deception, Silas needed a little bit of luck. Turning on to ███████████ Street,[1] he went to the middle of the block, searching for number ██, the build-

---

1. The address has been redacted for protection of the operative.

ing where Ricky O'Day, a computer programmer who did occasional work for the Agents, lived. He crossed his fingers, hoping that Ricky was home, and pressed the buzzer.

"What?" the voice on the intercom growled.

"Hey, Ricky. It's Silas. Let me in."

"I'm busy."

"Five minutes, Ricky. You owe me."

He buzzed. Silas stepped into the foyer and took the elevator up to the fourth floor.

Ricky opened the door and let Silas in without ever taking his eyes off the TV, which was blaring *How Far Will You Go?* at maximum volume. "Hey, man. You ever see this? It's hilarious."

Ignoring him, Silas went straight to the window overlooking the street and peeked around the curtain. It took him a minute, but he spotted Fallon standing between two cars and looking up at Ricky's building. Now the only questions that remained were: Did she *know* that Silas was on his way to see an agent? Did she already know about Andy? And if the answer to the second question was yes, *how* did she know? Was there another traitor in the Agency? It was unthinkable.

Ricky's sofa sagged beneath the weight of his shapeless, bloated body, which stretched from end to end. The coffee table between him and his massive TV was covered in potato chip crumbs, empty soda cans, and a half-eaten sausage and pepper pizza—the way it always was.

"What are you looking at?" he asked when a commercial interrupted the action on *How Far Will You Go?* "What's the big emergency?"

"What, can't I just stop by for a visit with my favorite geek? Love what you've done with the place, by the way." Silas pointed at the stacks of newspapers—several years' worth—piled from floor to ceiling.

"Thanks. I can get you the number of my decorator if you want. I have to warn you, though—she's expensive."

"I'll get back to you." He checked his watch and took another peek out the window; Fallon and the faux hipster had moved across the street, but the glow of a cell phone gave away her position. *If she still worked for the Agency,* Silas thought, *I'd be disappointed at such an amateur mistake.* "Well, it's been great seeing you, Ricky. Don't get up. I'll let myself out. And—"

"And if anybody asks, you were never here. I get it."

"Good-bye, Ricky." Silas took the stairs down, stopping between the first and second floors to make a call.

Mrs. Cardigan answered on the first ring. "Everything all right?"

"Yes. Just wanted to report that I unexpectedly ran into an old friend. She and her sidekick in the silly hat followed me."

"I see. You tell me all about it tomorrow at the Loom. How is *our* young man, by the way? Anything I need to know?"

"I was on my way to see him," Silas said, "but I think

now I'll wait. He's ready for tomorrow. All the usual doubts and confusion, maybe even a little paranoia, but nothing I can't handle."

"Any problem about the photographs?"

"No—the kid's already a pro. He got rid of the journal he was keeping on his computer as I asked, but he already started a hard copy. I think I'll let it go for a while. He has a great hiding place for it. He did ask his mother an interesting question. He didn't mention any names or any specifics, thankfully. Just wanted to know how he could tell if he could trust somebody."

"And you think he was talking about you."

"Well, it makes perfect sense. He's a smart kid. It's only natural for him to be a little suspicious. If I were in his shoes, I don't know if I would trust me."

21

Silas met with Andy at the bodega before school, "gluing" the earpiece into place well inside Andy's ear and showing him how the camera worked. His final instructions were to pretend to be enthusiastic about everything and to move around as much as possible, listening and observing. It was, Silas reminded him, an opportunity for the Agents to gain some much-needed intelligence on the inner workings of their greatest enemy.

"Most importantly, listen to what I tell you. Keep an eye on Winter. Stay close, so I can *hear* her, too. And take pictures of everyone she talks to."

"Don't forget—I'm going to be with Jensen, too," said Andy. "I don't think she's very good at blending in. And she hates that Decameron lady."

"Right. Jensen's not exactly a potted plant, is she? I have to admit, I'm a fan. Her reviews of the NTRP reality shows are *classic*. This could turn out to be an interesting day."

"It's already been kind of interesting."

"What do you mean?"

"Somebody was following me. He was waiting across the street from my apartment building. I think I surprised him, coming down earlier than usual. I'm pretty sure it's the same guy as before. I was going to take a picture, but he was gone before I had a chance."

Biting his knuckle, Silas took a deep breath. "And this happened on your way here this morning? Just now? Why did you wait so long to tell me?"

"I'm sorry—I didn't think it was that important. There wasn't anything to tell. I barely saw the guy."

"Do me a favor. Let me decide what's important, all right?"

Andy stared at his shoes and mumbled, "I said I was sorry."

"Okay, let's drop it. We can talk about it later. You need to get moving."

Without a word, Andy pulled on his jacket and started to go.

"Wait," said Silas. "I shouldn't have snapped like that. I know you're doing the best you can, and this is all still really new for you, and you still have lots of doubts about what we're doing. It's not fair. I'm asking you to trust me completely, but there's still lots I haven't told you, lots I *can't* tell you—at least not for now. So, are we okay?"

Andy looked Silas directly in the eyes and nodded.

"Great. Good luck today."

◆ ◆ ◆

A black limousine, courtesy of Deanna Decameron, picked up Andy, Jensen, and Winter at Wellbourne Academy and whisked them off to the NTRP building at Park Avenue and Forty-Fifth Street. Silas, meanwhile, was sitting with his back to a wall in a coffee shop on Forty-Third Street, watching and listening to the feed from Andy's audiovisual equipment.

"Right this way," said Decameron, taking them through the security checkpoint, where bags were opened and pockets emptied before they passed through a metal detector.

"Put the pen in the tray with your phone and watch," Silas told Andy through his earpiece. He smiled to himself as the boy spun around instinctively, forgetting for a moment that Silas was *inside* his head. Andy stepped through the detector, replaced the pen in his pocket, and then kneeled, pretending to tie a shoelace.

"Is that right?" he whispered.

"You're good to go," Silas said. "If you have a problem, just tap on the pen twice and I'll try to figure something out."

"Sandy, you coming?" nagged Jensen. "Try to keep up with me."

In the luxurious, wood-paneled elevator, Decameron pushed the button for the sixty-fifth floor, and they began their ascent.

Jensen broke the usual elevator silence: "What does NTRP have to do with education, anyway?"

"You may think of us only as a TV network, but we're so much more. NTRP is an international conglomerate—into a little bit of everything," said Decameron, looking straight ahead. "Our executives are true visionaries. They invest in companies that . . . share their vision of the future."

Jensen's eyebrows lurched upward. "What does that vision look like?"

Forcing a smile, Decameron turned to Jensen. "That's what you're here to find out. But it's all about building a better world for you . . . and your kids and grandkids."

"And the money to do . . . whatever it is they do . . . comes from all those god-awful reality shows? Their 'quality programming'?" Jensen asked, punctuating her final words with air quotes.

"Technically, from the advertising revenues that those programs generate, yes. You'll see representatives from several of the advertisers here today. In fact, you'll probably get some great stuff from them."

"I'm not here to 'get stuff,'" Jensen grumbled. "I'm here to do a story. You remember what that was like, don't you, from when you were a journalist?"

"Jensen!" said Winter. "That is so . . . rude."

Decameron smiled, waving off the insult. "Don't worry, Winter. I'm used to it. Jensen, say what you want about our programs, but the fact is that our ratings go up every week. We're giving the people what they want."

"Hmph," said Jensen.

"The website says that this building has sixty-six floors," said Andy, eager to change the subject. "I looked last night. How come the buttons stop at sixty-five?"

"That's very observant," said Decameron. "You're right: There *are* sixty-six floors. The executive offices are on the top floor, but you need a special key to get the elevator to stop there."

"Is that the only way up there?" Andy asked.

"There must be stairs, too, I'd imagine," said Decameron.

"Have you ever been up there?"

Decameron glanced at him, her head tilted to the left, measuring him. "A few times. Ah, here we are." The elevator doors opened, and they found themselves in an enormous room marked by a wall of floor-to-ceiling windows that stretched the entire width of the building.

Even Jensen was impressed. "Whoa. Check that out."

It was an ideal October day—paint-box-blue sky, pristine white clouds, and clear, clean air—and the view out over the Hudson River and New York Harbor went on for miles and miles.

"Pretty cool, huh?" said Winter, elbowing Andy in a friendly manner. "I wouldn't mind having an office up here someday."

"Not if we have anything to do with it," Silas whispered in Andy's ear.

"Okay, that's enough looking," said Jensen, returning to her usual state. "Where's the food? Ms. Albemarle promised that they would feed us."

At that moment, a set of double doors swung open, revealing a buffet table drooping under the weight of all the food on it.

Decameron pushed them toward the table. "Dig in. Who knows, there might even be enough variety to make Miss Huntley happy."

"I wouldn't count on it," said Andy.

◆ ◆ ◆

The first surprise of the morning came quickly. Victor Plante, the head of television programming at NTRP, spoke briefly about his network's commitment to improving the education system, even bragging a bit about the pilot program at Wellbourne Academy. Without mentioning them by name, he pointed out that student journalists from Wellbourne were present, and he encouraged the other "big shots" at the conference to seek them out and to take a few minutes to interview with them. And then he invited NTRP's "shining new star," as he called him, up to the podium to be introduced. A man in the first row of seats bounded to his feet and jogged to the front of the room.

"Oh, no," said Andy, not believing his own eyes. "What is *he* doing here?"

"Do you *know* him?" Winter asked.

"It's my . . . father."

Victor Plante greeted Howard Llewellyn at the podium with an exaggerated smile and a two-handed handshake. "NTRP is proud—no, make that *thrilled*—to announce that Howard Twopenny and his radio program will be joining our little family, effective immediately! And we're moving him up to a premium time slot. Starting at nine o'clock tomorrow morning, he will be tellin' it like it is on our network of radio stations from coast to coast. And here's the best part: Howard and our creative team are working on a talk show with an exciting new format . . . for NTRP TV! We're hoping to roll it out in January."

Winter beamed at Andy. "Howard Twopenny is your *father?* That is so . . . cool. Why didn't you tell me? My mom loves his show. He's so . . . honest, you know what I mean? He says what everybody else is thinking. And he's *famous.*"

"Um, yeah," he mumbled. "That's my dad. Tellin' it like it is, even when he has no idea what he's talking about."

"My, this is an interesting turn of events, don't you

think?" Silas said in Andy's ear as the audience rose, ready to move on to the mini-seminars scattered throughout the four conference rooms on the sixty-fifth floor. "Your father working for the very company that you're trying to stop. You'd better go congratulate him and introduce everyone."

"Do I have to?" Andy murmured softly.

"Can you introduce me to your dad?" Winter asked.

"There's your answer," Silas said.

Howard was charming a group of NTRP flunkies as Andy approached, with Jensen and Winter a half step behind. His shocked expression at seeing his son in that setting quickly gave way to a bewildered smile.

"Hey, look who's here!" he bellowed in his Radio Dad voice. "This some kind of school trip?"

"I guess this is the surprise that Mom mentioned. Why didn't you tell me that you got a new job?"

Ignoring the question for the moment, Howard looked over Andy's shoulder. "These friends of yours?"

Winter stepped forward, hand outstretched. "Mr. Twopenny, so nice to meet you. My name is Winter Neale. I *love* your show. I was just telling Andy that we listen to you at home all the time."

"Thank you, Winter. That's a great name, by the way. You're obviously a young woman with impeccable taste." He turned to look at Jensen. "And you are . . ."

No gushing, no offer to shake his hand, not even a smile. "Jensen. Huntley. Hihowyadoin'?"

Howard grimaced and placed his hand over his heart as if he'd been shot. "*Ouch.* I guess you're *not* a fan."

Jensen shrugged and shook her head ever so slightly. "Yeah, no."

Howard roared with laughter. "That's all right. That's why there's a dial to change stations. If you don't like me, you don't have to listen. Well, until we put the competition out of business, that is." Making a show of checking his massive gold watch, he added, "Time for me to hit the road. Big meeting with some creative types. What do you think of this watch, An? Gift from Victor. Hey, speak of the devil, there he is! And . . . there he goes."

Andy twisted around in time to see Victor Plante nod and half smile at Howard before turning and heading for the exit, where a thin man, all in gray, waited for him.

As Winter was taking a selfie with Howard, Jensen whispered to Andy, "Did you see who that was, over by the exit?"

"Uh-huh. The guy from the pictures. Ponytail. You see where he went?"

"Sort of. Let's go—maybe we can get an interview."

Andy waved at Howard. "See you at home, I guess."

Howard pulled him close. "We'll talk later," he whispered in his ear.

"Let's *go,*" Jensen insisted, jerking Andy away.

"Where are you two going?" Winter asked.

"We'll be right back," said Jensen.

"Well . . . shouldn't I come with you?"

Jensen summoned her bossy producer voice: "No. Go set up some interviews. Important people. No lackeys. I want to talk to somebody who actually knows what goes on in this dump—and is willing to talk about it."

Winter looked suspicious, but let them race off without further argument. Silas had his own doubts about the decision to ditch Winter for the moment, but he was curious to see where the trail led them, so he didn't try to stop Andy.

"There!" cried Jensen, spotting the heel of a man's shoe disappearing around a corner. By the time they got to that corner, though, he had slipped through one of the three unmarked doors that lined the hallway. Andy, sensing an opportunity, executed a feetfirst slide in an attempt to get (literally!) a foot in the still-closing door. He missed by inches, and the door clanged shut.

"Yer out!" cried Jensen in a perfect impersonation of an umpire. She reached down and yanked him to his feet. "Gutsy attempt, though, Jeter. Half a point for the effort."

"Now what?" Andy asked. He tried the door handle; it was locked, and so were the other two.

"I guess we find Winter and shoot some interviews— get that out of the way. There's got to be somebody willing to tell the truth about this place. It can't be that hard. We just have to find that person and ask the right questions."

"All right, but I need to find a restroom first. I think I saw a sign back there. Meet you in the big auditorium."

"Okay, Howie."

"Hilarious."

22

A few minutes later, as he was about to exit the restroom, with its expanses of polished marble and dark wood paneling (probably cut from an endangered species of tree, he decided), Andy noticed something odd. On the wall to the right of the door, one edge of a single section of the paneling looked as if it had sprung loose from the rest. What really caught his attention, though, was the sliver of light sneaking out from behind the wall. He ran his fingers down the long edge and then gently pulled the panel toward him. To his surprise, the panel swung open; it was a hidden door—no knob, no visible hinges, absolutely nothing to give away its true identity. If it had been properly closed, he never would have seen it.

He leaned his head and shoulders inside to see where the door led.

"What do you see?" Silas asked.

"It's kind of like a deep closet. Looks like it goes back about ten feet. After that, I can't tell if it ends or makes a— Uh-oh, someone's coming into the bathroom." He stepped all the way inside and pulled the door closed with the handle on the back.

"What are you doing?" Silas asked, slightly panicky at the thought of him getting stuck. "I've lost the picture. Did you turn the light out?"

"It went out by itself. There must be a switch here somewhere." There was a pause of a few seconds while Andy groped around in the dark, looking for it.

"Use your phone," said Silas.

"Good idea . . . Ah!"

The picture returned to Silas's screen as Andy flipped the light switch. "Much better. Just wait until whoever it is leaves, and then get out of there."

"Mm-hmm. Hold on." Andy crept silently to the end of the "closet." "Hey, it's not the end," he whispered. "It turns and goes about ten feet, and then I can see stairs going up."

"Say that again. *What* do you see?"

"Stairs."

It was too soon, Silas felt, to ask Andy to do what he was about to ask, but these were extraordinary circumstances that he simply could not ignore. An agent—one who was unknown to anyone outside the Agents of the Glass— was *inside* NTRP headquarters, and he had stumbled into a secret passage that appeared to lead to the sixty-sixth floor, home to the offices of the leaders of the organization. To stop him now was to waste an opportunity that the Agency might not see again for years, if ever. If Andy were an experienced agent, Silas thought, he wouldn't even hesitate, but he had to face the facts. Andy was a kid with zero experience at this sort of thing. It would be foolish to put him in danger without knowing more about what *might* lie beyond that staircase; maybe it would be worth it, maybe not. Andy had already proven himself to be a valuable asset, but if he went forward and was caught snooping, his spying days would likely be over.

In the end, Andy made the decision easy.

"You want me to go up?" he asked.

"I do but I don't," Silas said. "I'll be honest. I would be thrilled if you went, but I don't want you to go if you don't feel ready. There's no way of telling what you might be walking into. If you get caught . . ."

"I won't. And if I do, I'll tell them I got lost."

"It may not be that"—but Andy was already halfway up the stairs—"easy."

A right turn at the top, another short passageway, and then a dead end and almost complete darkness. Andy used the light from his phone to search for a switch for the fixture directly over his head, but no luck.

"I can feel a handle," he said. "I'm going to open the door and peek out."

"Peek quietly. *Please.* And do me a favor—hold the pen in front of you so I have a better view. Keep the lens pointing out." Andy pushed gently on the door, opening it no more than an inch, and held the pen up to it. "Good, that's perfect. It looks like a small library. A few nice reading tables, bookcases all around. You'll have to be careful. Directly across from you is a glass door. . . . I can't see much so you're on your own."

"Okay, I'm going in," said Andy, slipping through the door.

"Wait! Don't close the door all the way, or you might not be able to open it. Block it open an inch or two. Just don't make it obvious."

Andy glanced around the room for something to prop the door open with as the aroma of musty leather-bound books hit him. There was nothing else within reach, so without a glance at the title, he pulled a thin volume from the nearest shelf, wedged it against the doorframe, and pushed the door closed. As he tiptoed around the perimeter of the room, he noticed two things about the books that filled every inch of shelf space: They were ancient, and almost all the titles he could read were foreign-sounding.

"Which way?" he asked, opening the glass door and looking up and down the hallway.

"Do you hear anything?"

He stuck his head out a bit farther. "Nothing. It's weird how quiet it is in here. Maybe everybody's downstairs at that boring conference." He turned left out of the library and hurried down the hall to the next glass door. "Empty office. Door's locked."

The next three doors were the same, so he kept going until he reached a set of sliding glass doors that caught him by surprise when they opened automatically, triggered by his approach. He ducked through the opening, cringing and waiting for the inevitable *clank* that would give him away as the two doors converged. But they came together with barely a *whishhh,* and he took a couple of deep breaths, trying to calm himself.

Spinning slowly where he stood, he counted six walls around him. The room was a perfect hexagon, and at the center of each wall was a set of doors exactly like the ones he had come through.

"They're all the same, and there's no numbers or marks on the doors or the walls. How am I going to find my way back?"

"You must have some way to make a mark. Use your shoes to scuff up the floor."

"It's not working. Hey, I know: *bread crumbs.*"

"What?"

"I stuck a bagel in my pocket earlier. You know, in case I got hungry later in the day." He tore it into pieces and scattered them around the door in front of him.

"Good thinking, Hansel. Are you sure you haven't done this before?"

"I think I'd remember. . . . Hey, I just saw something. I'm going to check it out."

He edged up to a set of glass doors, dashing through them as they opened. Halfway down the hall, he heard footsteps ahead and flattened himself against a windowless wooden door. Reaching behind his back, he twisted the brass handle, holding his breath and praying that it was unlocked and that there was no one inside. To his relief, the door clicked open, and he backed himself into a dark storage closet—or at least that was his first impression as he turned around to investigate, almost face-planting into a stack of cardboard boxes, marked with the years from 1967 to 1979. The room itself was maybe eight feet square, low-ceilinged, uncomfortably warm, and quite dark. The only light flickered through a narrow opening in one wall, about a foot high and four or five feet wide, in front of which was parked a pair of enormous film projectors, the kind you would find in a movie theater. They were covered in dust and long unused, but like nosy neighbors peering over a fence, their lenses continued to poke through the slot in the wall and onto the private screening room below.

When Andy peeked through the opening, he couldn't believe his eyes. The scene below him was like something from a movie star's home: a ceiling-mounted digital projector, a screen that took up an entire wall, five rows of plush leather seats, a popcorn machine on wheels, and every kind of liquor imaginable lined up on the shelves behind a glistening wooden bar.

"What's going on? Where are you? I can't see anything," Silas said. The lens of the spy pen, back in Andy's shirt pocket, was pressed against the wall.

"It's cool, like a miniature movie theater. I'm above it, in the projector room."

"Is there anybody there?"

"Five, no, six people. Looks like two women, and then two men right behind them, and then two more men by the door. Two *big* guys. The lights are on; there's nothing on the screen. They're just talking."

"I need to see them. The camera."

"Oh, right. I forgot." As he aimed the pen out through the opening, he recognized the girl on the right. "Hey, that's *Winter*. What is she doing up here?"

"Are you positive? My picture is a little grainy."

"Yep, that's her. She just turned around and said something to a guy with a beard. And a bow tie."

"Great. I know who he is. How about the other two . . . Wait . . . come on, turn a little more. That's it. . . . Why, hello, Fallon."

"Who's that?"

"An old friend. Remember when I told you about someone betraying us? You're looking at her. Fallon Mishra. Among other things, she's a ninth *dan* black belt in kendo. She's fascinating and brilliant and beautiful . . . and utterly treacherous. You and Jensen should try to get an interview. Just be careful."

"Sounds like you have a crush on her."

"No, but I *respect* what she's capable of doing. Now, how about the other man? He could be important. Try to get me a—What just happened? Why did my picture go dark?"

"Um . . . I kind of . . . dropped the pen."

23

"You what? Where?"

"Well . . . I, uh . . . It's on the floor. Down there. I was holding it out the opening, and it just slipped. Don't worry, it landed on the carpeting. It didn't make a sound."

Silas banged his head on the coffee-shop table and gritted his teeth. *Stay calm,* he reminded himself. *He's just a kid.* "Yes, but now I can't see. That was kind of important, Andy."

"I'm sorry. I didn't mean to . . ."

"It's done. Nothing we can do about it now. This kind of stuff happens all the time. You're *sure* nobody heard it drop?"

"Uh-huh. Nobody even turned around. Oh, the projector's on now; something's coming up on the screen. That's weird. It's a bunch of pictures of Karina Jellyby."

"The singer? That's interesting. She's a Wellbourne grad, you know."

"Yeah, Winter told me."

"Can you hear *anything*? Because I can't, unless you put your chest up to that opening. And that might be a bit hard to explain if somebody catches you."

Andy was silent for a long time, focused on completing his mission and trying not to mess anything else up. "Wow, they *really* don't like her. Talking about her influence on young people. Especially Operation THAW and how kids are starting to do nice stuff for people. You'd think she was a serial killer. Are they going to kill her?"

"That's not their style. That would only turn her into a martyr, and there's nothing they hate more than that. No, it will be something much more subtle."

"Uh-oh."

Silas choked on the last of his tea. "Now what?"

"They just put up a picture of you. It's the exact same one that was on Jensen's site, with my dad and the guy with the ponytail, except you're still in this one. That Fallon lady is pointing at it, saying something about the concert and . . . my dad. Yep, there's another picture of him at the radio station."

"Did Fallon say anything about me?" Silas asked, his body tensing.

"No. The way she was standing in front of the screen mostly blocked you out of the picture. Your face was only up for a couple of seconds."

"Really?" Silas was genuinely surprised. Fallon certainly must have recognized him; why didn't she speak up? A known Level 2 Agent sitting on a bench just yards away from an NTRP agent? It could hardly be dismissed as a coincidence.

"Okay, now everyone is leaving; everyone but Winter. She's alone, except for the bow tie guy. . . . No, wait. There's the guy with the ponytail. He came in from a . . . I'm not sure *where* he came from, actually. There must be a secret door. He just . . . appeared."

Silas sat up in his seat. "You're sure it's the same guy?"

"Positive. Long gray ponytail. Gray suit. Well, more like silver. It's him."

"Winter. It has been too long," said the man, his voice soothing, musical.

"He has a funny accent," whispered Andy. "Sort of British, but different."

"I've been following your directions, Mr. de Spere," said Winter. "Everything is going exactly the way you said it would. Do you remember my fifth birthday party? You told me that you had a raven as a pet. His name was Edgar. You said he could talk. I don't think I believed you. I should have known better. You've never lied to me."

"She called him Mr. Despair," said Andy.

Silas nodded to himself. St. John de Spere. The mystery man at the top of the NTRP pyramid, the man rarely seen in public. And now Andy Llewellyn, Level 1 Agent for all of a few weeks, was practically in the same room with him.

"That's right. You have an excellent memory," said de Spere.

"Do you still have him?"

"Sadly, no. Edgar passed a few years back, but I have another. Lenore. Much more talkative than he was. In fact, I have to be careful that she doesn't listen in on some of my conversations. She remembers everything, and she's not very discreet. A dangerous combination. Ah, but let's talk about you. I understand that Mr. Ickes and Ms. Mishra briefed you about the timing of the event," he said, nodding at the man in the bow tie.

"*Mr. Ick-eez?*" Andy whispered.

"That must be the guy in the bow tie."

"Yes. The Karina Jellyby concert. October thirtieth."

"Correct. Remember that date, Winter—it will go down in history. When you wake up the morning after that concert, you will have two hundred and fifty disciples, every one of them willing—no, *desperate*—to do whatever you ask. With your gift and my guidance . . . nothing can stand in our way. This is just the beginning." He moved toward the bar, pouring himself a seltzer water.

Winter lifted her chin and stared off into the distance, smiling. A *dangerous* smile, thought Andy, and *not* the smile he'd seen on that first morning at Wellbourne, a smile that had seemed so friendly and welcoming at the time.

"What's happening?" asked Silas.

"Winter's talking to the guy with the ponytail. It's kind of hard to hear."

With Winter and de Spere facing each other, white screen in the background, Andy got the idea to try out his Lucian Glass on them. He took the blue disk from beneath his shirt, brought it up to his right eye, and focused on her.

Seeing her *lumen* for the first time, he gasped before he could cover his mouth with his free hand. Through the sky-colored glass of the medallion, she appeared to be engulfed in flames. In places, the *lumen* extended several feet outward from her body, like tongues of fire flaring wildly, reaching and groping toward him, reminding him of pictures he'd seen of sunspots and storms on the surface of the sun. Terrified and fascinated at the same time, he turned his gaze to St. John de Spere, whose *lumen,* every bit as bright as Winter's, pulsed like a slow, steady heartbeat.

"I see that the Huntley girl is here with you today," said de Spere. "We put a tracker on her when she went through security, just to make sure she stayed out of trouble. Have you had any problems with her?"

"Nothing I can't handle," said Winter coolly. "She's arrogant and sloppy. Nobody listens to her, and nobody reads her secret blog, which isn't secret at all. Everybody knows about it. It's a joke, like her. And on top of that, she dresses like a bag lady. I think there must be something wrong with her neck, because I've never seen her without that horrible scarf wrapped around it."

Andy's mind flashed back to the incident in the

cafeteria—Winter threatening poor Craig Lessing—and he shivered. This was a side of Winter that he could no longer deny existed, and more than anything else, he felt disappointment. Despite everything that he had witnessed, and even after seeing her astonishing *lumen* for himself, part of him had stubbornly refused to believe that Winter was as bad as Silas and the other Agents insisted she was.

His view of her only went downhill from there.

"And the boy?"

"Andy Llewellyn. He's new at Wellbourne. A nobody. No, I shouldn't say that—I just found out he's Howard Twopenny's son. So maybe he won't turn out to be completely useless after all. At least he's cute. He'll be perfect as my personal assistant."

Andy felt as if he'd been punched in the gut. A nobody? Useless? Up to that moment, he had simply been doing his job, doing as Silas directed. But now it was personal.

"Come with me for a moment," de Spere said. "A more secure place to talk." He drew up his lanky frame from his seat and led Winter out of the screening room. The door slammed shut, and Andy took a much-needed deep breath.

"They're gone," he whispered to Silas a moment later. He was alone, left to chew on Winter's mocking words.

◆ ◆ ◆

"Morality is *dead*, Winter," said de Spere, staring out at the city street below. "And good riddance to it. If history proves anything, it is that mankind is most productive and creative and inventive when they are in a state of conflict. They were better off as a species before a few mediocre, would-be leaders decided that there was a difference between right and wrong. There is no difference; there is no *wrong*. There is only what is right for *me*, right *now*. Morality was invented for one simple reason: to keep people in line. If they do *right*, they are promised a *reward* at the end of life. If they do wrong, they will be punished for eternity. We are standing at the threshold of an electrifying, exhilarating new world, you and I and those who make the journey with us. An age of reason and rational thinking. Morality and the so-called virtues, like courage and integrity and dignity, are all obsolete. Selfishness is the only virtue that matters. Which is why we must make an example of these well-meaning but dangerously misguided musicians and their equally naïve fans. They worship at the altar of altruism, and they—and others like them—must be stopped. Encouraging people to help other people for no financial or any other type of gain is folly. Humans are naturally selfish, and the only way humans can survive the next hundred years is if they return to their true natures and rid themselves of foolish, outdated ideas like compassion and charity. Once we have eliminated them and *purified* the minds of the weak . . . then *real* human progress can begin again."

Winter was spellbound. She absorbed every word, every idea, every nugget of the man's philosophy, nodding in agreement as he spouted them. "I see what you mean. Now all the shows on NTRP make even more sense."

"Ah, the shows. That's just simple entertainment, like the Roman emperors'. As long as the people have bread and circuses—food and cheap entertainment—they're happy. And if we can start to gnaw away at a few tired, old ideas, all the better."

"But what about people who *don't* watch NTRP? How do you change the way they *think*?"

"Ah, yes. That is the real issue, isn't it? I'm happy to tell you that twenty years of research and experimentation has paid off. Are you familiar with the term *eugenics*?"

Winter shook her head. "Is it something to do with genetics?"

"It is, as a matter of fact. It is a movement dedicated to the improvement of the human race by . . . *controlling* certain hereditary factors."

"Like what?"

"Well, for example, if we wanted to create a race of very tall, thin, blond people, we would match tall, thin, blond men to women with the same characteristics."

"What if you're not tall, thin, and blond?" asked Winter.

"Simple. We don't let you reproduce."

"But . . . how? You can't stop people from having kids."

"Not the way the world is today. But times change. Besides, that was just an example—that's not what we're after. Eugenicists have been at it for centuries, but they all made the same fundamental mistake. They were all obsessed with how people *looked*—their physical traits. Most of them were crackpots trying to create a race of people who all looked alike. Frankly, I don't *care* what you look like. I'm only interested in *what* and *how* you *think*. NTRP's TV and radio programming is designed to help change the way people think, but it's too slow and too unpredictable. And, of course, some people, like young Miss Huntley, simply refuse to watch. Since my days at university, I have been working on something a little more . . . immediate, and a lot more *certain*. And now I have it. I'm still perfecting it, but my new process does in seconds what used to take years, and testing shows that it is ninety-five percent effective. My vision is about to be realized: a race of people free from the imperfections that have been plaguing mankind since the dawn of civilization."

"How is that possible?" Winter asked.

"I call it Operation Tailor," said de Spere. "As in, I can now *tailor* a person's personality to suit our needs. Simply a matter of a little genetic engineering. Ironically, we have the Agents of the Glass to thank. If they hadn't discovered the presence of the *lumen*, none of this would be possible. I examined the genes of hundreds of people with *lumens*—Syngians, in the terminology of our friends— and I discovered exactly *how* they differed. Once I identified the specific genes involved, all I had to do was figure out a way to target *just* those genes in ordinary humans, the kind who are slaves to their own emotions. Then it's like flipping switches on and off. One minute, you're generous; the next, you're greedy. I started small, just one person at a time. I made mistakes along the way. . . . There were casualties, collateral damage, but that's to be expected in any revolution."

"What happened to them?"

"It's probably better if you don't know the details. Then came the Halestrom Conference. That was almost a dozen at once—all in all, a tremendous success. But now the process is ready to be used on a much bigger scale. A few hundred. Then . . . who knows?"

"And so . . . the concert at Wellbourne? Will the . . . process be . . ."

"It's too perfect an opportunity to pass up," said de Spere. "And the irony of it all is just so *delicious*. You see, the word *eugenics* is from the Greek, meaning 'wellborn.' And here you have two hundred and fifty model citizens, the cream of the charitable crop at *Wellbourne* Academy, being congratulated for all their good work. We have our own reward in mind. A little *purification*."

De Spere checked his watch. "We'd better get you back downstairs, Winter. No need to raise any unnecessary questions. I'll be in touch."

24

Andy waited a few minutes after Winter and de Spere had left the room before making his move. He followed his trail of bagel crumbs to the right door, but then he somehow missed the turn into the library and ended up in front of the elevators. As he stood there, the door opened and he found himself face to face with Fallon Mishra.

Silas's words came rushing back to him as he stared openmouthed at a ninja warrior poised to take his head off with her bare hands: *ninth* dan *black belt in kendo . . . utterly treacherous.* She was as surprised by the situation as Andy, and she looked at him as if she couldn't believe somebody was actually *there.* He was frozen, so she grabbed him by the arm and yanked him into the elevator.

That's it. I'm dead, thought Andy. *They're not even going to find my body.*

"How did you get up here?" Fallon asked. "This floor is restricted. You really shouldn't be here."

"I didn't mean to—I was looking for my dad. . . ."

A moment before the door closed completely, somebody in the hall pushed the button and the door opened up again.

This time, it was St. John de Spere. His face expressionless, he scanned Andy's face. He spoke to Fallon without taking his eyes off Andy: "Is everything all right here, Ms. Mishra?"

"Yes, sir. Must be some kind of elevator malfunction. I don't know how else this young man could have reached this floor. I was going to take him down to the security office to fill out a report." She paused, waiting for a response that never came. "He's one of the visiting students . . . from Wellbourne Academy."

"I see," said de Spere, eyes still boring into Andy's. "And are you enjoying yourself, Mr. . . . uh, Llewellyn?"

Andy swallowed. *How does he know my name?* "I . . . uh . . . Yes, sir. I'm sorry. I . . . don't know how I ended up . . . I was looking for my dad. . . . He works here, and . . ." His voice trailed off.

The elevator stopped on the nineteenth floor, and de Spere stepped off without another word. As Andy sucked in a huge breath, he noticed the name tag stuck to the lapel of his blazer: *Andover Llewellyn, Wellbourne Academy.* He couldn't help smiling, even though he still had Fallon Mishra to deal with.

When they reached the ground floor and the door

opened, she pushed the button for the sixty-fifth floor and stepped off the elevator.

"I'll take care of the report," she said. "You go back with your group. And no more wandering. Got it?"

"Yes, ma'am. I promise."

Thirty seconds after stepping onto the sixty-fifth floor, he ran into Jensen. From the look on her face, he *almost* wished he were back on the elevator, taking his chances with Fallon Mishra.

"Where were you?" she hissed.

"I . . . got lost. I took a wrong turn and ended up in another room . . . and I couldn't leave 'cause this lady was right in the middle of a speech. I didn't want to be rude."

Jensen examined his face closely, looking for signs that he was lying. "Why should I believe you? How do I know you didn't sneak off with your girlfriend someplace? If I find out that you two have been working on some secret story behind my back, I am going to—"

"We weren't together," said Andy. He pointed to the windows behind Jensen. "She's right there."

"Who's that woman she's talking to? Let's go check it out."

"Hey, guys!" said Winter. "Where have you been? I've been looking all over for you. This is Jill Clermont, one of the founders of 233dotcom."

Suddenly, Jensen was very interested, and a transformation occurred before Andy's eyes: Jensen Huntley the sullen teenager became Jensen Huntley the serious journalist.

"I have some questions for you," she said, setting up the video camera and microphone, "about 233 and NTRP, and what's going on in school libraries. And the old books—can you clarify what is happening to them? Could you do an interview? Right now?"

"I'm sorry, I really can't," said Jill. "I'm late for an appointment across town already. But here's my card. Send me an email, and I promise you an interview. Deal?"

Jensen grunted. "Okay. You guys heard her. She promised."

◆ ◆ ◆

On the way back to Wellbourne, Winter looked across the limousine at Andy and pointed at his shirt pocket. "What happened to your pen?"

"What?"

"Your pen. It looked like a nice one. I noticed it in your pocket on the way there this morning."

"Oh. Uh, yeah. I guess I, uh, lost it someplace. It was nothing special. I think it came from the radio station. I didn't give it to you, did I?" he asked Jensen.

She scowled. "No. I didn't take your pen. You must have lost it when you disappeared for half an hour. Thanks again for that, Sandy."

"Hey, check this out," said Winter, pulling a chartreuse NTRP T-shirt out of her goody bag. "It's even the right size. There's a hat, too!"

Jensen dug her shirt and hat out of the bag and threw them at Winter. "They're all yours. Like I'm gonna be a walking ad for those mouth breathers. In fact, take the whole thing. I don't want anybody questioning my integrity because I took ten bucks' worth of trash from them."

Andy peeked inside the canvas tote bag that he'd been handed on his way out the door of the NTRP building. He laughed as he held up his T-shirt for Winter and Jensen to see. Splashed across the front was a silk-screened photograph of Howard Twopenny, his mouth wide open in midrant, his eyes wild with anger.

"'Howard Twopenny tells it like it is,'" read Jensen. "*Niiice.* Now, *that* I would wear. Trade you for . . . Let's see, what else is in here? A giant chocolate bar? Just what I need. A flashlight . . . that doesn't actually work?"

"Here you go," said Andy. As he handed the shirt to her, something at the bottom of the bag caught his eye. It was his pen—or, to be accurate, *Silas's* pen—the one he had dropped into the screening room. "What the—"

"What's the matter?" Winter asked. "You look like you've seen a ghost."

"Oh . . . nothing. I was hoping for . . . one of those chocolate bars, but I got peanut brittle instead. I hate peanut brittle."

◆ ◆ ◆

It was after two-thirty in the morning when Silas finally arrived at his apartment. He let the finches out of their cage and dropped into his lone chair to stare at the painting on the easel. He hadn't touched the painting in days because his dreams had been more incomprehensible than usual, filled with disturbing images that evaporated from his memory the second he opened his eyes—except for one, of a girl about six. The face seemed so familiar that at first he was sure he was seeing a reflection of himself as a child, but something was not quite right. The girl in his dream had an odd expression, her mouth forming a smile but her eyes not quite cooperating.

"One more night," Silas said to the finches. "If I can get another look, maybe something will click."

As the finches chirped in agreement, he opened his laptop and clicked on Howard Twopenny's website in order to listen to the show recorded that morning. He'd received a message from Reza Benali that Howard had mentioned the concert at Wellbourne and Karina Jellyby.

Howard was in fine form: "Listen up, folks! Uncle Howard has some important news for you. I know you've all heard of this god-awful singer that goes by the name of Irena Jellyroll. No, wait, my producer Wally is shouting in my ear that that's not right. What? Karen Jellybean? No? Rena Jelly . . . bee? No *n* at the end? Are you sure? He's nodding. All right, then, Karina Jellyby. What the heck kind of name is that? Irregardless, a few weeks ago, this no-talent slacker started a contest to find the country's biggest losers. As if spending two hours a week working for nothing weren't punishment enough, if you want a chance to attend a 'special concert' with the Jellybean, you have to write a warm, fuzzy essay about your experience, too—about how those two hours a week helping losers changed your life. The poor schlub who has to read those sweet-as-sugar essays is probably in a diabetic coma someplace.

"Folks, I just can't let something that stupid go unchallenged. And so, I am proud to announce the first annual Charity Is for Losers contest. That's CIFL for short, and I expect to see those letters splashed all over the Internets tomorrow. Winning is easy. We want your horror stories about what really happens when people 'do good' but don't get paid for it, and what these charity cases do with all the dough us hardworking schlubs are handing out. Winners will be joining me in the front row of a very special concert featuring AS2, the legendary Air Supply tribute band that could teach Mizz Jellybean a thing or two about how to rock."

25

"It's really important that you don't act any differently around her," Silas told Andy over a root beer in the back room of YouNeedItWeGotIt! on a chilly Saturday morning. "A good spy has to set his personal feelings aside and do his job. Your job is to gather information."

"She called me a *nobody*."

"It sounds terrible, but it's actually *good* that she thinks that. It means that she doesn't suspect you at all. Which means that she might not be as careful as she ought to be. If she slips up, you're going to be there to catch it. Instead of being mad about it, *use* it."

Andy sighed. "Fine. I'll try. It just . . . I mean, she is so nice to my face. How can she be like that?"

"It's in her DNA. She's wired differently than you or me. I've seen others like her—not as strong as her, but still plenty dangerous—and everything they say, everything they do, is *calculated*. She's looking for the maximum advantage for herself in every situation. And that brings us to your assignment, assuming you and Penny don't have any other big plans for the day."

"I'm twelve. I don't have plans. I'm taking Penny to the park, and then I'm probably going to work on my ship model."

"How's that coming along?"

"Slow. It's more complicated than I thought."

"Maybe I can help. I'm pretty good with my hands."

"Yeah. Maybe. So what's the job? Who do I have to kill this time?" he asked, flashing a smile for the first time all morning.

"No hits today, thanks. Surveillance work. You're going to accidentally run into Winter and her parents outside the Metropolitan Museum in about an hour."

"Accidentally?"

"Mr. Neale is on the board of directors, and they're having brunch in the dining room later on, but first they're going for a little family outing. They'll be in the Conservatory Garden—are you familiar with it?"

"My mom loves it there. We go all the time."

"How is your mom, anyway? Any word on when she's coming back?"

Andy shrugged. "The date keeps changing. First it was going to be this week. Then she said it might be a few more days. Sounds like things are kind of messed up over there."

"Have you talked to her?"

"Oh, yeah. We Skype two or three times a week, and I get emails from her. It's fine. I'm fine. You don't have to worry about me," he added unconvincingly. "Now, what am I supposed to do after I accidentally run into Winter's family?"

"Well, first I want you to get close enough to get a good look at Mr. and Mrs. Neale through your glass in order to confirm what our earlier research tells us. We're trying to get a better understanding of how Winter came to be the way she is. Her mother, we know, is a Syngian, but we've never picked up any sign of the *lumen* on her father. And *that's* the strange part. You see, when a Syngian and a normal person have a baby, the kid is *always* normal. It's just the way it works out genetically. In the entire time we've been keeping track, there are no exceptions. Period."

"What if they're both Syngians?"

"Then the kid is guaranteed to be a Syngian."

"Maybe his *lumen* is just hard to see."

"It's possible, but not very likely. From everything we know about him, he's one of the good guys, you know what I mean? Anyway, get a good look from a little distance, and then bump into them so Penny can have a look, and a smell, too. We've never gotten a dog close to him, so this is the perfect opportunity. When you get to the garden, be extra careful. Whatever you do, don't let Winter catch you spying on her."

"What about Penny? Don't Syngians know about dogs like her? And what if Penny goes crazy or something?"

"They know that some dogs are able to identify them, but we still have the advantage because the dogs aren't all exactly alike. As far as they'll be able to tell, it's just a boy and his dog out for a Saturday stroll. As for Penny, there's a little secret I guess it's time you knew: If she sees a Syngian and starts to growl or act up, say the word Lapsang to her and she'll be fine."

"Lapsang? What's that mean?"

"You'll find out soon enough."

◆ ◆ ◆

Sawyer Ascutney Neale III, Winter's grandfather, was one of the richest people ever to live in New York City. He had inherited a small fortune, money that came from the sale of bullets and grenades and mortar shells during the two world wars, but it was his brainchild—the decision to start manufacturing and selling land mines—that took the Neales from the merely rich to the much more exclusive neighborhood of the truly *wealthy*.

Although it was a business whose success was measured in agony, death, and dismemberment, he never lost a moment's sleep. To anyone who dared question his ethics, he was fond of pointing out that he slept like a baby no matter where he laid his head—his penthouse on Central Park

South, the London town house, a ten-bedroom "cottage" in Nantucket, ski chalets in Chamonix and Aspen, or the family yacht. To his way of thinking, Neale Industries was merely providing products that the world wanted—no, *demanded*. "It's a simple calculation," he'd recently told the *Times*. "If we don't do it, someone else will."

Father and son, however, were as unlike as two humans who shared DNA could be, and on his twenty-first birthday, Winter's father, Sawyer IV, announced his decision: He wanted nothing to do with the family business. He was cashing in his shares in Neale Industries, giving up his future as an executive with the company, and dedicating his life and fortune to helping the victims of the very land mines his family sold. This, naturally, did not go over well with his father, and the two had not spoken in fifteen years. Despite that estrangement, Winter spent her summers with her mother and grandparents, flying back and forth between Nantucket and London on their private jet.

The Neales were right where Silas said they would be, and right on time. Andy and Penny were halfway into their second loop of the garden when he spotted Winter's unmistakable silhouette. He ducked behind the wisteria that formed a semicircle at the far west side of the garden, a hundred yards or more away, and set off on a path that would intersect with the family's and give him a chance for an up close look before the "accidental" meeting. Even at that distance, Penny knew something was up, and Andy had to add a second wrap of the leash around his hand, just to be safe. Andy found a perfect location for spying the moment before the Neales turned a corner and began coming toward him.

The first thing he noticed was how relaxed Mr. Neale looked. He was smiling, clearly enjoying the beauty of a fall day in the park, sauntering along a few steps behind the tense-looking Mrs. Neale and Winter, who had their heads down in a private, serious conversation.

Beside Andy, Penny emitted a soft growl.

"Easy, girl. It's okay." He leaned down to look her in the eyes. "Lapsang."

Penny's demeanor changed immediately. She licked his face and sat quietly.

"Wow. It worked. Good girl." He handed her a treat from his pocket and removed the sea-glass pendant from beneath his shirt. Winter's *lumen,* even in the bright sunlight, was impossible to miss. Even though he was prepared for it, its vividness and liveliness still caught him by surprise. When Mrs. Neale stopped and turned to say something to her husband, Andy got a clear look at her *lumen,* too. It had some of the same characteristics of Winter's—the tongues of fire reaching out several feet from her body— but it was noticeably less intense in color and brightness.

Finally, he directed his gaze at Mr. Neale, who was walking past a dark background, an ideal situation for *lumen* spotting. Andy turned the glass this way and that, but there was nothing to see. Mr. Neale was *lumen*-free.

Andy tucked the glass back into his shirt, took a deep

breath, and walked out from behind the trees, aiming right for the Neale family.

A few seconds later, Winter shouted, "Andy! Hi!"

He acted surprised to see her and, with one last reminder to Penny, waved and met them on the path.

"What are you doing here?" Winter asked. "Omigosh, is that your dog? She is beautiful. What's her name?"

"Penny. Thanks."

"Mom, Dad, this is Andy Llewellyn. He's the new kid at Wellbourne. I'm his SA."

"Hi, Andy," said Mr. Neale, shaking his hand. "Call me Sawyer. I'm a Wellbourne man myself."

"I'm Fontaine," added Mrs. Neale. "Everyone calls me Taney. It is *such* a pleasure to meet you. Winter has told us all about you. And she's right—you are a handsome young man."

Andy felt himself blushing but had a hard time looking away from Mrs. Neale. There was *something* about her that was oddly familiar, but he couldn't make the connection in his mind. Something about the eyes, he decided—but Winter pulled him away before he was able to get more specific.

"Mom! You're embarrassing him." She reached down to pet Penny, and Andy cringed, waiting for her to snap. Penny, however, didn't flinch and even wagged her tail—a little. "We're headed down to the museum—do you want to walk with us?" Winter asked.

"Uh, sure."

"Why don't you come to brunch with us? That would be okay, wouldn't it, Dad?"

"Fine by me," said Mr. Neale.

"Thanks, but I can't," said Andy. "With Penny and all . . ."

Winter put on a disappointed face. "Oh, right. Well, walk with us, anyway."

She took him by the arm and pulled him a few steps ahead of her parents. As they walked, she stared at Andy for several seconds, as if trying the words out in her mind before blurting them out.

Finally, she said, "I *know.*"

26

Andy's heart threatened to burst right through his ribs, but somehow he managed not to show how freaked out he was by Winter's casual remark.

"What do you mean?" he asked. A fast-motion film ran through his head, narrated by Winter's voice:

I know who you are.

I know who you're working for.

I know what you're trying to do.

I know all about the Agents.

I know what they told you about me.

I know . . .

"I know it was you . . . that day at the bank. You're the one who almost got killed and then gave the money back."

From the confident look in her eyes, Andy knew that there was no point in denying it.

"How did you find out? The police weren't supposed to tell anyone. That was part of the deal."

"It wasn't the police. I just put two and two together. The bandage on your head. New school, everybody being super nice to you. The bank never said who returned the money, but they did release a picture of the backpack, and guess what? It's the same one you have."

"You're not going to tell anyone, are you?" Andy asked.

"I don't understand why you're being so . . . humble about it all."

"Because I didn't really do anything except almost get killed and give back something that didn't belong to me in the first place."

"Well, that's better than actually *getting* killed, isn't it? I heard there was a homeless guy who disappeared, like it was a magic trick. Kablooey and—pffft—he's gone!"

"It's not funny," said Andy, realizing for the first time that Winter's name was perfect for her: She was cold as January in New Hampshire, as his mom would say. "Geez. Maybe he was homeless, but that was a person. He was somebody's friend. Maybe even somebody's brother. He *died*. I don't think we should be joking about that."

He thought for a moment that he had made her mad by criticizing her, but she just laughed it off. "Oh, right. Sorry. Sometimes, I just blurt out stuff like that without thinking. No, you're absolutely right. I probably shouldn't do it. I mean, I *definitely* shouldn't."

She didn't sound convincing at all to Andy.

"Anyway, back to you and the money. I mean, *why*? What made you want to give it back? You're not, like, filthy rich, are you?"

"Psshhht. No. Definitely not."

"Then . . . I don't get it. I'm trying to understand, really, I am."

Andy couldn't help noticing the expression of utter confusion on her face at that moment. The thought of doing something that had no direct benefit to her was completely foreign to her.

"You sound like my dad," he said. And then he did something unusual: He lied. Or, as he would tell Silas later, he merely "stretched the truth" about his father, letting Winter believe that the Howard Twopenny she heard on the radio was the same person as Howard Llewellyn. "He doesn't get it, either. After I gave the money back, he cut off my allowance completely. He won't even give me money for lunch. Luckily, my mom sneaks it into my backpack when he isn't around. I don't know what else I can tell you. The money didn't belong to me. It belongs to the people at the bank and their customers."

"Yeah, but you could have been killed! One step closer and you'd have been a goner."

"It's not the bank's fault that some wacko decided to blow himself up in their lobby."

"Look, Andy, Ms. Albemarle really likes you. She says you're perfect for the control room. If we're going to be working together, we need to get to know each other better.

So here's the thing: I want to do a news story about you. I already told Deanna Decameron about you, and she said it sounded like a great piece. If we do a good job, they'll run it on the network! That's national television, Andy. You'll be famous."

"No way. I am not going on TV. Ever. Even if I wanted to, my dad would kill me."

"Don't forget—he works for NTRP now. I'm sure he could be talked into it."

"It's not going to happen."

"But, Andy, you're a *hero*. The people want to hear your story. They need stuff like that to give them hope that the world isn't as bad as they think. They need *you*."

"Yeah, to humiliate me. They're not looking for people who do good things. Look around, Winter. The most popular show on TV right now is *How Far Will You Go?* Last week, the woman who ended up in second place—and I only know this because my dad told me about it—shaved her own kid's head and forced her to pretend that she had cancer so she could start this fake charity. And she was only *second* place! Do you know what that means? There was somebody worse than her! So, no thanks."

"Wow, you're serious, aren't you? I like this side of you. Kind of fierce, you know? But I'm not giving up. I am *so* going to talk you into this."

27

At the end of a long day of classes, Andy sat cross-legged on the floor next to his locker, weeding through a stack of textbooks and corresponding notebooks. "Don't need. Need. Need. Need. Don't need," he chanted. When he finished, he stuffed the need pile, which was nearly a foot high, into his backpack and returned the don't-need pile to the bottom shelf of the locker.

"Having a nice chat with all your friends?" asked Jensen, who had been watching and listening from a doorway a few yards away.

Andy closed his eyes and swore under his breath; he had hoped to sneak out of the building without running into anyone he knew. All he wanted was to go home, take Penny for a walk, and then get started on the several hours of homework that lay ahead. It was a few more seconds before he got Jensen's little poke at him. "Oh. All my friends. That's funny." He was too tired to smile.

"What's *your* problem?"

He held up his planner, pointing to the list of assignments.

Jensen shrugged. "Welcome to Wellbourne. So, remember that woman I met at that stupid NTRP conference?"

"No. Should I?"

"If you're serious about being a journalist, yes. Jill Clermont. From 233dotcom. She started the company with a couple of friends when they were still in college. But here's the thing: I asked her what the *233* stood for, and she didn't know. It was called GlobalBooks when she owned it. Anyway, things were going well, they were starting to make money, and then NTRP came along and bought the whole company. And changed the name to 233dotcom."

"So?"

"So, I met with her yesterday, and she was very cool. I mean, I'm still not crazy about the idea that books are going to disappear when the computer grid crashes, but when GlobalBooks started out, they actually had some good intentions. The only books they were replacing were the older, less used ones that had been sitting on the shelves for years without anybody checking out. The schools traded the old books for digital copies, and then GlobalBooks sent the paper ones to schools all over the world. Anything newer or more popular, they left alone."

"But *all* the books are gone from our library," said Andy.

"That's just it. When I told her about that, she *freaked* out, and it was the real thing. Nobody is that good an actor. She went *white*—like, even whiter than you. NTRP had promised to keep doing the old-book exchange and leave all the new stuff alone, but they obviously have other plans. So come on. Get your stuff. It's time."

"Time for what?"

"We're going on a little field trip."

"No. We're not."

"Yes. We are. Our school library is now in the hands of the network that proudly fills every hour of the day with the worst garbage imaginable. Do you really trust them to do *anything* that they say they will? Either to provide the digital books they say they will or to do something worthwhile with the ones they boxed up? And don't worry, you'll be home in plenty of time to get your homework done. Scout's honor." She held up her left hand, fingers spread in the Vulcan live-long-and-prosper salute.

"I don't think that's the Scout . . . I really can't go. I'm already . . . and my parents . . ."

He went.[1]

Which explains how Andy came to be trespassing at a warehouse on Willis Avenue in the Bronx—standing on a Dumpster and looking through the grimy windows—on

---

1. But then you knew he would, didn't you?

a school night. It had taken twice as long to get there as Jensen had promised, and Andy was already anxious about the time.

"I don't get it. Why are we here?" he asked. "So what. It's a warehouse."

"Remember all those boxes of books in the library?"

"What about them?"

"There they are."

"What are they doing here?"

"We're about to find out. Keep your head down—someone's coming."

"How did you *find* this place?"

A sly grin appeared on Jensen's face. "While they were loading up their truck, I, uh . . . *borrowed* their clipboard for a few minutes, long enough to get the address. Hey, what's going . . . Oh . . . my . . . God."

Andy stood on his tiptoes and pressed his face against the glass. A man in gray coveralls with the NTRP logo embroidered on the front was using a box cutter to open a carton of books labeled *B*. He held up a copy of Charlotte Brontë's classic novel *Jane Eyre,* smirking at the art on the cover that marked it as a work of serious literature. Meanwhile, another worker in the same coveralls, along with a pair of fireproof gloves, opened the heavy iron door of an incinerator, stepping back as the blast of heat hit him in the face.

"No. No, no, no," Jensen cried, loudly enough that Andy thought for sure that the men inside would hear.

They watched in horror as the first man wound up as if he were on the mound at Yankee Stadium and pitched *Jane Eyre* into the fire. "They can't . . . That's my favorite book. Why are they doing this?"

Wuthering Heights went into the flames next, followed by an armful of books by *B* authors: Blake, Browning, Buck, Byron, Burns, Boswell, and on and on. When the guys in coveralls got tired of digging in the box, they dumped the rest on the floor and began to toss them, three or four at a time, into the fire raging within the incinerator.

"I swear to God, if I could get in there, I would kill them both with my bare hands," said Jensen, and Andy believed her.

One of the men returned to the stack of cartons, accidentally kicking a dog-eared paperback across the floor. Around and around it spun, finally coming to rest directly beneath Jensen and Andy.

" '*Fahrenheit 451*. Ray Bradbury,' " Andy read from the front cover.

As angry as she was, Jensen laughed almost involuntarily. "Now, *that's* ironic."

"What do you mean?"

"Have you read it? *Fahrenheit 451*? It was dystopian before dystopian was cool. It's set in the future, and the government has outlawed books. They have these guys called firemen who go around burning all the books they find. Four hundred and fifty-one degrees is the temperature where paper starts to burn."

"Why did they outlaw books?"

"Because they want people to be stupid," said Jensen. "Stupid people don't question . . . Oh, my God. I think I just . . ." She took her phone from her pocket and tapped furiously for a few seconds. "You're not going to believe this. Guess what temperature four hundred and fifty-one degrees Fahrenheit is in Celsius."

She and Andy answered at the same time.

"Two hundred and thirty-three."

◆ ◆ ◆

Jensen Huntley wasn't the only one piecing together a story. When Andy told Silas what he had witnessed at the warehouse in the Bronx, and about the realization that 451 degrees Fahrenheit is equal to 233 degrees Celsius, something clicked in Silas's brain. The company, 233dotcom, had been mentioned, he was certain, in an article in the *New York Inquirer* a few months earlier, but when he searched online, the story had disappeared without a trace. That made him even more curious, so an hour later, he was once again pressing the buzzer to Ricky O'Day's apartment. He was the only person Silas knew who actually read the *Inquirer,* and even better, he never threw them out. In addition to being a computer genius, Ricky was a world-class hoarder.

"Now what?" he asked, opening his door.

Silas pointed at a stack of newspapers that reached the ceiling. "Are those organized?"

"Of course. They'd be kind of useless if they weren't in order."

"I'm looking for something from a few months ago. Probably April or May. Maybe March."

Ricky, his head tilted, glared at him. "I thought you said this was all a waste. That I would never need it. In fact, you said, and I quote, that *no one* would ever look at them, that ten minutes after they found my dead body, the entire contents of my apartment would be in a Dumpster. You called me a hoarder and inferred that I needed psychiatric help."

"I assume you mean that I *implied* it, but that's not right, either. I have *begged* you to seek help on a number of occasions. But now I see just how wrong I was, judging you like that. And, more important, how *right* you were, Ricky. I should have listened to you. You're not crazy. Now just show me where to look."

"That's all I wanted to hear," Ricky said with a triumphant grin. He patted a six-foot-tall pile of yellowing *Inquirer*s. "Here ya go." He returned to his sagging, smelly couch and within minutes was snoring loudly.

Silas went through twenty-three newspapers before he found what he was looking for, a short piece on page seventeen, under the byline Zhariah Davis. "Yes!" he shouted, waking Ricky, who jumped to his feet faster than one would have thought possible for someone his size.

"Oh, it's you. Forgot you were here," he said, breathing heavily.

On his way out the door, Silas turned and said, "You

don't mind if I take this, right? Great. See you around. Oh, and one more thing. I *was* right. For Pete's sake, Ricky, get some help. You look terrible."

Ricky swore at him and threw a half-full plastic soda bottle across the room, which Silas blocked with the door. "And get rid of all those newspapers!" Silas shouted before ducking down the stairs.

Pausing on the stoop of Ricky's building, he called Andy. "Sorry to call so late, kid, but it's important. Tomorrow morning, go to your locker and open up your history textbook. There's a section about John Paul Jones, the first—"

"I know who he is."

"Right. Of course. The model ships. You know your naval heroes. You're going to find an envelope with a copy of an article from the *New York Inquirer*. I'll make it look like something *you* printed out from a website. I want you to read it and then share it with your friend Jensen, but nobody else, okay? But here's the thing: You have to make her believe that you found it online, even though that would be impossible. This article has somehow disappeared from the paper's online archives."

"Then how did you get it?"

"I have a friend who has a little problem with throwing things away."

"A hoarder? Cool."

"Yeah . . . no. Nothing about Ricky is cool."

"What's the article about?"

"Philanthropy."

"What's that?"

"Philanthropists are people who give away their money to charitable causes. People like Winter's father."

"What does that have to do with me and Jensen?"

"Here's the short version: Last September, a dozen of the country's richest and most important philanthropists got together for a conference at a hotel here in New York. Since that meeting, eleven of the twelve have completely stopped giving to charity. Somebody at the *Inquirer* put it all together and wrote a piece about it, but the article was buried in the middle of the paper, and there was no follow-up, at least not that I'm aware of. And then, like I said, it disappeared completely."

"Why'd they stop?"

"That's what I want you to find out. One more thing: 233dotcom is connected . . . somehow, which means that NTRP is, too. Looks like a lot of companies presented new products at the conference, but the fact that they were there seems like a strange coincidence. If there's one thing NTRP hates, it's charity. Worth having you look into it, at least."

"How . . . where are we supposed to start?"

"You and Jensen are journalists. Start with the reporter. And remember, *quietly*."

28

Luckily for Andy, Jensen didn't ask too many questions about where he got the article. As expected, the brief mention of 233dotcom got her attention, and after dismissal they trekked across town to the dingy offices of the *New York Inquirer* on West Forty-Third Street in search of the reporter who had written the story. They signed in at the desk in the lobby and took the elevator to the nineteenth floor.

Jensen's face broke into a huge smile when the elevator door opened and they found themselves facing a bustling newsroom with more than thirty desks jammed together so closely that reporters and editors could barely squeeze between them. The floor itself was a snake pit of wires and cables connecting outdated, oversized computers with green flickering monitors and noisy printers. At a desk in the back corner, farthest from the door, an elderly man wearing a mismatched bow tie and suspenders pounded away on an enormous typewriter.

Jensen elbowed Andy. "Geez. I thought dinosaurs were extinct. A typewriter! And look at his *phone*. That thing must be from the sixties. It has a *dial*. This place is *awesome*."

"Maybe that elevator was really a time machine," said Andy, checking his watch, which, in a strange coincidence, had stopped a minute or two earlier.

From the doorway of a tiny office across the room, a chubby, red-faced man in a spaghetti-sauce-stained white shirt pointed accusingly at them. "What do *you* want?"

"I'm looking for Zhariah Davis," said Jensen, not at all intimidated.

"Who? There's nobody here with a crazy name like—"

A black woman in her mid-twenties sitting at the desk closest to Jensen cut him off. "Shut up, Louie. I've been here for three years." She pushed her chair back, cursing quietly at the thick cable catching the wheels for the zillionth time. She was tall—nearly six feet, with heels adding another three inches and the pile of braids on top of her head adding twice that—and she towered over both Jensen and Andy by almost a foot. "That's Louie. The city editor. He's an idiot. I'm Zhariah Davis. What can I do for you?"

Jensen showed her the article.

"Let's go in here a second," said Zhariah, leading them

into a small break room that reeked of burned coffee. "Can I ask . . . where you got this? It's not supposed to be . . ."

Jensen pointed at Andy. "He found it. He's kind of a hacker."

"I'm not a hacker," said Andy.

"Anyway," Jensen continued, "we're from Wellbourne Academy uptown, and we're working on a story for our school news show. This company that's mentioned at the end—233dotcom—is . . . well, they're supposedly replacing all the books in our library with digital copies, but . . ."

"But . . . what?" Zhariah asked, her eyes narrowing as her interest level increased.

"I . . . we followed them yesterday. They were supposed to be taking all the books to their warehouse, but when we got there, these guys in NTRP coveralls were *burning* them. Hundreds—thousands—of perfectly good books. Beautiful books. They burned *Jane Eyre*. Seriously, I may never recover from seeing that. It was like witnessing an execution."

"I hate that book," Zhariah said. "Poor little white girl has a tough childhood. Boo hoo. But whatever. Burning books is just . . . wrong. I knew they were dirty as soon as I found out they were connected to NTRP, but nobody believed me. Do you have proof?"

Jensen took out her phone and showed Zhariah the pictures she had taken through the warehouse window.

"This is horrible. I didn't think . . . It's like a real-life *Fahrenheit 451*," Zhariah whispered.

"Funny you should say that," said Jensen. "Guess what temperature four hundred fifty-one degrees Fahrenheit is equal to in Celsius? Two thirty-three."

Zhariah swore under her breath. "Are you sure? Science wasn't exactly my thing."

"Positive," Andy said.

"What are they up to?" Zhariah asked.

"That's what we were hoping to find out from you," said Jensen. "One day they're meeting with a bunch of charities, and the next they're burning a whole library's worth of books? Why did you stop covering this story?"

"I didn't want to, trust me. Do you have any idea how hard it was to get this far?" she asked, pointing at the article. "*Weeks*. A couple of hundred phone calls and emails, ninety-nine percent unanswered. But then, after the story was published, somebody must have come down hard on Louie, because he told me that if I *didn't* stop digging, I was going to lose my job. It had to be somebody above him. A bunch of suits came over and put the pressure on him, and he folded."

"Suits?" asked Andy.

"From the company that owns this little slice of paradise," said Zhariah, her arm sweeping to take in the entire dilapidated newsroom.

"Who's that?"

"Guess."

"NTRP?" Jensen and Andy asked together.

"Exactly," said Zhariah.

"They own everything," said Jensen. "And what they don't own, they're trying to buy."

"Well, whoever they are, they did their best to make the story disappear. Deleted it from my computer when I was out and had the tech guys take it down from the website. Even took my notes right out of my desk. That's why I was so surprised to see the article when you came in."

Jensen couldn't stop shaking her head. "This is crazy. Why are they so desperate to hide this story? It's interesting, but it doesn't seem *that* huge. I mean, is it really so shocking when people stop giving to charity? It must happen all the time." She turned to Andy. "And by the way, if it was deleted, how did *you* find it?"

"I, uh, I don't know. All of a sudden it was just there. Maybe it was an old copy. I don't remember exactly."

"You are such a bad liar," said Jensen. "Why can't you just admit that you're a hacker?"

"It doesn't matter," said Zhariah. "Something big is going on. I'm getting back on this story, I don't care what Louie says. Somebody who was at that conference has to be willing to talk. Something important happened there, something bad. People don't just stop giving to charities for no reason. The charities that they gave to didn't do anything wrong, and none of the rich people were going broke. I checked them out—they're all doing just fine."

"In your article, you said that one of them hadn't stopped. Have you talked to him?" Andy asked.

"*Her.* Her name is Ilene Porter, and she's the heir to

the Porter Paper fortune. She was out of the country when I wrote the story, and I couldn't get in touch with her. By the time she returned, I had been shut down. But as far as I know, she's still giving away money. She's still attending charity events, at least."

"Has she ever said anything publicly . . . about what she thinks happened?" asked Jensen.

"Not that I know of."

A voice shouted at Zhariah from the newsroom. "Davis! Line four! Someone from city hall! Mayor's office!"

"Be right there. I have to take this call, but thanks, guys. Email the pictures you took, if you don't mind."

"Okay, but we want to help, too," said Jensen.

Zhariah looked at her skeptically. "Look, I appreciate you—"

"You can trust us."

"It's not that. It's . . . you're kids, and I can't be responsible for—"

"You won't be," said Jensen. "Nobody has to know. You cover your story, we'll cover ours, and if we can help each other, we will. The fact that we're kids could help you. No offense, but nobody trusts reporters. As far as the world is concerned, Andy and I are just kids, and everybody knows that kids are apathetic losers. All they care about is themselves. And video games. And Instagram. We can *use* that."

Zhariah looked them up and down, chewing on her lip. "One word: Halestrom."

29

Andy stared out the rain-spattered window of the taxi as it sped west on Seventy-Ninth Street through Central Park. "Where are we going, anyway?" he asked without turning to look at Silas. He sounded tired and as if he was afraid of what Silas might tell him. "I have a lot of homework. I think I'm failing math. And English. I can barely keep up with all the reading. Between you and Jensen, I'm never home. And when I am, I hardly ever see my dad because of his new schedule. My mom is *still* in Africa, and I don't know when she's coming home, to be honest."

"I'm sure it's hard for her, too, being away for so long."

"Yeah, sure. She was just about ready, but then something *else* happened—she couldn't say what. She's as bad as you about all these secrets. When I ask her, she just tells me it will be soon."

"Sorry. That must be hard. I'm sure she's ready to come home, too. The first thing is for you to stop worrying so much. You're not failing anything at school. I've been keeping track. As a matter of fact, right now you're in the top twenty percent of your English and math classes."

"How do you . . . Oh, right."

"By the way, you got a ninety-one on the science quiz today. Third-highest grade in the class. Although I'm a little surprised that you confused igneous and metamorphic rock."

That little bit of good news had no effect on Andy's mood. He kept right on staring out the window of the taxi, so Silas tried again: "Look, Andy, I know this is hard sometimes, but what we—what *you*—are doing is important. If it weren't for people like you, the world would be . . . well, a lot worse than it is. We're almost there. Here, take this. Buy something for your mom—a welcome-home present. She likes to knit, right?" He handed Andy two crisp twenties as the taxi pulled up in front of a storefront on Ninety-First Street. "That should get you enough for a scarf. If you need more, just charge it. Your credit is good here."

"Enough . . . what?" he asked, trying unsuccessfully to read the sign outside the shop.

"Yarn, of course. What else would you knit with?"

"Wait. Where am I going? What . . . who's here?"

"Mrs. Cardigan, for one. You must have noticed her knitting the day you met her down at the Mission. This is her shop. There's someone else, too. A surprise. Someone who wants to meet you."

"In a *yarn* shop?"

Silas shrugged. "What can I say? She likes to knit."

The door jangled as Silas led Andy inside Marner's Wool Goods, which, according to a plaque hanging behind the cash register, was established in 1977. A quick glance around the room assured Silas that they had the place to themselves, which didn't surprise him. He'd been in that shop a hundred times and had seen actual customers maybe twice. If Mrs. Cardigan had actually had to depend on selling yarn to stay in business, she wouldn't have made it past 1978. A devoted, talented knitter herself, she had admitted on a number of occasions that she was her own best customer.

The walls in the narrow, claustrophobia-inducing space were lined with row upon row of dark wood shelves, the lowest at knee level and the highest requiring a ladder to reach. Every square inch of shelf space was stacked with skeins of yarn, thousands and thousands of them, in every color imaginable and in many that were, frankly, *unimaginable*.

Mrs. Cardigan sat in a wing chair upholstered in fabric that mimicked the symphony of colors that surrounded her. She looked up and smiled when Silas and Andy came in. Her kindly, deep-set eyes sparkled with intelligence and wit, but her knitting needles clicked on; they never stopped moving. Hanging from them was a sock in a deep, rich green with two narrow purple stripes.

"Great color combination," Silas said. "Who are they for?"

She smiled up at him. "Thank you. I agree. I wasn't sure at first, but the colors are growing on me. There. Finished."

Silas noted that she hadn't answered his question, and he knew her well enough to know that she had no intention of doing so. Rather than pursuing the subject, he pushed Andy toward her. "Mrs. Cardigan, you remember Andy."

"Of course. How are you, Andover? Thank you for coming out tonight. I'm sure you have lots and lots of schoolwork that you could be doing."

"Oh, no . . . I'm okay," he lied.

"Hmm. That's not the story I got," said Silas, smiling. "Andy, I think I should tell you a little about Mrs. Cardigan's personal philosophy. She believes—strongly—that nothing bad will happen to a person who wears wool socks, so she knits them for everyone she knows. It's not as crazy as it sounds. According to her logic, a person whose feet are properly attired is probably well prepared in *every* way— 'ready for anything,' as she is fond of saying."

"Thank you, Silas," said Mrs. Cardigan. "You're learning." She removed the half-glasses she wore and let them fall to her chest, where they dangled from a chain. Deliberately, she laid her knitting on the arm of the chair and stood to address Andy. "There's someone I want you to meet. Someone you're going to be working with." She guided his eyes to the second armchair. Squished against the back of it, with her feet tucked completely beneath her, sat a much younger woman, her cropped black hair punctuated by a comma of bright orange curling around her left ear.

"Hey," she said, springing to her feet while still on the chair and then hopping to the floor in front of a very surprised Andy. "I'm Karina Jellyby. I hear you go to Wellbourne. Great school. Wow. You were right, Mrs. C.—he's *cute*. Look, I'm making him blush."

"Easy, Karina," Silas said. "We don't want to scare him off. Winter Neale is making him uncomfortable enough."

Andy had met a few sort-of-famous people at the radio station, but Karina was his first honest-to-God celebrity, and he seemed to be frozen in place. Finally, his mouth started to work again. "Wh-what are you doing . . . *here?*" He glanced up at the miles of yarn. "Don't you have a concert, like, every night?"

"I've got a gig downtown later. But we don't go on until ten or ten-thirty. In the meantime, Mrs. Cardigan is teaching me to knit." She held up her knitting needles, which held the first two inches of a red wool sock. "What do you think?"

Mrs. Cardigan lifted her glasses to her eyes for a closer look. "Not bad. I know it's a school night, and I don't want to keep you out too late, so what do you say we have a cup of tea and a little chat? We'd better move into the back room, just to be safe. Is everyone okay with Lapsang?"

Andy's ears perked up at the mention of Penny's "magic word" and watched as Mrs. Cardigan spooned loose black stuff into a cast-iron teapot and poured boiling water over it. He turned to Silas and whispered, "What is it?"

"It's a kind of tea. It's a tradition around here. You'll . . . learn to like it."

"Lapsang souchong," said Mrs. Cardigan as the smoky scent filled the air. "My favorite. Have you ever had it?"

"I . . . I don't think so."

"You're in for a treat, then. This comes from one of the finest estates in China. All handpicked leaves. This tin was a gift from an agent in Hong Kong."

"It's smoked over pinewood branches. At first, I thought it was a bit funky," Karina admitted, "but now I love it—the smell reminds me of the beach parties we had up on the coast of Maine when I was a kid."

"Supposedly, it was Winston Churchill's favorite," Silas added as Mrs. Cardigan filled a mug for Andy. "Try it with milk and sugar first."

Andy made a face when he tasted it and then added two more sugar cubes and another splash of milk. "That's better."

The back room at Marner's Wool Goods is about as different from the front as can be. Instead of shelves of yarn, knitting needles, and instruction books, the walls are covered from floor to ceiling with electronic equipment. Dozens of television screens and computer monitors show locations all over New York City, with banks of flashing lights seeming to insist on proving how hard they are working at whatever it is they're doing.

"Whoa. What is this place?" asked Andy.

"Not exactly what you were expecting, is it?" Karina said. "I remember my first time."

"We call it the Loom," said Mrs. Cardigan, motioning to Andy to sit between her and Karina at the long, narrow table. "A loom, as I'm sure you know, is a machine used to weave yarn into cloth. In this room, information is our raw material. We gather it and piece it together and, we hope, weave it into something useful."

Andy glanced up at the screen directly across the table from him. "Hey, I've been there. That's the entrance to the NTRP building. What are all those blue dots down at the bottom?"

"Each one of those dots represents a Syngian *inside* the building," said Silas. "We've been tracking it twenty-four/ seven, three hundred sixty-five days a year, since 2009. There was a gas leak in the area, and the entire building had to be evacuated. When the fire department let people back inside, we started counting, and we've been counting ever since. We have every exit and entrance covered, so we always know exactly how many Syngians are inside at any moment. We have some . . . new technology that picks up where Lucian Glass and the dogs like Penny leave off. That's what the number at the bottom left is."

"So, there's *exactly* thirty-nine of them in there right now? Why do you need to know that?"

Everyone in the room turned to Mrs. Cardigan, who smiled. "The operation started out as a way to keep track of the other side's important operatives—when they left, where they went, whom they met, and so on. But then we began to notice a pattern. There were more Syngians leaving the building than had gone in. At first, we thought it was an instrument malfunction, but over the past year, we have confirmed our worst fear: NTRP has learned how to inoculate people with the *lumen lucidus,* almost as if it were a virus. It changes them permanently."

"Th-they can? How?"

"We don't know yet, but we do know that they're getting better at it. We think it might be similar to what happens to domesticated pigs who escape captivity. In just a few weeks without human contact, they start to turn wild again. Not only their behavior—they change physically, too. They start to resemble wild boars. Their hair grows longer. They grow tusks. And they become very, very dangerous. It's quite an astonishing transformation."

"So . . . you're saying that people are like pigs?" said Andy.

"Well, not exactly. Think of your brain as a bank of switches—thousands of them—that regulate how you look, what you like, everything about who you are. Each switch is either on or off; it's that simple."

"We're learning about that in school," said Andy. "That's how computers think. Everything is either zero or one."

"Exactly—a binary code. The things that make us

civilized—our language, our ability to feel love and com-passion for others—those are switches, too. NTRP, it seems, has learned how to flip those switches from on to off. Right now the only thing we know for sure is that it's top-secret, even within NTRP. They call it Opera-tion Tailor—we think it's called that because they're do-ing *alterations* to the person's personality, maybe even their DNA. Only the people at the top seem to know much about it. When we first noticed what was going on, they were al-tering only one or two people a month on average. Now they're up to thirty—about one a day—and the rate is in-creasing quickly."

"And it's all the work of this man," Silas said, sliding St. John de Spere's file down the table.

Andy picked it up and glanced at the photo inside. "Hey, this is the guy who was talking to Winter. His first name is Saint John? That's weird."

"It's pronounced *Sinjin*. It's a British thing. Not that he's remotely British. From the little we've gathered about him, he appears to be from the Midwest. Ohio, maybe. The name St. John, we think, is a pun, just him having a little fun at our expense—St. John, Syngian."

Andy's eyebrows arched. "You mean he knows about . . . all this? All of you? All of *us*?"

"He knows we're watching," Mrs. Cardigan an-swered. "Just like we know they're watching us. Unfor-tunately, ninety-nine percent of what we learn is garbage, information that, on purpose, just *happens* to slip out. Naturally, we do the same to them. That's how it's been for a long, long time."

"But thanks to you, we finally have some hard information right from the horse's mouth," said Karina, reaching over to pat Andy on the shoulder. "These guys told me about your little adventure on the sixty-sixth floor. Nice work. Of course, I'm not exactly thrilled that I'm their target."

"Couldn't you just ... cancel the concert?" Andy asked. After a moment of silence in which everyone looked at one another, he added, "I mean, if you *know* something bad is going to happen."

"We considered that," said Mrs. Cardigan. "However, the concert represents a unique opportunity, a controlled environment. For once, they have no idea that we know they're planning something. If we stop now, that window closes, maybe forever."

Karina continued: "A couple of weeks ago, I met with Dr. Everly and others from Wellbourne, along with NTRP's Deanna Decameron. NTRP is especially eager to use the concert to show off what they're calling a new education tool. They won't say much about it except that it involves holograms and that it is going to change video presentations forever."

"As you can imagine, we're quite skeptical about their commitment to education," said Mrs. Cardigan. "It's very likely that this machine of theirs has something to do with what's going on inside the NTRP tower, but until we see it in action, there's not much we can do about it."

"The risk," Silas explained, "is that we don't know *enough*. We know the when and the where—it's Friday in Wellbourne's auditorium—but we don't know what they're planning or how they're going to do it. It's possible that we won't be able to prevent the attack. That is the real risk. The Agents, however, have unanimously agreed that it is worth taking."

"And that's why you're here tonight, Andy," said Mrs. Cardigan. "There are only a few days until the concert. Keep your eyes and ears open for anything unusual. If there's a way to be close to Winter, do it, even if you don't want to. Take advantage of the fact that she trusts you. Believe me, if the situation were reversed, if she knew who *you* were, she would attach herself to you at the hip."

"I'm going to set up an interview at the school," Karina said. "And we'll make sure that you and Winter get the assignment. Keep doing what you've been doing and you'll be fine, Andy. You're a natural at this stuff. When I was your age, there was no way I could have done what you're doing."

"I couldn't agree more," added Mrs. Cardigan. "And remember, we're here to help you. If anything is bothering you or if something doesn't feel quite right or if you just need someone to talk to, call us or send us a text—doesn't matter what time it is or how unimportant you think it might be. Okay?"

Andy nodded. "I will. I don't want to, you know, let you guys—and Brother Lucian—down."

Mrs. Cardigan took his shoulders in her hands. "You won't."

Maybe it was Mrs. Cardigan, who has a habit of bringing out the best in people, or maybe it was Karina, who shot him the smile that a million teenage boys would have killed for. Then again, maybe it was the image of Winter's *lumen lucidus* that had been burned onto his retinas. Whatever it was, at that moment, everyone in that room saw the look in his eyes and knew—*knew* that Andy was truly one of them.

◆ ◆ ◆

In St. John de Spere's penthouse on the other side of town, another meeting was taking place. After a vegan dinner prepared by his private chef, de Spere passed his guests a box of chocolates from a famous London department store.

"I have it on the highest authority that these are the Queen's favorites," he said, nibbling at one with a candied violet on top.

"The Queen must not have any taste buds," said Winter, shuddering. "It tastes like *soap*."

Fontaine Neale laughed aloud. "That's because they're made from flowers. An acquired taste, perhaps. Your father shares your opinion of them."

"Ah, speaking of your dearly beloved," said de Spere,

"where is the great man tonight? Handing out millions to orphans in Cambodia? Building a hospital in Zimbabwe? One never knows with him. So much money, so little time to give it away."

Fontaine rolled her eyes at the mention of her husband. "Who knows? Yesterday, he called from some hellhole in Africa. He rambled on for a while about a civil war, and there was something about land mines—isn't there always? I tuned him out after a while. He's so *predictable*."

"Hey, that's my *father* you're mocking," said Winter, not bothering to hide her wicked grin. "You won't be laughing when he wins the Nobel Peace Prize."

"Oh, *please*," said Fontaine. "As if he isn't insufferable enough already."

"Don't complain too much," said de Spere. "Since I brought you two together, your standard of living has been elevated several notches. Of course, now that Winter has come of age and her powers are exceeding even our wildest dreams—thanks in part to him, don't forget—perhaps it is time to bring him over to our side. That event at the Halestrom was supposed to have taken care of this unhealthy appetite for helping people." He chose another chocolate, this one topped with a rose petal, and turned his gaze to Eugene Ickes, his hipster henchman.

"There were circumstances beyond my control," said Ickes. "No one knew that a volcano in Iceland would cause his flight to be delayed. It's not a problem. We can take care of him whenever we want. Will he be at the concert?"

"No, he's not due back until a few days afterward," said Fontaine.

"It doesn't matter," said de Spere. "A minor concern in the grand scheme of things. We need to focus on the job at hand. Karina Jellyby will be a modern-day Pied Piper, leading two hundred and fifty lambs to the slaughter, and the beautiful thing is, she won't even know she's doing it. Eugene here is in charge of setting up my equipment before the concert."

"What about the loose end from the Halestrom Conference?" Fontaine asked.

St. John de Spere sighed. "Ah. Ilene Porter. I can't explain why she wasn't affected. I've tested the equipment over and over, and it all checks out. She was sitting between two of the others. I'm more concerned with that nosy reporter from the school—Jensen Huntley. Somehow, she found her and is asking questions."

"Is it going to be a problem?" asked Fontaine.

"No, ma'am," said Ickes. "I have the situation under control."

I'VE BEEN WEARING WOOL SOCKS FOR YEARS, IN CASE YOU'RE WONDERING. AND AS I WRITE THIS, A PAIR IS BEING KNIT FOR YOU, TOO. I HOPE YOU LIKE BLUE. WHAT AM I SAYING? OF COURSE YOU DO—IT'S YOUR FAVORITE COLOR

30

Jensen stood in front of Wellbourne's impressive bronze doors, her arms crossed, scowling at everyone who attempted to be friendly to her and stubbornly ignoring the raindrops that spattered the pavement at her feet. When she spotted Andy hurrying to cross the street against the light, she stiffened, pressing herself against one of the Ionic columns that framed the front doors, ready to pounce. With his hands deep in his pockets and the hood of his sweatshirt pulled over his head, he bounded up the steps two at a time, eager to get out of the rain. Poor Andy. He didn't know that he was running headlong into Tropical Storm Jensen.

She threw out an arm, clotheslining him and all but knocking him off his feet.

He backed away, shaking his head and holding his throat

where she'd caught him. "What the . . . What is *wrong* with you?"

"Why didn't you answer my text?"

"What are you . . . What text?"

"Don't play dumb. The one I sent you last night."

Andy pulled out his phone and pulled up his recent text messages. "I didn't get . . . I checked before I went to bed. Oh, here it is. I swear, I didn't see it."

"Right."

"Wait. You sent this at one o'clock in the morning."

"So?"

"I went to sleep at ten-thirty. I'm not like you, Jensen. I actually need sleep. What does this mean, anyway? 'I found her'—found who?"

"I don't know if I want to tell you now. God, you're such a *baby*. I didn't realize you had a *bedtime*."

"It's not my bedtime. It's when I choose to go to bed. I can't help it if I actually want to do good in school."

"*Well,*" said Jensen, cracking a smile.

"Well, what? What's so funny?"

"You. Mr. All Holier-Than-Thou. I think you meant to say that you want to do *well* in school."

Andy stood there a second, openmouthed. "It's like you're *trying* to get me to not like you. Guess what? It's working. You're like Jekyll and Hyde."

"Oh, lighten up. I texted you because I trust you, Sandy. I *found* her."

From the look on his face, it was obvious Andy didn't know who "her" was.

"The lady from the article? Ilene Porter? Remember? The Halestrom Conference? Geez. It's true; being in love does make you stupid."

"I'm not—"

"Right. Anyway, she checked in to a hotel down in the Village, and she has a lunch reservation in their restaurant for tomorrow at one-thirty—don't ask how I know. So, right after school, we are going to boogie on down there. Just you and me. I figure that if we get there by three, she'll still be there. Do you *know* how huge this is? Well, that is, it *will be* if we can talk her into an interview." Jensen pinched his cheek. "But how could she resist this bee-yoo-tee-ful face?"

Andy brushed her hand off and backed away from Jensen in preparation for the second wave. "I can't."

"You can't . . . what?"

"Go with you. Tomorrow. After school."

"Why not?"

"I'm, uh, doing an interview here . . . in the studio . . . with Winter. Now, before you explode, Ms. Albemarle asked me."

Jensen's scowl returned. "Who are you interviewing?"

"It's kind of a secret, so you can't tell anybody." He looked over Jensen's shoulders, then behind him, to make sure no one was listening. "Karina Jellyby."

Jensen, her face turning eggplant purple, squeezed her eyes shut and spit out the name through gritted teeth: "Karina Jellyby. A celebrity interview. And here I was, thinking you were serious about journalism. You're just like the rest of them."

Without another word, she turned her back on him and walked away.

◆ ◆ ◆

Their paths crossed twice more that day in the Wellbourne halls. Andy tried to get her attention, but Jensen continued on her way, her eyes never meeting his. As he stood there looking like a lost puppy for the second time, he felt a tap on his shoulder.

"Hey," said Winter.

"Oh. Hi."

Winter motioned down the hall with her chin. "What's wrong with Jensen?"

"It's a long story."

She took him by the arm, walking him down the hall. "So, have you thought any more about letting me interview you? I'm sorry if I came on kind of strong in the park that day, but it is *such* a good story."

Though he had no intention of doing the interview, Andy decided it would be best if he kept her hope alive. "I'm thinking about it."

"You are? That's great! I'm making progress. You've

gone from no way to maybe. I promise not to bug you about it every day, but promise me that you'll let me know if you change your mind, okay?"

"Okay. I don't think I will, but . . . I promise."

"So—did you hear the other news? The Karina Jellyby concert is going to be *here at Wellbourne*! How awesome is that?"

Andy smiled and pretended to be impressed by the news, even though he had known about it for over a week.

"And Karina has asked to do an exclusive interview with *me*. I guess Deanna Decameron told her all about me, so she had her publicist get in touch with Ms. Albemarle over the weekend and set the whole thing up. And now the really good news. Well, I think it's good, anyway. You might disagree. Ms. A. wants us to work together. Isn't that amazing?"

"Uh, yeah."

"You don't exactly seem thrilled. I thought you were a fan."

"I was. I am."

"You'd just rather not work with me." Winter stuck her bottom lip out, pretending to be sad. "Come on. I promise to behave myself. Cross my heart. I won't even mention that other story—at least until we finish this one."

"What other story?"

"You know—*your* story."

"Oh. Right. So, if I agree to do this, will I get to meet Karina?"

"Of course! Come on, let's get started right now. I have a million ideas. For the intro segment, we're going to pull together some old videos from when she was a student here. She was in all the musicals, I've heard. She was Dorothy in *The Wizard of Oz* and Éponine in *Les Misérables*. I already checked with Mr. Brookings in the library, and he's pulling them for me . . . us. And then we need to come up with a million questions. Maybe two million. We'd better get to work."

"I thought you didn't like her music."

"Who told you *that*? I *love* it."

"The first day I met you, when I said I was listening to her, you were like, 'She's okay.'"

"I must have been trying to impress you," she said, touching him lightly on the arm and flashing a dazzling smile. "You know, like Jensen and those other cool, hip kids who only listen to bands nobody's ever heard of. And as soon as you *have* heard of them, they suddenly don't like them anymore because they 'sold out' by making music that somebody actually wants to listen to."

Andy didn't respond. The fact is, Winter's description of Jensen's listening habits was spot on.

31

Jensen continued to ignore Andy's attempts to communicate in person or by electronic means for the next two days. He logged on to her website to read her latest anti-NTRP rant but only made it halfway through before he was bumped off. When he tried to log in again, a message flashed on his screen: *ACCESS DENIED. GO AWAY. THERE'S NOTHING ABOUT CELEBRITIES HERE.*

"Let me see what I can do," Silas said when Andy told him what was going on. "I'll send someone to keep an eye on her. If she's making progress on that Halestrom story, I want to know about it. I can't imagine that this woman— Ilene Porter—is going to talk to a conspiracy nut with a blog that she won't let anyone read, but you never know. Stranger things have happened. In the meantime, I'll get you access to her website, and she won't be able to tell that it's you. In fact, she won't even know that anyone is looking."

◆ ◆ ◆

At the Brink with Jensen Huntley

It's a school night and I should be studying for a big chemistry exam, but I'm
still riding a wave of adrenaline, and
won't be able to concentrate until I get
something down in writing.

Yesterday, I met with someone who attended a meeting of some of the country's
richest and most generous philanthropists
at the Halestrom Hotel a few months back.
She gave me a very strange account of what
happened during a presentation by one of
the sponsoring companies. But that's only
half of the story. What you probably don't
know (because it's been COVERED UP!) is
that in the short time since that conference, every attendee (except my source)
has STOPPED writing checks for charities.
I don't know what really happened that
day, but I'm going to find out. And if my

hunch is right, this will be the biggest
story since Watergate.

The end isn't near. It's here.

◆ ◆ ◆

Silas's go-to computer guy, Ricky O'Day, had no trouble
finding a way into Jensen's website, so Silas saw that blog
entry only a few minutes after she posted it, and he immediately had a bad feeling about it. Mostly, he was afraid
for Ilene Porter and Jensen, and with good reason. When
Ricky was snooping around the site, he was able to get
a look at a list of its regular visitors. There weren't that
many, so Silas had him track them down to see who they
were, what other sites they visited, that sort of thing.
Everybody checked out okay except the visitor who logged
in as THESAINT.

"He's good, whoever he is," said Ricky, a note of ad-
miration in his voice. "He didn't wanna be tracked. He left
behind a winding, twisted trail that bounces from computer
to computer, on and on."

Ricky, however, is as tenacious as a bloodhound on the
trail of a fugitive from a chain gang. After guzzling the last
third of a huge bottle of cola spiked with extra caffeine,
he leaned back in his chair and pointed at the map on his
enormous monitor.

"That's as close as I can get," he said. "THESAINT logged in from a computer in the building at the corner of Park and Forty-Fifth."

The muscles in Silas's face tightened, and he forgot to breathe for a long time as he stared at the screen, where a green arrow blinked, pointing accusingly at the NTRP Broadcast Center.

"Ricky, listen carefully. I want you to clear your search history right now so there's absolutely no trace of any of this information on your computer. It's for your own safety. You've never heard of Jensen Huntley, and you've never seen her website. And I was never here. Do you understand?"

Ricky cocked his head, not sure if Silas was serious until he saw the look on his face. "Like, you're serious. Okay. You're the boss." He seemed a bit frazzled after that, but he wiped the last half hour of activity from his hard drive. "All done."

"One more thing," Silas added on his way out the door. "Your parents have a place down on the beach in South Carolina, right? This might be a good time for a visit."

"Are you serious?"

"Just for a few days, until this blows over."

Or blows up, he thought.

◆ ◆ ◆

Silas really wanted to talk to Jensen Huntley, but he knew that she would never tell a total stranger whatever it was that Ilene Porter had told her. Not that he could blame her. She worked hard to get the story—why shouldn't she be suspicious of someone appearing from nowhere and asking questions. So, after leaving Ricky's apartment on the Upper East Side, he hurried downtown to the Newgate Hotel, where, according to Billy Newcomb (who had followed her on Silas's orders), Jensen had, in fact, met with Ms. Porter.

The uniformed doorman greeted him as he strolled into the slice of old-time New York that is the Newgate Hotel lobby. Crystal chandeliers shimmered, polished black-and-white marble floors shone, and the grand piano glistened, its keys tickled by an ancient, frowning man whose toupee appeared to be sliding off the back of his head. Silas took a seat at the bar and ordered a club soda, casually mentioning to the bartender that he was a few minutes early for a meeting with a guest at the hotel. From where he sat, he could see the lone desk clerk, and when she turned away to answer the phone, he slipped off his barstool and into the elevator. He got off on the twenty-eighth floor and stood for a second outside room 2801, listening. When he raised his hand to knock, though, he saw that the door wasn't closed all the way. Something on the floor—a plaid wool scarf—had prevented the door from latching.

He knocked quietly once, then again. No answer.

"Ms. Porter? Hello?" Still nothing, so he took a breath and stuck his head through the door. "Ms.

Porter?" The room was completely dark, so he reached in and hit the light switch on the wall, expecting to hear her cry out any second. But there was no cry, or any other sound.

Ilene Porter was dead.

32

Ironically, Silas had gone to the Newgate to tell Ilene Porter that there was a *small* possibility that her life might be in danger and that she might want to take the same advice he'd offered Ricky: to lie low for a while, until whatever was about to happen happened. Obviously, he had underestimated the danger—not that it mattered to her now.

As he evaluated the situation, Silas considered the possibility—for about half a second—that it was all a coincidence, that Ilene Porter had died of natural causes. "Right," he muttered. "And I'll be heading back uptown in a chariot pulled by a team of subway rats."

He was not surprised when his quick inspection revealed no signs of foul play. There wasn't a mark on her body, and he was willing to bet that nothing unusual would show up on blood tests in a coroner's report, either. None of that meant she hadn't been murdered, only that she'd been done in by professionals—the kind of people who worked for St. John de Spere.

She was on the floor, between the bed and the desk, on her side. Silas's first guess was that she had been crawling toward the telephone, but he quickly changed his mind about that when he saw the corner of a cell phone sticking out from beneath her body, inches from her left hand. It was reckless, he knew, to stay in that room a second longer, but he just had to check that phone. He slipped on a pair of thin cotton gloves and used Ilene Porter's index finger to press the on button and to do the swipe across the phone to unlock it, breathing a sigh of relief when it didn't ask for a password. The screen revealed a text message exchange she'd had with Jensen earlier in the day. Nothing caught his attention until Jensen's last text:

Send me a postcard from Africa. My address is ████████ ████████.

"Oh, Jensen. You foolish, foolish girl."

◆ ◆ ◆

Silas was already out of the Newgate and on his phone to Andy when he remembered that he had forgotten to wipe his own fingerprint from the light switch. He swore silently. A small mistake, but a mistake just the same, and he knew that in his business anything less than perfect could spell disaster. However, he also knew how foolish it would be to risk a return to Ilene Porter's room, so he put it out of his mind for the moment.

"Andy. Listen, I need you to do something right now. . . . I know it's late, I know it's a school night, but this is really, really important. Can you get out of your apartment?"

"I don't know—"

"It's Jensen. She's in danger. Serious danger."

"What? Why?"

"I don't have time to explain it now. She needs to get out of her apartment—fast. I would do it, but I'm all the way downtown. And besides, she doesn't know me."

"Okay, okay, I'll do it. I'll tell my dad I'm taking Penny for a walk. What do you want me to do when I get there? What if she won't come down? She's still mad at me. She won't answer her phone. And what if her parents are there?"

"Just get her out of the apartment, whatever it takes. Tell her you're in trouble at school and you really need to talk to someone. You'll think of something. Take her up to Eighty-Sixth Street and wait outside Burgers&Burritos— you know the place, right? Try to blend into the crowd, and wait there until you hear from me."

"I'm on my way."

Andy and Penny ran the seven blocks to Jensen's, stopping in front of a beautiful prewar building. "Okay, Penny. This is it." After catching his breath, he stepped into the lobby and announced to the doorman, with all the confidence he could muster, "I'm here to see Jensen Huntley."

"You and everybody else," said the doorman. "She's a popular kid tonight. Had a feeling somebody'd figure it out sooner or later."

"Wh-what do you mean? Figure what out? Who?"

"The cops." He pointed at a security monitor behind his desk. "Here they come now."

Andy and Penny backed up as two burly uniformed policemen, one on each side of Jensen, half led and half pulled her into the lobby.

Her eyes met his in silent but clear warning not to say anything as she twisted away from the cops. She kneeled, throwing her arms around Penny's neck, and looked up at Andy. "Omigosh, I love this dog. It's so strange—you live in the building, but I haven't seen you for so long."

"Hey, let's go," said the bigger of the two cops, roughly pulling Jensen away from Penny, whose posture and attitude changed immediately. She snarled at him, baring her teeth to show that she meant business.

"Easy, Pen," said Andy, caught by surprise. He'd never seen her behave like that before, toward anyone, and didn't want to add to Jensen's problems, whatever they were, by having Penny attack the police, so he whispered the magic word in her ear: "Lapsang."

"Step aside, kid," said the second cop, jabbing a meaty finger right in Andy's chest. "Now. And keep that mutt under control, or I'll have the dogcatcher down here."

Penny twitched under Andy's hand but kept her cool, to Andy's relief. *Good girl.*

With all the attention on Jensen, Andy dared to take a quick peek through his glass medallion. Two cops, two *lumens*. They're *everywhere.*

The doorman followed the two cops and Jensen out the door to their waiting car. "Miss Huntley, do you want me to call . . . anyone?"

Jensen turned around to answer him but looked directly at Andy. "There's no one to call."

Then four hands pushed her into the backseat of a black sedan—not a regular police car—which disappeared into the night.

"What did she mean, there's no one to call?" Andy asked the doorman. "Where are her parents?"

"This is just between you and me, right? Her parents ain't been here for five, six months. They're in Shanghai or Singapore, 'bout a million miles from here, on some kind of big business deal. Jen's on her own. A few of us keep an eye on her, help her out if she needs a hand. I guess they send her money, 'cause she ain't starving."

◆ ◆ ◆

"Well, that answers a lot of questions about Jensen," Silas said when Andy and Penny showed up outside Burgers&Burritos without her.

"What's going to happen to her?" Andy asked. "I don't get it. What did she do wrong? The cops ought to arrest her *parents*. Well, I guess she's not in danger, anyway, as long as she's with the police."

"Those weren't cops."

"Wh-what do you mean? They had uniforms. And badges."

"I'm sure they did."

Andy scrunched his lips to one side as he thought back to their *lumens* and connected the dots. "They're . . . Syngians? So . . . Jensen's not . . . out of danger?"

"Not even close. I'm sure if I check the security cameras at her building, we'll see two NTRP employees dressed up like cops." He pulled up Jensen's last blog post on his phone. "This made *somebody* nervous. She spent a lot of time the past couple of days talking to Ilene Porter. According to this, she was going to spill the whole story sometime tomorrow. But I'm afraid that even if she already wrote it and set up a timed release of the story on her website, there's no way NTRP is going to let that happen. Every trace of her website will be gone within the hour. And Ilene Porter . . ."

"What?"

Silas hesitated. He had to tell Andy the truth—he owed him that much—but he was afraid of how the poor kid might react. "Ilene Porter is dead. I went to her hotel to warn her, but somebody else got there first."

His face turning white, Andy stammered, "I—I

was supposed to go with Jensen to see her. I *should* have gone, except I was doing what you told me I had to do—babysitting Winter, who still hasn't actually *done* anything wrong, as far as I can see. And now she's . . . Are they going to kill Jensen, too?" He started to back away from Silas, shaking his head in disbelief. "What am I doing? I should be . . . doing homework or playing video games like a normal kid. I don't even know you. You tell me a story about Syngians and pieces of old glass, but you don't even give me your real name. Well, I'm done. I quit. But I'm keeping Penny."

He turned and ran down the sidewalk, with Penny at his side. Silas didn't try to stop him.

33

Fifty-eight minutes later, when Silas was in the Loom, scanning the previous twenty-four hours of security video from the lobby of the Newgate Hotel, his phone vibrated loudly against the wood tabletop: Andy.

"Hey."

"Hey."

"You okay?"

"Yeah. Forget what I said. I was just mad about . . . Look, I found something. Something important. A flash drive. You know, I thought it was weird when Jensen kneeled down to pet Penny. She'd never even seen her before, but she was acting like they were best friends. She must have clipped it onto her collar."

Feeling a surge of relief—for too many reasons to count—Silas sat up straight in his chair. "Have you looked at it?"

"Uh-huh. It's the notes from her meeting with Ilene Porter. There are audio files, too. She must have recorded everything, because they take up a bunch of space on the drive."

Silas whistled. "Okay. Listen carefully. Sooner or later, someone's going to remember that the kid with the dog is the same kid who was with Jensen in the NTRP building and . . . You need to send me the files ASAP and then get rid of the flash drive, okay? Get it out of your apartment—tonight. Okay?"

When the contents of the drive landed in Silas's in-box, he clicked through them to make sure the documents were readable and the audio files worked.

"Perfect," he said. "That's everything, right? Good. Clear your email, and then take care of the flash drive."

"Can I do it in the morning?"

"No, do it now. Destroy it. Take your frustration with me out on it. Tomorrow's Saturday, right? Meet me at the bodega at seven-thirty. No, make it seven-forty-five. You did some good work today. And don't worry—we'll find Jensen."

◆ ◆ ◆

Excerpt from Transcript of Interview with Ilene Porter by Jensen Huntley
Newgate Hotel, NY

JH: Thanks again, Ms. Porter. Like I told you, Zhariah Davis gave me your name.

IP: She left me several messages when I was in Greece. I called her when I got back in the country—I always return calls—but she never answered or returned mine.

JH: Yeah, um, her editor took her off the story. He said it wasn't interesting enough—

IP: But you disagree. How old are you? I was expecting someone—

JH: I'm old enough to know an important story when I see one. Something strange happened at that conference. You're my only chance to learn the truth so I can tell the rest of the world. I know I'm young, but you can trust me completely. I just want to know why all these important people suddenly stopped giving money away.

IP: That makes two of us. It can't be a coincidence, so many drastic about-faces. One or two, perhaps, but eleven? I keep asking myself, *What made them change . . . but not me?*

JH: Let's go back to the beginning. How did you first find out about the conference? Were you invited, or . . .

IP: One of the sponsors contacted me—a non-profit that distributes water filters in areas where the drinking water is unsafe. When she told me the names of the others who would be attending the conference, I agreed immediately. Those eleven, as individuals and as heads of companies and organizations, were responsible for hundreds of millions of dollars in charity. Billions, even.

JH: What about the companies pitching ideas—how many of them were there?

IP: Oh, lots. Dozens. Pitching everything from computer programs and mosquito nets to shoes made from recycled tires. I brought you a tote filled with a few of the goodies. You're welcome to it all.

JH: This was all . . . free? Wait, there's a tablet in here. I can't take that—it's worth—

IP: Take it. You'll see, it's not a tablet—it's one of those e-reader devices for people who don't read real books. The paper kind, I mean. This company, 233dotcom, is planning to hand them out the way companies used to hand out key chains. They have a solar panel, so they never need batteries. Clever.

JH: Let's skip to the part you mentioned over the phone—something strange happened during the conference?

IP: Ah, yes. The NTRP presentation. Quite a show. Presented by a woman . . . Sorry, I don't remember her name. Dianna, maybe?

JH: Deanna Decameron, most likely.

IP: Yes, that's the name. In any case, I don't know how practical it is, especially in poor communities, but from a purely technological standpoint, it was very impressive—like something from a science fiction movie. I have no idea how to explain what I saw except that suddenly the room was filled with people from history floating here and there. Shakespeare, Napoleon, George Washington, Michelangelo, Beethoven, Rembrandt—there were hundreds of them. As real-looking as you are to me right now.

JH: I don't understand. They were just . . . floating? Like, pictures of them?

IP: Yes, but three-dimensional. They looked alive. And not like in a 3-D movie, but like you could reach out and touch them. And that was just the warm-up. Those people all disappeared, and then, a second later, there was this scene from the signing of the Declaration of Independence on the stage. All these men standing around and talking about King George. . . . It was absolutely astonishing. I've seen a lot of new things in my sixty-three years, but nothing prepared me for that.

JH: Where were the images coming from? Was there a projector of some kind?

IP: I have no idea. They were just . . . there.

JH: Then what?

IP: It must have been a malfunction. The images just started flashing, hundreds of them, going by too fast to really see them. Like an old black-and-white movie but brighter, jerkier, and all in this incredible three-dimensional world. Made me a bit dizzy. I had to look away, and that's when I noticed . . .

JH: What?

IP: Well, I could barely stand to keep my eyes open while the pictures were flashing, but when I looked around the room, everyone else was . . .

captivated, as if they couldn't bear to take their eyes off any of it for so much as a second.

JH: Did anyone say anything?

IP: Not at the time. Later, when I asked the others about it, they spoke of it as if it had lasted only a second or two. But it was much longer than that— more than a minute.

JH: You're sure?

IP: Positive. It was uncomfortable.

JH: What was Deanna doing all this time? Did she say anything?

IP: Only that it was merely a programming bug, and that they were working on it.

JH: And then what?

IP: And then . . . nothing. Everything went back to normal. The signers of the Declaration were back in their places.

JH: How did you feel? Did you notice anything different?

IP: Nothing. The rest of the conference went on without any further problems. Before we checked out, the twelve of us met privately to talk about the future, and everyone seemed perfectly normal. No one seemed disillusioned or angry or fed up. Quite the contrary; we were all energized by what we'd seen and heard. We were ready to get back to work.

JH: How long was it until you knew something was wrong?

IP: Three weeks, give or take a day. I got word that Roscoe Mertyn had shut down his charity. My first thought was that he was in some kind of financial trouble. With all the ups and downs of the economy, he wouldn't have been the first. Then, two days later, Sylvia Langhorne joined him. Within a week, the other nine had done the same thing. No big announcements, no political agendas—they simply stopped writing checks. What went wrong? And why them and not me?

34

Faster than Silas would have believed possible for someone so small, Andy polished off two bacon-and-egg sandwiches, a large order of home fries, and a pint of fresh-squeezed orange juice in the back room of YouNeedItWeGotIt! on Saturday morning.

"Flash drive taken care of?"

Andy nodded, still chewing.

"Hard drive wiped?"

More nodding, more chewing.

"Good. I have a plan. We need to get the police interested in Jensen. The real police. There are over thirty thousand cops in New York—they'll find her. I'm going to do a little snooping into Ilene Porter's background. The notes from that interview have given me some ideas that I need to check out. Meanwhile, you're going to pay a visit to your old friend at the Nineteenth Precinct—where you turned in that big bag of money."

"Detective Cunningham?"

"You liked him, right?"

"Yeah, he was okay. He's kind of . . . loud. When he laughs, I mean."

"Well, you certainly impressed him, so he won't think you're a nut or a stalker. He'll take some action. If Jensen's parents really are overseas and not in regular communication with her, no one may report her missing until she doesn't show up for school on Monday."

"Should I tell him about the guys who dragged her away?"

"I think you have to. Doormen gossip. There's no telling how many people know about it by now. You tell Cunningham that you showed up there last night as the police were taking her away, and you just want to make sure she's okay—you know, act like you're worried about her."

"I *am* worried about her."

"I know. Sorry. I didn't mean . . . I'm worried, too. Really."

"Can I say something?"

"Of course."

Andy pulled the disk of Lucian Glass from beneath his shirt and swung it back and forth in front of Silas's face. "For somebody who's supposed to be . . . to have all these qualities—compassion and courage and discipline and all the others—you're not always exactly, you know, *nice*."

Rubbing his eyes, Silas acknowledged Andy's criticism with a single nod. "You're absolutely right. It's no excuse, but my own childhood wasn't like yours. I was . . ." His voice and his focus drifted off to a faraway place, and for a few uncomfortable seconds, there was silence.

"Sorry, I didn't mean to . . . ," said Andy, trying hard to decipher even one layer of the secrecy and complexity that made up Silas. For all the time they had spent together, he realized that he knew nothing personal about him. Admitting that to himself made him ashamed. His parents, especially his mother, had taught him better.

"Being a good friend is like being a good reporter," she had told him. "You have to ask the right questions."

He would start asking questions, Andy promised himself.

Silas snapped out of his reverie. "What? No, don't be sorry. Let's get back to work."

The questions can wait till tomorrow, Andy decided.

◆ ◆ ◆

Detective Greg Cunningham listened to the story of Jensen's "arrest" and then asked Andy to wait in one of the chairs outside his office while he made a few calls to various precincts around the city. Ten minutes passed. Fifteen. Andy drank a root beer from the vending machine. After twenty minutes, the door finally opened.

"You'd better tell me again. From the beginning,"

said the detective, his brow deeply furrowed. "Every little detail—it might be important."

For a second time, Andy told him what had happened, leaving out only the details of the flash drive and that he knew the two guys in uniform weren't really cops.

Cunningham, scratching his goatee, announced, "We've got a little problem. I asked around, checked with all the precincts in the area, looked in the computer. No Jensen Huntley in the system. Since she's a minor, there ought to be red flags waving all over town. There ain't even a red handkerchief out there." He took a blazer from the hook on the back of his door and stuck a long arm into a sleeve. "We'd better check it out. You have some time?"

"Y-yeah!" said Andy. "Really? You want me to come?"

"Why not? You know where she lives. I want you to show me exactly where everything went down last night."

◆ ◆ ◆

For a teenager living alone for months at a time, Jensen kept the apartment remarkably clean and neat. So neat, in fact, that Detective Cunningham had a difficult time believing that her parents had been away for nearly six months—a fact that two doormen and the building handyman confirmed.

"Don't touch anything," the detective cautioned, slipping on a pair of latex gloves. "Just in case . . ."

"That's her laptop, there on the kitchen counter," said Andy.

Cunningham pressed the power button and waited a few seconds. When nothing happened, he pressed it a second time. Still nothing. He checked the cord; it was plugged into the wall outlet. "Doesn't look damaged."

"Turn it over," Andy suggested. "Maybe there's . . . Ohhh. Whoa. The hard drive is *gone.*"

"I've got to call this in," said Cunningham, putting his phone to his ear.

Andy, meanwhile, peeked around a corner, pushing Jensen's bedroom door open. Her backpack was unzipped and turned inside out, its contents scattered around the room: an organic chemistry textbook, several notebooks, a calculator, a paperback of *The Motorcycle Diaries,* and the aluminum water bottle that she carried everywhere.

"Somebody was looking for something," said Detective Cunningham, peering over his shoulder. "What's she like? Is she . . . involved in anything illegal? How well do you know her?"

Andy shrugged. "I don't know—I just met her at the beginning of the year, when I started at Wellbourne."

"You're in, what, seventh grade? And she's in eleventh? Are you two . . . How do you know her? Sorry, it's just kind of odd, the age-difference thing. Is she your—"

"No. No! It's not like that. We're both in the Broadcast Club. We were working on a story together. I think . . . this could have something to do with that. We were supposed to interview some lady, but I got assigned to a different story. Jensen was *really* mad at me. Said she would do it herself. That was the last time I talked to her. She was right. I should have gone with her. It's an important story."

"What lady? Where?"

"Her name is Ilene Porter. She's a phila . . . a philth . . . uh, she's involved in a bunch of charities. She's staying at the . . . the . . . uh . . . New . . . gate Hotel. The thing is, I know Jensen talked to her. She put something up on her website. I checked today, though, and her site is gone. Like it was never there."

Detective Cunningham shook his head. "Maybe I'd better have a talk with this Ilene Porter. The Newgate, you say?"

"Uh-huh. Room 2801."

◆ ◆ ◆

The woman behind the desk at the Newgate Hotel checked her computer screen, frowning. Then she typed for a few more seconds and frowned again. "This is very strange." She caught the eye of another desk clerk—a slight, bored-looking man with a shaved head and frameless glasses. "Emilio, could you take a look at this?"

He glided over to her, and as he did, Andy felt a chill run up the back of his neck. Rubbing the spot, he felt the knot in the cord that held his disk of Lucian Glass.

"This is Detective Cunningham from the NYPD. He's

looking for a woman named Ilene Porter. Room 2801. When I call it up, I get a different name."

"*Perhaps* you have the wrong room, Detective," said Emilio in a voice that gave Andy another case of what his mom called the jeebies. "Or *perhaps* Ms. Porter is using another name. Many of our guests are important people who don't want to be bothered by . . . anyone."

"Well, you see, that's just it," said the woman. "I remember Ms. Porter. I helped her check in. Room 2801, I'm *positive*."

Emilio shrugged—a great, exaggerated shrug with a facial expression to match. "Ah, but you see, the computer . . . it does not lie."

"*Perhaps,*" said Detective Cunningham, visibly annoyed with Emilio, "I'll just take a look for myself." He marched to the elevator, with Andy trailing behind.

"Just a second," said Andy, stopping to retie a shoelace that didn't need to be retied. As he kneeled down, he sneaked a peek through his Lucian Glass at Emilio, who was already typing a text message on his phone. "I knew it," he said under his breath, and then ran to catch up to Detective Cunningham, who was holding the elevator door for him.

A woman answered the door to room 2801. She was in her late twenties, blond, model-beautiful, and dressed head to toe in red leather.

"Oh, hello," she said. Her accent was unfamiliar to

Andy. Somewhere in Europe, he thought, but he couldn't narrow it down any further.

Detective Cunningham held out his NYPD shield. "Good morning, ma'am. Sorry to bother you. Are you Ms. Porter? Ilene Porter?"

Her eyes darted from Cunningham to Andy, then back to the shield. "No. My name is Alicia Rondell."

"Are you a friend of Ms. Porter's?"

"No . . . I'm sorry, what's this all about? I don't know anyone by that name. Who is she?"

"Just someone we'd like to talk to. She was registered in this room. Can I ask how long you've been here?"

"Just the one night. I checked in yesterday afternoon, about four-thirty."

"Has there been anyone else . . . asking about her?"

Ms. Rondell shook her head.

"Well, there seems to be a bit of a mix-up down at the desk. Would you mind if I—we—took a quick look inside? We'll only be a second."

She stepped to the side and let them in. "There's not much to see."

Andy stayed near the door while the detective poked his head into the bathroom, then looked out the window at the city spread out beneath him. "You're right. Not much to look at. Sorry to have bothered you." He handed her a card. "If you hear anything—a phone message intended for her, whatever—give me a call, okay?"

"Sure. Hope you find what you're looking for."

Andy turned to leave but stopped suddenly when Ms. Rondell reached for the doorknob. Hanging on the back of the door was Jensen's scarf—that ratty plaid thing that she wore constantly.

"Wait. That's—" He paused, debating whether to continue.

"What is it? The scarf? Have you seen it before?" asked Detective Cunningham.

"It's Jensen's."

"Are you sure?" Cunningham turned to Ms. Rondell. "Is this yours?"

She laughed. "*That* thing? I'm *quite* sure it's not mine. I think you'll agree that it's not exactly my style. You're welcome to it. In fact, *please* take it. I wouldn't want anyone to think it was mine."

"Jensen never goes anywhere without that thing," said Andy. He squeezed his eyes shut, trying to remember whether she had been wearing it as she was being dragged away. "Except yesterday. She didn't have it on. I'm positive."

35

"I can't believe you're actually here," Winter gushed to Karina Jellyby in the Wellbourne broadcast studio. "Thank you *so* much. I *love* your music. This is Andy. He's my assistant. . . . Ha-ha. Actually, he's my producer, *and* he's a huge fan. The first time I met him, he was listening to one of your songs."

Karina gave him a firm handshake and, when she was sure Winter wasn't looking, a wink. "What's up, Andy? Nice to meet you."

"Yeah, you too." Even though he had already met her, he didn't exactly have to pretend to be awestruck by her. He pinched his arm to stop himself from staring at her. "Do you, uh, need anything?"

"No, no. I'm fine. Man, this brings back a lot of memories," Karina said, looking around. "I was in the BC, too. I loved it down here. Life was . . . so simple then. Although I'm sure I didn't think so at the time." She slapped herself hard across the face, surprising Winter and Andy. "Snap out of it, Karina! You're not here for a stroll down Nostalgia Boulevard. Let's get to work."

Winter pointed to the guest's chair on the set. "Okay, right, let's go. You can sit over there, and we'll get started."

With Karina in place, sound and lighting checks completed, and Winter's "Welcome back to Wellbourne" out of the way, the real interview began.

◆ ◆ ◆

Excerpt from Transcript of Interview with Karina Jellyby by Winter Neale
Wellbourne Academy, NY

WN: Let's talk about the Wellbourne concert and those two hundred and fifty fans.

KJ: Those guys aren't just fans—they're unstoppable, a force of nature. Like a hurricane, but one that does good. An inspiration. I mean that. We asked kids to write about their Operation THAW experiences, and we were absolutely blown away. You hear a lot of bad stuff about today's kids—that they're selfish, they're lazy, all they care about is their phone. Maybe that's true about some kids, but not the ones we heard from. They are *GETTING IT DONE,* Winter. We seriously considered moving the concert to a larger venue so we could invite more, but Wellbourne is special to me. . . . I really had my heart set on it.

WN: We're just SO psyched that you decided to keep it here! Could you tell us about some of the contest winners?

KJ: Are you kidding? I'd love to! I have to warn you, though. Once I get started, you might have to stuff a sock in my mouth to make me shut up. Might as well start with Parker and Patricia Elmsford. They're twin sisters here at Wellbourne who organized a food donation program. It started in their apartment building, but now they're collecting from four other buildings in their neighborhood. With a little help from an older cousin who's a carpenter, they designed and built these beautiful wooden chests that go in the lobbies where everyone can see them. And seriously, these kids are whip-smart; they paint the chests the same colors as the lobbies, so they look right at home. Twice a week, rain or shine, Parker and Patricia borrow grocery carts and deliver—and then sort and organize!—hundreds of cans and boxes to a local church, where the food is distributed to people who need a little extra help. Those two kids are working their butts off. And what's really wonderful is that their attitude is absolutely contagious. Donations are still increasing every month, and more and more buildings are *asking* for donation boxes for their lobbies. Buying an extra can of soup or an extra box of pasta has become a habit for the people who live in those buildings, thanks to the Elmsford twins. In their essay, they wrote about their belief that all people are basically good—they just need an occasional reminder that not everyone is as fortunate as they are. Two hours a week. Not so much to ask, is it?

WN: Wow, that's an awesome story. Now let's talk for a minute about your critics. Not everyone is a fan of your music or Operation THAW. A lot of people think it's wrong to pressure—or, in some cases, *require*—kids to do community service. They say that the whole idea is un-American, that it sounds like socialism, that it's sending the wrong message to people who need help. How do you respond to that?

KJ: [*Laughs.*] Ah, you're talking about my old friend Howard Twopenny. Look, I'd love to live in Howard's world—at least the way he thinks it is, a black-and-white place where everyone starts out equally and the hardworking rise to the top and the lazy end up on the bottom of the heap. But that's just not the way it is, Winter. I've seen plenty of hardworking people out there struggling to make ends meet. And plenty of lazy ones who are doing just fine. The folks at NTRP have gotten rich by focusing their cameras and microphones on all the worst aspects of human nature and completely ignoring the rest. I know I'm wearing some serious rose-colored glasses, but I think—no, I *know*—they're wrong.

WN: But why is it up to kids to fix the problem?

KJ: I wouldn't say that it's "up to" kids. If Howard Twopenny doesn't want his kid to spend two hours a week volunteering, that's fine. But if you ask me, kids need to get out there and see the world for themselves—the good *and* the bad—and let's face it, sometimes kids need a little push. I know I would have when I was that age.

WN: Funny you should mention Howard Twopenny's kid. He's a student right here at good old Wellbourne: our producer, Andy [Llewellyn]. Hey, Andy, could you come out here? Here he is. Howard Twopenny *is* your dad, right?

AL: Yep. That's him, all right.

WN: So, whose side are you on, Andy? Your dad's or Karina's?

KJ: Oh, let's not put him on the spot here. Tell you what, though. Andy, you tell your dad that I want him to be my personal guest at the concert Friday. I mean it. I would love for him to come and see for himself. To hear some of the stories—not just about what these kids have done, but about how they have been changed by volunteering a couple of hours a week. Will you ask him for me?

AL: Um, okay. You're serious?

KJ: Absolutely. I'll leave two tickets for him at the door. You tell him that I am going to be *so* disappointed if he doesn't show.

WN: Do you think he'll come, Andy? . . . He's shrugging. Well, I guess we'll just have to wait and see. Getting back to the concert: Karina, you kept the location under wraps for a long time—any secrets you're willing to share about Friday?

KJ: Hmm. I guess it would be all right to let the cat out of the bag—the goody bag, that is. Before the concert, we're throwing an all-you-can-eat pizza party, and everyone is going to get a tote bag *packed* with goodies.

WN: Lucky kids! We're just about out of time, so let me thank you again, Karina. It's been such a thrill, and I can't wait for Friday.

◆ ◆ ◆

When Winter called for him to join her on the set, Andy had been in the process of snooping through her email, which she had left open on her tablet in the control room. Unfortunately, he was caught off guard when he heard his name, and he left a message open when he stood to go on to the set. To make matters worse, the moment the interview was over, Winter asked one of the boys in the control room to bring her the tablet so she could take a picture with Karina.

"I'll get it," said Andy, rushing into the room.

"Too late," said Luke Toller, a ninth-grade computer whiz with a major crush on Winter. "I've got it, *Howie Junior.*"

Luckily for Andy, Karina saw the look on his face when Luke started to hand the tablet to Winter.

She reacted quickly, taking a step toward Luke and pretending to trip on the rug at the same time. Her left hand flung forward into his, sending the tablet flying across the room and onto the hard tile floor, where it landed with an unhealthy *crunch*. An awkward silence followed as every-one cringed, waiting for Winter's reaction.

"You . . . *idiot*," she snarled at Luke, who seemed to be shrinking into the floor.

"It was totally my fault," said Karina, picking up the tablet. "Ouch. That doesn't look good." The shattered screen had gone completely black. "Let me get you a new one. And I have a guy who can retrieve everything you have on this one. He's amazing. Used to work for the government, real hush-hush kind of stuff. Okay? Come on. Let's not end the day on such a bummer. It's just a tablet, right? Not nearly as important as a friend."

Winter forced a smile and even apologized to Luke. "Sorry I freaked out on you like that. It's . . . I mean, my *life* is on that thing." She took the remains of the tablet from Karina. "Thanks, but you don't have to replace it. It was an accident. My . . . dad is pretty good with stuff like this. He'll be able to get what I need from it."

◆ ◆ ◆

"It was quick thinking on Karina's part," said Silas when Andy told him about the incident with Winter's tablet. "She's always been like that. Now tell me about the email."

"I only saw it for a second," said Andy. "Maybe not even a whole second. It was from a weird address—just a long list of random numbers and letters. Impossible to memorize. The message was . . . 'Cotwo delivery at WA cafeteria on Friday afternoon. More details to follow.' That was it."

"Cotwo delivery? You're sure? With a *c* or a *k*?"

"*C. C-O-T-W-O.*"

"All right, I'll check it out. Maybe it's the name of a delivery service. Anything on Jensen yet? Heard from Detective Cunningham?"

"He's supposed to call me. . . . Here he is right now."

Andy answered his phone, hitting the speaker button so Silas could hear.

"This a good time?"

"Yeah, it's cool. Did you find Jensen? Is she okay?"

"Slow down. We haven't found her, but I have some news."

Andy sat, expecting the worst. "Oh, no."

"She's in California. At least that's what she says in her letter."

"Letter?"

"Arrived here at the precinct yesterday, finally made it into my hands an hour ago. Looks legit. I haven't had the experts look yet, but the handwriting seems to match the sample you gave me."

"What did she say?"

"The whole thing was staged, she says, to make it look like she was being arrested. She wanted to create a little drama—those are her words, not mine—and give the people in her building something to talk about, so she hired a couple of actors. She claims she's going to visit relatives in California for a while. We're waiting to hear back from her parents to confirm that. We checked the airlines, trains, buses. No sign of her yet."

"It's a fake," said Andy. "She would never use the word *drama* like that. She *hates* people who do that almost as much as she hates her uncle—and everything about California, for that matter."

◆ ◆ ◆

(*New York Inquirer,* Around the City news brief)

PHILANTHROPIST MISSING

Noted philanthropist Ilene Porter, the Porter Paper heiress with an estimated worth of nearly three billion dollars, was reported missing yesterday by her personal assistant. Although few details have been made available, a source revealed that police have reviewed security camera footage from the Newgate Hotel and have a number of "persons of interest" in the case. —Zhariah Davis

◆ ◆ ◆

I'm fairly certain that I'm included in the list of "persons of interest" mentioned by Ms. Davis—not an ideal situation in the middle of an already complicated situation. The last thing I need is to be dragged into a police station for questioning. Not that it would be the first time. Or, likely, the last. Don't worry, when you get into trouble—and you will—the entire army of Agents will be there to back you up. Remember, we have friends everywhere.

36

Andy left his building early Tuesday for Penny's morning walk, but as he made the turn onto York Avenue, he spotted Billy Newcomb and Silas, waiting for him in the Twenty-First Street Mission van.

"Get in out of the rain," Silas said.

"I don't have time. I'll be late to school. And Penny hasn't eaten."

"You're taking the day off. At least the morning. We'll feed Penny."

"I have a math test today! I studied two hours for it."

"You can make it up later. I wouldn't ask if it wasn't important. Come on."

Grumbling, Andy slid the side door open and climbed into the middle seat in the back. Penny hopped in after him, excited at the prospect of a ride.

"Don't you want to know where we're going?"

"Does it matter? It's not like I have a choice."

"What if I told you it might help us find Jensen?"

Andy grunted. "How?"

"You're going to visit your dad at the NTRP Broadcast Center. He goes on the air in a few minutes."

"I guess that explains why he was in such a hurry. Wait . . . how is *that* going to help find Jensen?"

"There are some interesting guests scheduled for today: Roscoe Mertyn and Sylvia Langhorne, two philanthropists from the Halestrom Conference—*former* philanthropists, that is. Billionaires, both of them, and *not* people who are easy to get close to. I'm dying to hear what they have to say, but even more important, I want to know what Penny thinks of them. And don't take any unnecessary risks, but if you can sneak a peek at them through your Lucian Glass, that would be helpful, too. I have a hunch about something, and you're going to help prove it."

"You think that NTRP got to them with Operation Tailor?"

"So, you *have* been paying attention," said Silas. "That's what I'm thinking, yes. Last night, after I found out who the guests were, I went through a ton of records and found something helpful. They both attended an event where Mr. Nakahara—remember him from the meeting at the Mission?—was present with his dog. No *lumen*. He's sure."

"So, if they have one now . . ."

"Exactly."

♦ ♦ ♦

The security guard inside the NTRP Broadcast Center eyed Andy up and down, then pointed at Penny with a scowl. "Where're you goin', kid? You can't bring that mutt in here."

"I'm here to see my dad . . . Howard Llewell—er, Twopenny?"

Instant backtracking by the guard. "Wha . . . you're Howard's kid? I'm really . . . Come on in. Sorry, son," he babbled. "Can you just sign in right here? Thanks." He reached down and awkwardly patted Penny on the top of her head. "Really sorry about that, boy."

"She's a girl." Andy was enjoying the moment, this feeling of power that he had simply because of who he was—a very dangerous feeling.

"Oh, right. Of course. Sorry, she's a beauty, too. Take the elevator to the fifth floor. I'll tell the receptionist that you're on your way."

It took Andy and Penny under a minute to reach the studio on the fifth floor, but the greeting they received there was very different from the one they'd first gotten at the front door.

The receptionist (gorgeous, familiar-looking) met him at the elevator as if she were greeting the Queen of England. "Andy! It is *so* nice to finally meet you. Your dad has told us so much about you."

"Oh, yeah? Like what?" said Andy. He really did wonder what his dad had said about him.

She forced a laugh and ignored the question. "I'm Gerri—that's with an *i*—and this beautiful girl must be Penny. Omigosh, she is so *sweet*. Can I get you anything, Andy? A Coke? Blueberry muffin?"

"No thanks. I'm just here to see my dad. Can you take me to the studio where he does the show? I haven't even seen it yet. Isn't there a place where you can watch what's going on, you know, without being heard?"

"Absolutely. Follow me." She glanced at the clock. "I'm afraid he's about to go on the air, so you won't be able to talk to him until the news break on the half hour."

"That's all right. I just want to watch for a while."

Gerri-with-an-*i* led him through a set of heavy soundproof doors and into an empty auditorium-style room with thirty or forty seats facing the glass studio wall. In an enormous, thronelike chair behind the glass sat the man himself, Howard Twopenny, with his two guests. He didn't see Andy and Penny enter, which was just fine with Andy, who wanted to give Penny a chance to get a good look at the guests.

"What do you think, Pen?" he whispered.

It didn't take her long to decide. As she stared at Roscoe Mertyn, her lip began to quiver and she gradually bared her teeth, emitting a low growl.

"Easy, girl." He checked the room again, making sure

no one could see him, and pulled his Lucian Glass from beneath his shirt. A quick glance through it confirmed what Silas had suspected and Penny had just told him: Mertyn had a clear *lumen lucidus*. To Andy, a newcomer to the world of the *lumen*, it seemed pale and weak compared to Winter's, but there was no doubt it was there.

During a commercial break, Sylvia Langhorne stood and moved close to the glass wall, her back to Andy. Penny had the same reaction, and the Lucian Glass again established the existence of the *lumen lucidus*. Two for two.

So it was true. Mrs. Cardigan, Silas, and the Agents had all been clinging to the hope that NTRP's ability to create the *lumen* was limited to the weak-minded or those who were seriously lacking in any of the eight qualities that the Agents regarded as essential, but now that hope seemed to be dead and buried. If NTRP was able to "flip" two of the most generous people in the nation, was anyone safe?

THAT SUMS IT UP PRETTY NICELY, DON'T YOU THINK?

37

Just how serious the situation was became apparent a few minutes later, when Howard Twopenny's show went on the air.

"Folks," he began, "I think you all know how I feel about charity. I've made myself pretty clear: It's for *losers.*"

Cringing, Andy sank lower in his seat.

Howard continued: "If you still have doubts, go to my website and read a few of the entries in my *world*-famous Charity Is for Losers contest. If you're still not convinced, I have a feeling that today's guests might bring you over to my team. Until very recently, they were at the very top of the list of the most generous people in America. Over the past twenty years, they gave *millions*—tens of millions—to charities of all shapes and sizes. But *no más, amigos.* Both of my guests, along with a number of their formerly generous friends, have turned off the money spigot, and they're here today to tell us about it and to talk some sense into those of you out there who are still intent on giving away your money to losers who can't take care of themselves. Welcome, Mr. Roscoe Mertyn and Ms. Sylvia Langhorne."

"Thank you, Howard," said Sylvia.

"Glad to be here," added Roscoe.

"Let's cut right to the chase. A lot of people are wondering, What happened? Why the sudden change of heart? Ladies first."

"At some point, it all becomes pointless," Sylvia said. "You give a million dollars to an organization, and six months later, they're back, asking for more. Nothing ever changes. I'm a very successful person, and I'm not going to apologize for that. Yes, I started out life with a little money, but I've worked hard, and you know what? I like getting results. I'm *used* to it. I simply got tired of feeling that *I* didn't matter. Only my money."

"But surely you must have done some good, made a few lives better."

"Perhaps. A few months back, I was listening to bright-eyed eager-to-do-gooders pitch their ideas, clinging to this naïve belief that *their* generation would be the one to wipe out poverty and corruption and suffering and unfairness, and then . . . something . . . *happened* to me. I don't want to say it was a bolt from the blue, but it happened almost that fast. One morning, I woke up and I knew that I had donated my last dollar."

"How about you, Roscoe?" asked Howard. "Similar experience?"

"I've never quit at anything in my life, but the fact is, this is a battle we *can't* win. It's impossible, like a high school basketball team trying to beat the Los Angeles Lakers. At some point, it becomes useless even to try. So I decided to sit this game out, so to speak."

Silas, listening in the van, cringed as he listened to Roscoe and Sylvia. Despite what they were saying, he still felt sorry for them, because he knew that it wasn't real; they had been manipulated, possibly genetically altered. As he began to wonder if the process was reversible, the show took an interesting turn.

"Before any of you liberal dingbats call in and accuse me of telling only one side of the story, let me bring on my next guest, Mr. Sawyer Neale the Fourth. Is that right? The *Fourth?*"

Winter's father, who had been waiting in the green-room, sprang into the studio, shaking hands and smiling like a politician. "Thanks for having me on, Howard. My wife is a big fan."

"But not you, I'll bet," said Howard, grinning.

"I think you're very . . . entertaining," Sawyer said.

"Ah, a diplomat. Fair enough. Well, you've been listening to what Roscoe and Sylvia have to say about charity—what do you think? Let's see, my producer wrote down some figures here. . . . According to public records, your foundation gave away about seventy-five million last year. Will you be joining these two on the sidelines?"

"No, I won't, Howard," said Sawyer. "Look, I can sympathize with Roscoe and Sylvia, feeling that it's all uphill, all the time, but that's no reason to quit. My daughter mocks me mercilessly, says I'm a hopeless optimist. I can live with that. She also complains about the service requirements at her school, but you know what? It's good for her to see firsthand how people who aren't as fortunate as her live."

"Oh, goody," said Howard. "*Service*. The big lie. I'm so glad you brought that up. As far as I'm concerned, it's a modern-day plague. Forcing kids to work for free. And then you have these rich celebrities, like this Jellybean person—"

If there had been a post nearby, Andy would have banged his head against it. Part of him wanted to jump up and shout (for the hundredth time), "It's *Jellyby*!" but instead he laughed out loud, quickly covering his mouth. That wasn't his dad up there blustering into his microphone—it was Howard Twopenny, star of the highest-rated radio talk show in America.

"It's sad to see," chimed in Sylvia. "Their hearts are in the right place, I suppose, but it's all very misguided. I think that instead of requiring and encouraging service, the leaders of these schools should be requiring kids to find paying jobs so they can really understand how the system is *supposed* to work. I doubt that Miss Jellyby has ever worked a day in her life."

"I'm sure you're right," said Howard. "But we need to take a break for the news. You're listening to Howard Twopenny tellin' it like it is. And we will be back in exactly five minutes."

Andy was on his feet, being waved into the studio by Howard.

"What are you doing here? Shouldn't you be in school? With what that place charges, you should be there seven days a week. And you have Penny with you."

Penny looked up into Andy's eyes at the mention of her name. Being in a tight space with two Syngians was making her a bit jumpy, so Andy pulled her close to him, slipping his fingers under her collar in case she decided that she'd had enough of Roscoe Mertyn and Sylvia Langhorne.

"It's a, um, a special service day. I was on my way down to the Twenty-First Street Mission, but I was early, so I figured I would stop by and see the studio. And you."

Howard clapped him on the back. "Well, I'm glad you did. Everyone, this is my kid."

"Nice to see you again, Andy," said Sawyer.

"You two know each other?" asked Howard, flabbergasted.

"Our kids are friends. Winter is at Wellbourne, too."

"You met her, Dad. She took a selfie with you. Now, can I say something about Karina Jellyby?" Andy asked. "She worked *lots* of real jobs. She's not from a rich family at all." He knew all the details of her bio, including where she worked (Canavale's Pizza) when she was at Wellbourne, and he wasn't afraid to use them.

"How do you know so much about her?" Howard asked.

"I know her," said Andy. "I met her at school. She went to Wellbourne. We just interviewed her."

"Well, la-di-da," Howard said. "So you met one celebrity. Oh, God. Don't tell me that you won tickets to her concert. It's bad enough that you're even taking part in this ridiculous Warm Up America project; please don't humiliate me any further by being really *good* at it."

"What are you *talking* about? Warm Up America?"

"You know, that whole two-hours-a-week nonsense. Heat Up America? Is that it?"

"Not even close. It's Operation THAW, Dad."

"Oh, I wasn't that far off. I knew it had something to do with that global-warming silliness."

"Actually, it doesn't. *Thaw. T-H-A-W.* It stands for Two Hours a Week. Oh, and by the way, we're *both* going to the concert. Mom, too, if she's home by then."

Howard held a cupped hand up to his ear. "I'm sorry, it sounded like you said that I'm going to the Jellybean concert."

"That's a good one, Dad. You're going. Winter—Mr. Neale's daughter—told Karina that you're my dad, and she told me to invite you to the concert."

"I think I'm busy that night."

"I haven't told you when it is yet."

Sawyer, who had been watching with an amused expression, chuckled. "I think he's got your number, Howard. Looks like you're going to a concert. Don't forget your earplugs."

"Karina doesn't care what you say about her or her music. She just wants you to see and listen to the kids who won the contest. They're *amazing*. They make *me* feel like such a slacker. Anyway, if you're serious, it's Friday night. There will be two tickets waiting for you. You should take Mom."

"I think you should go, Howard," said Roscoe, piling on. "It'll be good for a laugh, if nothing else. And you can't beat the price."

Howard threw his arms up in mock surrender. "All right, I'm outnumbered. You win. Tell the Jelly Bear that I'll be there. Just don't expect me to break down in tears when I hear some little bleeding heart tell the story about how reading books to the deaf or finger-painting with blind kids has changed her life."

"I think you got that backward, Dad," said Andy.

38

With just two days to the concert at Wellbourne, Silas felt the pressure increasing and went to the Loom to do some serious research. Though he was desperate for sleep, he didn't dare close his eyes until he had answers to some of the questions that had been tormenting him, which he had scribbled on the whiteboard above his desk.

WHAT HAPPENED AT THE HALESTROM CONFERENCE?

WHAT DO THOSE 3-D IMAGES HAVE TO DO WITH THE
  PROCESS THAT NTRP IS USING?

WHY WASN'T ILENE PORTER AFFECTED? WHO KILLED
  HER? WHY?

MEANING OF "COTWO DELIVERY" IN MESSAGE TO WINTER?

WHO IS ST. JOHN DE SPERE, REALLY?

WHY DOES HE LOOK FAMILIAR?

While he stared at the board and mumbled to himself, Mrs. Cardigan, knitting a burgundy-and-cream sock, entered the Loom. One step behind was Reza Benali, her head covered with her traditional hijab. Originally from Morocco, she had earned several advanced degrees in computer science and designed the systems in the Loom. Her dark, intense eyes seemed to light up whenever she entered that secret world. She loved it there.

"Let's start with Halestrom," said Mrs. Cardigan, glancing at Silas's questions. "Let's take another look at the Huntley girl's notes and see if we can sort out what went on."

"Here's exactly what Ilene Porter said about it." Silas read aloud from the transcript of Jensen's interview with her: " 'It must have been a malfunction. The images just started flashing, hundreds of them, going by too fast . . . in this incredible three-dimensional world. Made me a bit dizzy. I had to look away, and that's when I noticed . . . everyone else was . . . captivated, as if they couldn't bear to take their eyes off any of it.' "

"Sounds like subliminal messages," Reza said. "An attack on the subconscious. There's a reason they're illegal in advertising."

"There has to be more to it than that," said Mrs. Cardigan. "Subliminal messages can be powerful, certainly, but these people have undergone some kind of chemical change, not merely a psychological one. There must be another aspect to the process, something we're missing. A drug? Electrical shock? And what about video? Is it even conceivable in this day and age that there is no recording of the event? Silas, why don't you start with that?"

"If it's here, I'll find it," said Silas, drifting off to the opposite side of the room.

Mrs. Cardigan looked over Reza's shoulder at the white-board and pointed at the fifth question written there: *Who is St. John de Spere, really?* "Let's you and I take a stab at this one. Something tells me that once we know the *answer*, the others will unravel themselves."

"Like a wool sock?"

"Certainly not one that *I* made, but, yes, that's the idea. Now tell me about this program that you and Martin are so excited about. Does it have a name?"

Reza leaned in close. "Officially, no. In fact, there are only a handful of people in the world who even know it exists. Unofficially, it's called Otis."

"Is that an acronym?"

"No, it was the name of the creator's dog—a beagle. The idea is that the program is like a hound that's on the scent of something and won't give up until it finds it. We upload every photograph of this guy that we have, and Otis searches every nook and cranny of the Internet: library collections, newspaper and television archives, private collections, just about anyplace you can imagine—a lot of places that Google and other search engines have no access to."

"All *legal* places?" Mrs. Cardigan asked. "We don't want to open *that* can of worms."

"Absolutely. Everything it finds will have been part of a public record somewhere, at some time. That's the other beautiful thing about Otis—it also creates its own age progression photos. Say, for example, that all of the photos we have are from twenty years ago. Otis will take all the information and create accurate images of how the person looks now. That way, it can search more accurately. It works the other way, too. If I take a picture of you and upload it, the program will determine how you looked at every age and will look for matching pictures."

"Is it ready for its debut?"

"Almost . . . uploading the last of the photos right now. There, it's searching."

"How long does . . . Otis . . . usually take?"

"Could be a few minutes, could be a few days. Depends on how much is out there and where it is."

"Well, we don't have a few days, so talk nice to it or something. Offer it a juicy bone if it hurries. In the meantime, we should have tea."

◆ ◆ ◆

Three hours and two pots of Lapsang souchong later, a single thread appeared, and the edges of the mystery began to fray.

"Mrs. Cardigan, take a look at this," said Reza, pointing at an image of a grainy photograph. "This is from the Grootman College newspaper, twenty years ago. The caption reads, 'Professor Roger Bursten presents award to Grootman students.' That's Oxford, right?"

Mrs. Cardigan squinted at the picture, trying to make it appear clearly, but her eyes weren't the problem—the picture was decidedly fuzzy, the men's faces obscured by shadows and smudges. "Cambridge," she said, her voice distant and dreamlike. "Not Oxford. How on earth did Otis find this?"

"What is it? Do you know about this?"

Across the room, Silas looked up from the screen he'd been staring at for hours. When he saw the look in Mrs. Cardigan's eyes, he rushed around the table to see the photograph.

"Oh . . . my. Now I see him," said Reza. "That's really him, isn't it?"

Without taking her eyes off the picture, Mrs. Cardigan nodded.

"Is someone going to tell me what's going on?" said Silas. "Who are these people?"

"Read, starting *here*," Mrs. Cardigan said, sitting back in her seat. "Aloud."

Silas read: " 'A team of three Grootman College graduate students received a grant of £100,000 from the National Science Fund to continue their research on the topic of permanently altering human behavior through manipulation of a person's DNA. According to Corinne Apfeldt, one of the recipients of the grant, criminal behavior can become a thing of the past. "With the proper mix of chemical and environmental stimulation," she said, "we can change the fundamental way a person thinks, their very nature. And this is just the beginning." Added Yuri Yevgenev, another recipient: "It truly is a brave new world." ' "

Silas looked puzzled. "I don't get it. How is this helpful? This sounds like the anti-NTRP. Is that it? Did they do something to stop this research?"

"Not exactly," said Mrs. Cardigan. "The article mentions Corinne Apfeldt and Yuri Yevgenev. Does it give the name of the third student?"

Silas scanned the rest of the article. "Ah, here it is. But I'm betting that you already know his name, don't you?"

"James Thorneside," Mrs. Cardigan answered softly. "I haven't said that name aloud for a long, long time. You know him as St. John de Spere. They're the same person, I'm afraid."

Silas scrutinized the identified face in the photograph. "You're sure this is him? This picture is not exactly clear."

"I'm positive," said Mrs. Cardigan.

"You knew him . . . when he was Thorneside?"

"I knew *of* him. I never met him. And no one I'm aware of has seen him in twenty years. I was under the assumption that he was probably dead. Only because he has been so quiet for so long. The other option didn't make sense."

"Other option?"

"The possibility that he was living in the suburbs with a wife, two and a half kids, and a beige minivan," said Mrs. Cardigan.

"So . . . what happened?" Silas asked. "Why did he disappear? And change his name? Was he in some kind of trouble?"

"You could say that. Six months after that picture was taken, Corinne Apfeldt was dead and the other two had been arrested. There was an incident at the college . . . in the science labs. Hundreds of lab rats and dozens of other animals—and Miss Apfeldt—were killed when an experiment went wrong. Something involving the release of a gas that was intended to alter their behavior. The three had broken into the lab to conduct the experiment because their advisor had forbidden them to go forward with it. She said it was too dangerous, too untested."

Reza clicked on a link to a London newspaper. "Here's a follow-up story, from a few days after the incident at Grootman. It was ruled a tragic accident. The charges against Thorneside and Yevgenev were dropped, but they were both expelled from the university. That seems . . . crazy. A young woman dies, along with hundreds of animals, and their only punishment is that they got *expelled*? Who did they know?"

Mrs. Cardigan swallowed the last of her tea. "A better question is, What madness has he been up to for the past twenty years?"

39

Mrs. Cardigan pushed her chair back from the table. Neither Silas nor Reza had ever seen her look so worried.

"This is very troubling," she said. "James Thorneside—or St. John de Spere, if you prefer—is not someone to be taken lightly. He's not like us. What I mean is that he's not like *anyone*. He's brilliant and creative but utterly unpredictable because he doesn't feel emotions. He *can't*. The story is that he had almost no human contact for the first ten years of his life. He was the subject of a bizarre psychological experiment. His parents were scientists. Quite mad ones, I'm afraid. They kept him in a room without windows and controlled every aspect of his life."

"But I've seen him smile," said Silas. "In fact, he's smiling in almost every picture we have."

"It's an illusion, that's all. I wouldn't be surprised if he could cry on command, too. He imitates; he pretends. Look a little closer at that so-called smile. It's as if a machine taught him. The mechanics of a smile are all there—the teeth, upturned lips—but his eyes are cold, unfeeling . . . the eyes of a reptile. The truth is, he's no different from those lab animals he destroyed twenty years ago. He's a monster, the laboratory creation of twisted minds who were *obsessed* with eugenics—using genetics to create the perfect human. Clearly, he has picked up right where his parents left off. And to say that his idea of the perfect human and ours are different would be the understatement of the century."

"If you never met him, how do you know so much about him?" Silas asked.

"Do you remember the file I showed you the day you brought Andy to the Mission for the first time? The one that surprised you so?"

"Yes, of course. What does she have to . . ."

"Twenty years ago, she was a postgraduate student at Grootman College. She was the advisor who refused to allow the experiment that went wrong."

Silas whistled. "No kidding. Do you think he knows. . ."

"I hope not, for her sake. For everyone's sake. She's in a different field and has a new name, too—but for a very different reason. She changed hers when she got married. Lots of water under the bridge since then."

◆ ◆ ◆

Although virtually no one outside the Llewellyn family knew it, Howard was an excellent cook.[1] Andy actually preferred his dad's cooking because he stuck to the basics. Nothing fancy, no weird vegetables or fish that he'd never heard of. Chicken. Beef. Occasionally, pasta. As Andy worked on his *Indefatigable* model, which was spread out over half of the kitchen table, trying his best *not* to think about Winter or the Agents of the Glass or NTRP or the fast-approaching concert, Howard sautéed chicken to go on top of a Caesar salad.

"How's the model coming along?" Howard asked over his shoulder as he shook the frying pan back and forth. "Looks like a lot of pieces. How many are there?"

"Like, a thousand or something," Andy answered. "This first part is the hardest, because you have to make sure everything is straight. If you're not careful, the hull turns out twisted."

Andy stood up to show him how the individual wood planks were attached to the framework.

"Holy cow. I didn't realize it was so . . . It's like you're building a real boat. How long is it going to take?"

"The instructions say about a hundred hours. But probably longer for me, since I've never done one like this before."

"Well, no one can say you're not patient. Hold on a sec." With a flick of the wrist, he flipped the chicken in the air like a pancake. "So tell me, whose ship is this again?"

---

1. It was certainly *not* something he would want his listeners to know.

"Horatio Hornblower. I mean, he's not real, but the *Indefatigable* was a real ship."

Howard smiled. "*Indefatigable.* I like that. Seems perfect for someone else I know."

"Mom?"

"Actually, I was thinking of you, but now that you mention it, it fits her pretty well, too. And speaking of your mom, I have a little surprise for you. She's on her way—she'll be home a day earlier than she thought. She'll be here in time for dinner on Saturday. I'm sure you're ready for a little break from my cooking."

"No, your cooking is great."

"*But . . .*"

"No *but.* It's just . . . I . . . Can I ask you a question? About your job, I mean?"

"Of course. Anything."

"Why do you have to be so . . . negative? It's like you can't ever like anything that's good. You know, like the Karina Jellyby thing. It really is amazing what some of those kids are doing."

"I know."

"But . . . then . . . why?"

"The short answer is: It's what people want."

"But you're not like that. And what about Mom? Her whole life is all about helping people. When you're on the radio, you make it sound like she's wasting her time."

"I'm playing a character, Andy. There are a lot of people out there who think that Howard Twopenny is right.

People who buy products from our advertisers. Who pay the station a *lot* of money for those commercials."

"So you don't believe what you're saying? Doesn't that make you—"

"A hypocrite? Sure. You could say that. But it's more complicated than that. It's not just about the money. The world you believe in—your mom's world, Karina Jellyby's world—is locked in a battle with the world of people like Howard Twopenny. A battle that the good guys are losing at the moment. At least part of the reason for that is that they don't truly understand the nature of the enemy. It's hard to defeat an enemy you don't understand. I like to think that I help make that perfectly clear."

"Oh, I think you're doing that," said Andy. "A lot of people *hate* you. Doesn't that bother you?"

"Ah, but they hate Howard *Twopenny*. To me, he's like a ventriloquist's dummy. At the end of the show, I stuff him back into a suitcase. You know, I think that's the best thing about radio. I'm a voice, not a face. That's why I've been resisting my boss's plan to put my show on TV. That all make sense?"

"I guess."

"Good. So now it's my turn. What's the real reason you showed up at the studio?"

Andy hesitated and sat down. How much more could he reveal without having to explain *everything*? "It's . . . we're . . . I'm working on this story at school, you know, in the Broadcast Club. I can't tell you all the details because some of it is a surprise, but it has something to do with the Karina Jellyby concert. Are you really going to come?"

"Wouldn't miss it. Are you kidding? Me and Jelly-bean, breathing the same air. Of course, I'll probably have to listen to a speech about how that air is being replaced by CO_2—she's really into that whole global-warming, carbon-footprint mumbo jumbo."

Andy sat bolt upright in his chair, transfixed. "Wait. That's it! CO_2! Carbon dioxide. Not *cotwo*. God, I'm an idiot. Sorry, Dad. I need to make a call right now."

"What are you talking about? What's so important about CO_2?"

"I can't explain—all I can say is: It could be a matter of life or death!"

40

Mrs. Cardigan's brow was furrowed, and her knitting needles were clicking and clacking as her fingers flew, wrapping burgundy yarn this way and that. When she reached the end of the row, she looked up. "Whatever happened at Halestrom, NTRP is planning the same thing for the concert at Wellbourne. Just think: two hundred and fifty bright, young, idealistic minds. De Spere must be licking his lips at the thought of it."

"I have something here," said Silas, his fingers still tapping furiously at the keyboard, in search of video from the Halestrom Conference. "When I—" He stopped as his phone, vibrating, scooted across the table. He held it up for all to see that it was Andy.

"Hi, Andy. Everything okay? I'm putting you up on the big screen for Mrs. Cardigan and Reza."

"Yeah, okay. Listen, I was wrong. The email to Winter. It's not a *cotwo* delivery—it's CO_2. Carbon dioxide. The stuff they use to make soda fizzy. So simple. I'm sorry, I should have thought of it before."

"But why would they be telling Winter about a . . . Holy smokes! Andy, you're a genius."

"What's going on?" Mrs. Cardigan asked. "What's so unusual about a delivery of carbon dioxide?"

"Because it's *not* carbon dioxide. The tanks are filled with the gas they used at the Halestrom," Reza explained. "Which is, I'm guessing, a more refined version of the gas that was used in the Grootman College disaster twenty years ago. And that's how they get it into the building, no questions asked. Every bar and concession stand uses tanks of CO_2."

"You have no idea how big this is, Andy," said Silas, holding his phone in front of the monitor he'd been working on so Andy could see it. "You need to see this, too. Somebody was very clever and turned off all the video feeds from inside the Halestrom Hotel—well, *almost* all the feeds. I found one camera that is not part of the security system or their closed-circuit TV network. This one was installed by the heating and air-conditioning contractor to monitor equipment. It's an easy, cheap way for them to see what's going on remotely. Fortunately for us, the thing it's aimed at only takes up about a quarter of the screen . . . and it's high-def video, so I was able to slow it down and blow up the individual images. In this first part, you can see the people Ilene Porter was talking about. That's George Washington, and there's Beethoven. Now I'm going to fast-forward to when things start to go crazy."

"Right," said Reza. "She said that the figures were coming and going so fast that she couldn't tell what she was seeing. Like a flickering movie, I think she said."

With a final tap on his keyboard, Silas sat back in his chair. "I was able to isolate that section of the video and examine it frame by frame. What's interesting is that they've alternated pictures of various types of scenes with printed messages and super-bright colors—that's why it looked like flashing lights to Ms. Porter. But there's a definite pattern to it, a rhythm."

Reza and Mrs. Cardigan stared at the screen as Silas gradually slowed down the parade of 3-D images until they could see them in detail. The first to appear clearly was of a young girl begging on the side of the road, her clothes tattered, her face unwashed, her eyes dark and lifeless. Then an entire family huddling in a culvert, the mother holding a baby close to her chest. Rows of abandoned houses and shuttered factories. Emaciated farm animals. Puppies and kittens in crowded, filthy cages. An overturned boat with hundreds of desperate people in the water around it. Poverty. The poor. The starving. The beaten down. The miserable. Thousands of photographs of humans and animals drained of any value or importance or dignity they once had. It was a slide show intended to do one thing: evoke pity and sympathy in anyone who viewed it. Yet, in the midst of all that misery, one face appeared again and again.

Smiling. Confident. Beautiful.

Winter Neale.

Mrs. Cardigan touched Silas gently on the arm. "Turn it off, please. So that's what it's all about. St. John de Spere is offering them Winter Neale. He's setting her up to be the empress of his warped, soulless world."

"I don't understand," said Silas. "If he wants a world without positive qualities like sympathy, what's the point of manipulating people with these images?"

"Maybe he's trying to show that the world isn't merely in trouble but is past the point of being able to be fixed," said Reza.

"No, it's more than that," said Mrs. Cardigan. "Those pictures are part of the process. They're very *deliberate*." She closed her eyes, deep in thought.

Silas clicked the monitor off, and the Loom was silent for several seconds before he said, "By my calculation, it's something like five hundred images per second. At that speed, they're flashing by so quickly that they don't register on a conscious level."

Reza nodded, adding, "Subconsciously, however, the human brain has amazing abilities, and it's processing the images one by one and storing them away somewhere."

Mrs. Cardigan opened her eyes. "By themselves, the images would have no lasting effect. Same thing with the flashing colors. But similar series of flashing color plates have been used to stimulate certain parts of the brain, creating a state of hypnosis. In those circumstances, the mind could become more . . . *suggestible*."

"Where does the gas fit in?" asked Andy.

"Without a sample, there's no way to tell," answered Mrs. Cardigan. "Clearly, the rules of the game have changed. We have some catching up to do."

"We should consider canceling the concert," said Reza. "There are too many variables outside of our control. It's too dangerous."

"With all due respect, I disagree, Reza," Silas said. "There are risks, but I'm working on a plan that I think will work. That I *know* will work. If we're going to find a way to fight back against *this*—this gas, this entire process—we need to get our hands on some of it. Analyze it. Develop an antidote. A vaccine. And don't forget, we have the advantage of surprise. NTRP thinks we're clueless about all this, so their guards will be down."

"But these are kids," said Reza. "*Good* kids. Exceptional, even. What if we fail? I'm a computer person; the world is made up of zeros and ones. You're certain we'll succeed. NTRP is just as certain that they will. Yet, logically, someone has to be wrong. Are we prepared for the *possibility*, no matter how slight, that that could be us? Are we prepared to sacrifice two hundred and fifty kids? Or even one, for that matter?"

"In one night, we stand to learn as much real, hard information about NTRP and its plans as we would with five years of spying. It's too good to pass up," said Silas. "And besides, we have a secret weapon, too." He pointed at Andy's face, projected on the screen before them.

"Mrs. Cardigan, what do you think?" asked Reza.

A true leader, Mrs. Cardigan did not hesitate. "Let's move forward with the plan. There's risk in everything we do, but every morsel of information we have helps us to minimize it. So, we keep digging and evaluate the situation every six hours. Anything new comes directly here to the Loom. Andy, can you come by tomorrow for a final briefing? Good. In the meantime, keep your eyes and ears open, and be extra careful. And . . . everyone? Wool socks. Andy, do you have a pair?"

"I . . . uh . . . There's a bunch of socks in my drawer, but I don't know *what* they're made out of."

"Well, that won't do," said Mrs. Cardigan. "I'll see to it that you're properly equipped."

"Just one more question," Reza said. "Why now? And why Wellbourne, of all places?"

"I have a theory about that," said Mrs. Cardigan. "St. John de Spere cannot resist a pun. *Eugenics* comes from the Greek, meaning 'good breeding.' You see, the whole point of eugenics is to create a race of people who are born with *exactly* the right qualities—who are, in other words, *wellborn*."

41

Andy's phone buzzed while he and Penny were taking their final walk of the day, around nine-thirty. When he saw that it was Winter, part of him wanted to ignore it—he just wasn't in the mood to deal with her—but Mrs. Cardigan's words about minimizing the risk of the operation rang in his ears, so he took a deep breath and answered.

"Andy! Hi! You weren't sleeping, were you?"

He breathed in deeply again before answering. "No. I'm outside, walking Penny. What's up?"

"I was just wondering . . . what's going on with Jensen? I heard she ran away. That she's in California. Figures. She's so *weird*."

"What? California? No way. She hates California. She has a relative there, and she hates him. Where did you hear *that*?"

"I had a meeting with Deanna Decameron—you know, from NTRP—about this story they want me to do, and while I was there, I saw video of one of their reporters talking to a cop. I don't know the reporter, but the cop's name was Cunningham. Super handsome. Really nice suit. Loudest laugh I ever heard, I swear."

"Oh, yeah? Huh. Well, I haven't heard anything like that," said Andy, staring at his phone and smiling at the realization that Winter obviously knew everything he did. "I haven't heard from her, but I just figured she still wasn't talking to me because she was mad about the whole Karina Jellyby interview thing. But I still don't believe she's in California."

A long silence followed, finally broken by Winter. "So, what's going on, Andy? Why are you acting so . . . you know, cold? I thought we were friends. I mean, I've had fun working with you. And we were great together on the Karina piece. What is it? Did I do something to offend you?"

Her sincerity was so realistic that Andy *almost* believed it. He was relieved that they were talking by phone; in person, it would be harder to resist her charms. It wasn't hard to imagine those remarkable pale eyes pleading with him, her hand touching his just so, her voice oozing fake genuineness. Despite all of Silas's talk of his unusual ability to resist the power that Syngians have over mere mortals, Andy didn't trust himself completely, and he touched the glass circle hanging around his neck to remind himself of the importance of his mission.

"I'm . . . You didn't do anything. I just . . . have a lot on my mind, that's all," he answered. "We *are* friends, at least I hope so."

Two can play this game, he thought. *I can pretend to be charming, too.*

"That's good to hear, because I really like working with you, and now that we're going to be working at . . . Well, I can't tell you because I promised not to tell anyone until after the concert, but I can't wait." She laughed, adding, "The whole world will be a better place when it's over."

"What do you mean?"

"You'll just have to wait and see like everybody else. See you tomorrow?"

"Yeah, sure."

◆ ◆ ◆

A few blocks away, Detective Cunningham was having coffee with Zhariah Davis, the reporter from the *Inquirer.* Since meeting Jensen and Andy, she had been spending most of her spare time (as well as most of her spare money) on the Halestrom story—unofficially, because her editor threatened to fire her if she asked him so much as one more question about the story. Cunningham was the lead detective on the Ilene Porter case, so she'd waited for him outside the Nineteenth

Precinct and offered to buy him a coffee if he would let her ask some questions. At least he couldn't fire her.

"You can ask all you want, but a cup of coffee doesn't necessarily buy you any answers."

"Fair enough. Let's start with Ilene Porter. Do you know the cause of death yet?"

"We would have to have a body to know that," he said. "That's why it's a missing-persons case. There's no evidence of anything more than that. No signs of foul play, as you reporters like to say. But maybe you have information that you want to share. Shed some light on this case for me, please. Is it a kidnapping? That seems logical—rich lady, single, no security."

She held his gaze for a few seconds before answering. "I don't have anything concrete, but I don't think it's an ordinary kidnapping, if that's what you're saying. When you look at the big picture—you know, the timing and all that—her, um, disappearance is . . . *unusual,* to say the least. She meets with a bunch of charity bigwigs at this swanky hotel, and then, they all stop giving away their money. Except her. And then . . ."

"And then what? Nothing. It's all circumstantial. She comes to New York, she's at the Newgate . . . and then she isn't. She's worth in the neighborhood of a billion dollars. If she wanted to disappear for a while, she could afford to do it right. An island in the Caribbean. A little place in Provence. Maybe she's thinking about it."

"Thinking about what?"

"About whether to stop giving *her* money away, too. Maybe they all just got tired of fighting a losing battle."

"Geez, you sound like that nut on the radio. Howard somebody."

"Twopenny? Ouch. You know how to hurt a guy."

"How do you explain Jensen Huntley?"

"Who?"

"Oh, nobody. Only the girl who just happened to interview Ilene Porter just before the alleged *disappearance*."

"Ah. Jensen. You asked how I explain her. The words *conspiracy nut* come to mind. She's a troubled teen. We had her listed as missing, but that's all been cleared up."

"Oh, *wake* up, Detective! She's not a nut—or *troubled*, whatever that means—and nothing has been cleared up. She came to me with a friend, said they were working on a story for their school news program. About this company 233dotcom, which, according to those two, took all the books from their school library and *burned* them. They saw it with their own eyes. She was going to interview Ilene Porter and send me her notes, but . . . nothing. Her website's gone. She hasn't been in school. I bribed the doorman in her building, and he told me that the police dragged her away. Only, it turns out, it wasn't the police. I have *other* contacts who are cops, and they confirmed that. So where is she?"

"Finally. A question I can answer. California."

"California?"

"Yep. Big state. Left side of the country. Nice beaches. Ring any bells?"

"Why are you so sure she's there? She call you or something?"

"She wrote me a letter. With a stamp and everything. Very old-school."

"And you believed it? You know, Detective, just when I start to think that you're a smart guy, you go and say something like that. If Jensen Huntley is in California, I'll smear peanut butter on my phone and eat it. And I hate peanut butter."

"Ha! That I'd like to see. Look, I know you have a job to do, but so do I. Right now my number-one priority is finding Ilene Porter—*alive*, I hope. Look, there's a concert Friday night at Wellbourne Academy. I'm going to be there because . . . well, because. You interested? It's that Karina Jellyby—" He paused when he saw Zhariah looking at him with a strange expression. "Wait . . . no, I don't mean like it's a date or anything. . . . I just thought, you know, your story . . ."

"Sure, I'll go. Meet you there. Here's my number," Zhariah said, slipping a business card in his hand. "And don't worry—I don't date cops."

42

When Andy arrived at the Loom after school on Thursday, Mrs. Cardigan set down her knitting and rose from her chair to greet him. "Come in, come in. We have lots to talk about. But first, some tea." She filled a mug with smoky Lapsang souchong and handed it to him. "Everyone thinks better over tea, don't you agree? Now let's get you caught up on everything we discovered last night. When you called, we had just found these articles about some students at Grootman College—"

"Hey, my mom went there. Let me see."

Andy skimmed quickly through the articles as Silas filled in the missing pieces of the story. When they were finished, Mrs. Cardigan pointed to the large television screen on the wall. "Everyone, take a look. This is from a few minutes ago, the five o'clock news on NTRP. I got a message from our man inside the network that it's already generating a lot of buzz." She pressed play, and the video started.

"NTRP is proud to introduce a new segment today, called nTeens," the anchorman, Bill Betts, announced in his baritone voice. "Once a week, students from Wellbourne Academy will be writing and producing a special story for the younger viewers in our audience. Today, we are joined by Winter Neale, who brings us her interview with the musician Karina Jellyby, herself a graduate of Wellbourne. May I be the first to say, 'Welcome, Winter.' It's great to have you aboard as our first-ever junior correspondent."

"Thank you *so* much, Bill, and everyone here at NTRP, for giving me this opportunity," said Winter, her voice oozing sincerity. "I am really excited to be a part of something so big, and with such a great network. We have a wonderful tradition of journalism at Wellbourne, and it's amazing to have the chance to show the world what we can do."

Mrs. Cardigan clicked it off after the interview with Karina, which had been edited down to just under three minutes. Winter's face was on-screen longer than Karina's, which was no accident; NTRP wanted everyone staring into those hypnotic eyes for as long as possible.

A few seconds later, her phone buzzed with another update. "Our NTRP insider says that the phones are ringing nonstop and they got so many emails that their server crashed. Our biggest fear is about to come true: Winter Neale is going to be a media star. They're giving her a perfect platform to get started. How long till they decide to make this a daily thing? Imagine her as a regular on the morning news program. That show draws *millions* of viewers every day."

"We have to stop her," Reza said.

"Not as easy as it sounds," said Mrs. Cardigan. "She's dangerous, yes, but in the eyes of the world, she's a child. We have to be careful—one wrong move could expose us or set us back years. The mood of the country is difficult."

"Thanks to NTRP," Silas said. "Their sleazy programs created this monster and made it possible for Winter Neale to become their—"

"Savior?" offered Mrs. Cardigan, smiling wryly. "You're right, of course, but that doesn't change anything. But we have something that St. John de Spere doesn't—and that thing is *patience*. They're a little too eager to put their new technology to work and to push Winter onto the American public now. They're going to make mistakes . . . and we're going to capitalize on them. Now, can I get a minute with Andy, everyone?"

"Sure. Let's go get some coffee, Reza," said Silas. "There's a new place around the corner."

"You buying?"

"Sure. Andy, in case you're gone when I get back, I'll see you at two-thirty tomorrow. I'll be with the band." He paused, smiling. "Never thought I'd hear myself say those words."

When they had stepped out into the darkness, Mrs.

Cardigan stuck the CLOSED sign to the front door and invited Andy to sit in one of the wing chairs.

"Can I get you anything?"

"No thanks."

She poured herself another cup of tea and closed her eyes as she inhaled the pungent steam. "I'm sorry, you're waiting for me. There's so much to say, but I don't want to burden you with too much information on the eve of an important battle—yes, *battle*, because that's what this is, Andy. The Agents. NTRP. Good. Evil. It's that simple. You are one of us. For some people, it takes years, but not you. I can assure you that every one of the Agents, including those you have not yet met, is one hundred percent behind you."

"Even the scary guy who used to be a British spy?"

"Ha! That's a very accurate description of Mr. Gardner. But the answer is yes, even him. Now, I understand that your mother is on her way home from Africa—is that right?"

"Uh-huh. She'll be back the day after tomorrow."

"I'll bet you're excited. I'm sure you miss her. It's been a long time."

Andy nodded. "Yeah. A *long* time. But it's okay. I mean, I understand why she does it. She's helping people who really need help."

"That's a very mature attitude for someone so young. You're right. Her job is very important. I'm going to tell you something else about your mom—something that may surprise you. Has she ever talked to you about her time in England, when she was at Cambridge?"

"Not much. Just that she went to college there. And I think she was an assistant professor or something like that for a while. That's about it."

"Well, there's a little more to the story," said Mrs. Cardigan. "Something that was kept out of the newspapers. At the time of the tragedy at Cambridge that you just read about, St. John de Spere—his name was James Thorneside then—was under the supervision of an advisor at Grootman College. She was a postgraduate student, a brilliant scientist in her own right. Well, after winning that big grant, de Spere felt he was untouchable, that nothing was off-limits to him. When he approached his advisor with the plan for his experiment, she refused to allow him to use the labs. The proposed experiment was so irresponsible, so against *everything* that she and the university stood for, that she went directly to the department head, who suspended de Spere's lab privileges pending an investigation. The next night, he carried out the experiment anyway, and you know the rest." She paused, sipping her tea before dropping a bombshell: "What you don't know is that the graduate student who stood up to St. John de Spere was your mother."

"*What?* My mom knows him?"

"It was a long time ago. She *knew* him. Even though

she was completely exonerated of any blame, she felt that her name would forever be linked to the tragedy, so she left the university a few weeks later and came back home to America."

Andy's mind whirled as he pieced together the fragments of the story. "There's still one thing I don't understand. If the part about my mom was kept out of the papers . . . how do *you* know about it?"

"My, you *are* quick, aren't you?" Mrs. Cardigan said, her eyes glimmering. "Silas warned me about you—he says you're the best agent he's ever worked with, of any age. I was hoping to save this for later, but the answer to your question is that I knew your mother back then. We knew about de Spere's experiments, and we were interested in them . . . until his objectives changed. Much as you are doing, she worked for us, keeping us informed about his work."

"What about now? Is she still . . . Does she know that I'm . . . because I haven't told her. Silas told me not to tell anyone, even family."

Mrs. Cardigan raised her hand to stop him. "I promise that when all this is over, I'll tell you everything I can. Don't forget, this is your mother we're talking about— the person who knows you best in the world. Like every mother of every son, she knows more than you think. Let's just leave it at that. Right now, though, let's focus on tomorrow. Is there anything else you need?"

"Not that I know of."

"Is the plan clear? You know what to do in case of emergency?"

"All good," said Andy. "I'm as ready as I'll ever be."

"What are you doing with Penny?"

"She'll be with Karina in case I need her. I'm going to sneak her in right after school and put her in the greenroom backstage."

"Your Lucian Glass?"

Andy pulled on the cord around his neck and showed her the disk of glass.

"Wonderful. Now take a close look at it. What letter do you see at the top and the bottom of the circle?"

"It's a *C*." Andy's mind ran through the eight qualities. "Courage. And Compassion."

"That's right. Have you thought much about the points on the glass? Does the circle remind you of anything?"

"I don't . . . A clock? Although, now that I think about it, it's more like a compass."

"That's exactly right. Except that, in place of the four cardinal directions—north, south, east, and west—you will find what we call the cardinal qualities: Compassion, Courage, Integrity, and Discipline. The ordinal qualities—no less important, mind you—of Intelligence, Loyalty, Dignity, and Humility correspond to the ordinal directions of northeast, southwest, and so on. In the late 1500s, during the age of exploration, the Agents decided to call a person who has all eight qualities a Compass. And although we've been keeping track for hundreds of years, we still don't know by what accident of genetics a Compass comes to be. But I do know this, Andover James Llewellyn: You are one."

"But I'm . . . You hardly know me. I'm still a kid."

"Age has little to do with it. I was your age when I found out. Your mother was a little older."

"My mom? She's one, too?"

"Yes, which makes your case even more unusual. The child of a Compass is almost never one."

Andy sat up straight in his chair, squeezing his head between his hands. "Wait . . . I'm still trying to—this is too much for me to—you know my *mom*?"

"For many years," said Mrs. Cardigan, her eyes twinkling. "I still have a few surprises. Be patient. I promise that you'll know more very soon."

"And my mom—she's a . . . she's like me? Are there a lot . . . of us?"

"Not nearly enough, I'm afraid. And many have no idea that they are, including, strangely enough, Winter's father."

"What! If he's . . . how can Winter be . . ."

"It's because he is a Compass that Winter is what she is: a kind of super-Syngian. As Silas told you that day you saw them in the park, we've known that her mother is a Syngian, but thanks to your fieldwork, we now know the full truth about her father. That's how he's been able to resist her conniving and dangerous ways, at least so far, and how he was able to walk away from the Neale family business."

"So, when a Syngian and a Compass have a baby . . . you get . . . *Winter?*"

Mrs. Cardigan nodded. "A very dangerous combination, indeed. If we had known that Sawyer was a Compass, we would have done something to . . . well, to make sure he married somebody else."

"I don't get it. If he's a good person, why *would* he marry someone like that?"

"Don't forget that Syngians can be *very* persuasive. They don't have the same issues that normal people have with lying to get what they want. They don't understand guilt. And Winter's mother was taught by the very best. But enough about them. I want to talk about you."

Andy nervously rubbed his Lucian Glass between his thumb and index finger.

"Do you remember the first time you saw a compass? How, no matter which way you turned it, no matter how fast, it always kept its bearing. It always points north. Like you, Andy. Since the end of summer, your life has been spun like a top, and turned upside down and inside out, but you've never lost your way. You have a rare gift, and I want you to know how grateful we all are to you for sharing it with us and for the sacrifices you've made."

"I—I'm just trying to do what's right."

"Yes, I know. And that's a wonderful thing." Mrs. Cardigan paused, collecting her thoughts. "I'm getting old. I can't go on like this forever. Oh, don't worry—I'm not going anywhere for a while. What I'm trying to say is that you have given me hope. Hope that when I do step down one day in the not-too-distant future, Brother Lucian's dream of a better world will be in good hands."

A chill ran up and down Andy's spine, and he had to look away for a moment.

"Some final words of advice for tomorrow," said Mrs. Cardigan, breaking the silence. "The same advice I gave your mother twenty years ago. It's the advice I give Silas every time I send him out on a new mission. You're here tonight because of this advice: *It's all in the eyes.* Everything you need to know about a person is revealed through them. People can learn to beat lie detectors, they can pretend to be lots of things they aren't, but they can't fake the qualities that the letters on that glass circle stand for: Dignity. Loyalty. Integrity. Intelligence. Discipline. Humility. Courage. And most of all, that *C* at due north: Compassion. You have known the truth about Winter from the moment you looked into her eyes. You just weren't *certain* until we told you some things and you saw some for yourself. If the eyes truly are windows to the soul, then Winter's soul is a bleak place, empty of humanity. The hard part is learning to trust your own eyes and instincts when it comes to people. Penny and your Lucian Glass are helpful, but sometimes you really are on your own."

"Do you think that tomorrow . . ."

"I wish I could tell you what to expect besides the unexpected. But whatever happens at that concert, it will be only the beginning of a long and difficult battle. NTRP has amassed an army of its own, with weapons that we know little about."

"That's not exactly encouraging."

"I want *your* eyes to be wide open—literally and figuratively. You'd better be on your way. Try to get some sleep—tomorrow's going to be a long day."

Andy glanced around the Loom, taking it all in once more before turning for the door.

"What is it?" Mrs. Cardigan asked. "You have the strangest expression on your face."

"It's just . . . all this . . . and everything that's happened since that day at the bank. It's kind of hard to explain, but I've never really felt like I . . . *belonged* anywhere. Until now."

Mrs. Cardigan's eyes glistened as she handed him a small brown paper bag. "Open it. These are for tomorrow. I guessed at the colors. I hope you like them."

Inside was a pair of wool socks—blue with two narrow yellow stripes.

43

Meanwhile, on the east side of town, St. John de Spere stood on the terrace of the Neales' apartment, ignoring the chilly north breeze as he raised his glass of champagne. "To our success."

Winter's mother echoed his words and clinked glasses with him while Winter gazed out at the park, sipping sparkling water from her champagne glass.

"What's wrong, Winter?" de Spere asked. "This is it. Humanity gets a do-over, starting tomorrow night. And you're the one they'll be looking to for inspiration, for guidance."

"She's probably a little overwhelmed," offered Fontaine Neale. "You're putting a lot on her shoulders."

"I'm fine, Mom," said Winter, mildly annoyed that her

mother was making excuses for her. "I can handle it. I could have handled it when I was six."

"You know, I believe you could have," said de Spere. "But I'm glad we waited. The process is ready for prime time, if you will. The Halestrom Conference was the technological equivalent of stone knives and twisting a stick to make fire, compared to what you will see tomorrow. It's practically perfect."

"Practically?" Fontaine asked.

"Well, there's always room for improvement," said de Spere. "As technology improves, so will the process."

"How does it work?" Winter asked. "I mean, I know the concept, the general idea, but I want you to explain the science. How does this machine of yours change people without even touching them? And don't talk down to me. I hate it when adults do that. Explain it as if you were talking to a new laboratory assistant."

"Have you learned about ions yet?" de Spere asked.

"I've heard of them."

"It's pretty simple, really. Most of the time, an atom has the same number of electrons and protons, and they balance each other out—that is, there is no electrical charge. But if that atom picks up an extra electron, it's no longer neutral—it becomes an ion with a negative charge. Now, the thing about ions is, because they're *charged,* they are attracted to particles with the opposite charge—in this case, a *positive* charge."

"Where do those come from?"

"Ah, a good question. Positive-charged ions occur when a particle *loses* an electron. In other words, it has one more proton than it has electrons. Still with me?"

"Uh-huh."

"Good. Now comes the fun part. Have you ever noticed how attracted you are to the Llewellyn boy? Even though you no doubt find him ridiculous?"

Winter squirmed a bit in her chair. "I don't . . . He's not . . ."

"Don't be embarrassed," de Spere said with a wave of his hand. "You can't help it. Just like your father couldn't resist your mother. Those matchmaking companies that are always talking about the 'chemistry' involved in finding your perfect match don't even realize how literally right they are. Early in my research, I studied thousands of individuals using the most sophisticated medical instruments available—CAT and MRI scanners and even a brain-wave scanner invented by the Russians—and I made the discovery that changed everything. I found the real difference between people like Andy and your father and people like you and your mother comes down to a unique positive ion. Some people—your father, for instance—have it; you do not."

"What do you mean? Where is it?"

"In moments of extreme emotional distress, such as when a person is feeling compassion for a starving puppy, the body starts releasing this compound that is carried by the bloodstream to the brain and causes the person to *act* on those feelings."

"So you're saying that doesn't happen in my body?" Winter asked. "Why not?"

"The simple answer is that you're more evolved. Human evolution didn't just stop when we got to modern man; it's still happening."

"Why are you so sure it's *us* who are more evolved?" Fontaine asked. "Isn't it just as likely that it's *them*?"

"It's common sense, really," replied de Spere, a bit put off by the question. "Clearly, compassion and other useless qualities are doing nothing to ensure the survival of humans as a species—and that's what evolution is all about. Evolve or go extinct. And if mankind continues on its current path, I don't need to tell you where it's headed. Well-meaning people, like those fools, the Agents of the Glass, love to preach about having a 'moral compass' that keeps them pointed in the right direction, but I assure you that the only direction they're headed is for extinction."

"Okay, so I get it so far. That explains the difference between them and us, but how are you turning the Andys of the world into, you know, people like me?"

"It's a two-step process. In order for it to work, the part of their brain that feels compassion has to be working at maximum capacity. We do that with pictures of suffering people, especially children and animals—whatever we can throw at them. Mixed in with those are thousands of bright flashing colors that help to trigger even more brain activity, which is key for reasons we don't entirely understand. Then we hit them with Compass Ion gas—get it? Compass Ion, *compassion*. Basically, it's a synthetic version of the gas their body produces, but it's a *negative* ion. The molecules seek out the positive ions, neutralizing them, and then . . . well, that's it. When they snap out of the trance they're in, they feel exactly like they did before."

"And that's it—they're changed forever?"

"We've been keeping an eye on everyone who has been through the process, and so far the failure rate is only about one percent, which may simply be a matter of upping the dosage of the gas the next time. As I said, we're constantly tinkering."

St. John de Spere set his glass on the table and stood up to leave. "Thank you again for hosting tonight, Fontaine. And for the lovely champagne. A perfect night."

Winter said her good nights and went to her room as Fontaine walked with de Spere to the door. "Do I have your word that she's in no danger? I may not be in the running for mother of the year, but she is my daughter. I would be . . . unhappy if anything were to happen to her. Is . . . *he* still snooping around?"

St. John nodded, and a section of his long silver hair fell across his left eye. "After tomorrow, your brother will no longer be a problem."

44

Friday. Officially, Karina Jellyby Day at Wellbourne Academy. From seven-thirty to two-thirty, it was a regular school day, but by two-forty-five, serious preparations were under way and Silas was already inside. His visitor's badge identified him as a member of the band's road crew, responsible for setting up the sound and light systems—not that he knew the first thing about either one. With the brim of a baseball cap pulled down over his eyes, a fake beard, and thick-framed glasses, even Andy didn't recognize him at first.

One of the side effects of NTRP's broadcast of Winter's interview with Karina was that Ms. Albemarle assigned the same team of students to create a behind-the-scenes video of the concert, including all the before-and-after work by the crew. This gave Andy complete, unquestioned access to the auditorium and allowed him to keep a close eye on Winter. Luke Toller, the freshman with the crush on Winter, had volunteered to be her camera operator, but Ms. Albemarle came to Andy's rescue, giving him the job and assigning Luke to another reporter.

"Looks like it's you and me again, Andy," said Winter, so close to him that he smelled her minty-fresh breath as he stared up into her peculiar pale eyes.

It took everything he had, but he finally willed himself to look away, remembering Mrs. Cardigan's advice: *It's all in the eyes.*

"Uh, yeah . . . Are you ready? Where do you want to start?"

Winter checked her watch. "Let's head down to the service entrance off the alley. We need to hurry."

"Why? What's there?"

"That's where they're bringing in all the equipment. We can get some shots of that, and maybe talk to one of the roadies. They look . . . interesting. They have *lots* of tattoos."

She wasn't kidding about the tattoos, but her actual motive for hanging out near the service entrance was to be there when the CO_2 arrived. A young man in coveralls wheeled in a hand truck with two large tanks of compressed gas strapped to it. Andy examined them from across the room. He had seen tanks used to make soda, and these looked like the real thing to him. They were plain metal tanks, five feet tall and ten inches in diameter. Both had labels identifying them as carbon dioxide, with the usual warnings about the contents being under pressure and to avoid breathing the gas and so on. Except for a single stripe painted around the top of each tank—one in green, one in blue—the two tanks were identical.

The delivery guy looked around, then pulled a slip of yellow paper from his front pocket. "Hi. I've got the gas for the soda machine. I'm supposed to talk to . . . Winter Neale."

"That's me," said Winter. "You can just follow me to the concession stand."

"Why is he asking for you?" Andy asked, trailing a few feet behind her.

"Dr. Everly asked me to take care of it," Winter lied. "She knew I'd be here, and I was on the refreshments committee last year for the spring concert, so I know where stuff like that goes." She stopped at the concession stand door and turned to him, her head tilted in a way that reminded Andy of Penny. "Why do you ask?"

Andy shrugged. "It just seems weird, that's all."

"Just being helpful." She pulled the door open and held it for the guy to wheel the hand truck through. "The machine's over there."

He went right to work, disconnecting the old tanks and wrestling the new ones into place. After removing the plastic cap that protected the threads, he connected the gas line to the top of the tank with the blue stripe and tightened it with a crescent wrench. "You're all set. Just sign here."

"Andy, can you take care of that?" Winter said as she pretended to be reading an important message on her phone.

Andy was not thrilled with the idea of having his name connected to whatever was in those tanks. He glanced from her to the delivery guy and asked, "Is this okay? I mean, since her name was on the order?"

"It don't matter," the guy said as he strapped the two empty tanks to the dolly.

Andy scribbled something that didn't resemble his signature at all and handed the paper back.

"Thanks," said Winter, holding the door for the guy and pointing the way out. She turned to Andy, smiling mischievously. "Come on. Let's make sure it's working."

"Make sure *what* is working?"

"The soda machine, of course." Winter slipped behind the concession counter and filled two cups with ice. She pointed the soda gun at Andy. "What can I get you, sir? Your usual—a root beer, with extra ice?"

He looked around nervously. "Uh, are you sure it's okay?"

Winter waved off his concern. "It's just soda, Andy. And we're not stealing. When you put on a new tank, you have to run it for a few seconds to clear the lines. Everyone knows that. Besides, one of the sponsors is paying for all the food and soda. All the kids at the concert get to eat and drink all they want for free." She handed him the cup, overflowing with foamy GoodTimes root beer. Then she filled her own cup with cola and raised it to him in a toast. "What should we drink to? To the future. I think today is going to be a *very* special day."

◆ ◆ ◆

Their next stop was backstage, where a heavy black tarp with the NTRP logo covered an object nearly as tall as Winter. A thick steel cable running all the way from the middle of the auditorium's ceiling disappeared under the tarp, which carried this warning: EXTREMELY FRAGILE! TO BE HANDLED BY AUTHORIZED PERSONNEL ONLY!

"What's *that*?" Andy asked, his eyes following the path of the cable.

Winter shrugged. "Speakers, probably. C'mon, let's interview the roadies. I'll bet they have some great stories."

When she turned to look for Karina's road crew, Andy lifted a corner of the tarp with his toe. He caught a glimpse of shiny metal and glass, lots of wires, and something that looked like a lens sticking out before Winter nudged him and motioned toward the guy taking guitars out of their cases and setting them in stands.

"I'm going to talk to this guy. Why don't you try *him*? He looks important." She pointed across the stage at Silas, who was checking items off a list attached to a clipboard.

"Oh, okay," said Andy. "Catch up with you in five minutes."

He went to Silas, who led him to the far side of the stage, out of Winter's sight. "Anything to report yet?"

"A guy brought two big tanks into the concession stand," Andy whispered. "I think it really is just CO_2, though. He hooked one up to the soda machine, and it's normal. At least it tasted normal to me." He burped loudly, as if to prove his case. "Sorry, I had some root beer. . . ."

"You said there were two tanks."

"That's right."

"Where's the other one?"

"They're right next to each other."

"And they're identical?"

"Yeah, exactly. Except—"

"Except what?"

"Each one has a stripe painted around it at the top. One's green, the other's blue. He hooked up the tank with the blue stripe."

"Got it. Blue stripe. Is anyone in the concession stand now?"

"It was all clear about five minutes ago."

"Okay, good work. Anything else?"

"Just that thing," said Andy, pointing at the black tarp. "I peeked under the cover, but I still don't know what it is. I've never seen anything like it. Lots of wires and some lenses, I think."

"Yeah, I've been watching. It's going up to the ceiling— some kind of projector."

"Kind of scary-looking. Like something from a science fiction movie."

"Except this is real. Go on, you'd better get back over there with Winter. Report back here in exactly one hour. And take it easy on the root beer. That stuff will kill you."

45

When Andy rejoined Winter, Silas checked the time and then made his way to the concession stand, where he listened at the door before pulling it open and stepping inside.

Behind the counter, the tanks looked the way Andy had described them, except for one important difference: Now *both* tanks were connected. A clear plastic hose, three-quarters of an inch in diameter, was screwed into the top of the tank with the blue stripe and led directly to the soda machine. It was the second tank, though, that worried Silas. For one thing, the stripe painted around it was *red*, not green.

"What the . . . Didn't he say blue and green?" he wondered aloud. He reached up and turned the valve to open it ever so slightly. A pale green, lethal-looking gas began to creep along the transparent hose, and he quickly shut the valve, turning it until his hand ached.

Silas breathed in deeply and pulled up his wool socks, trying to maintain his own heart rate. It was really happening: NTRP was going after a bunch of kids. Snapping a picture of the hose and nozzle, he allowed himself a smile and sent it to Mrs. Cardigan with this message: *Not today, NTRP.*

With the help of his flashlight, he followed the hose, which ran under the counter for about eight feet and then turned downward, straight through the floor and into the basement. Silas had to be absolutely certain that the tank and the hose were exactly what he thought they were, so he got his bearings, measuring the approximate distance from the walls, and quietly slipped down the stairs. The basement was remarkably clean and well lit, and he set out to find the spot directly beneath the concession stand. He shone a flashlight at the ceiling above him. It was too high to reach, so he found a stepladder and climbed it. Poking his head up into the ductwork and conduit, he felt around for that plastic hose until he finally had it between the fingers of his left hand. Without letting go, he reached into his pocket and unfolded the small blade of his Swiss Army knife.

"Try a little to your right," said a man's voice.

Silas froze, grasping the hose and waiting for the ladder to be kicked out from under him.

"Don't stop now. You're so close," the man said. "Did you find it? It runs along the electrical conduit and then back up into the auditorium's ventilation system. But then you already knew that, didn't you? Now drop the pocket-knife. Nice and easy. No sudden moves."

Silas dropped the knife, and it clattered against the concrete floor. He cursed himself for allowing himself to be caught so completely off guard. His left hand still held on to the flimsy plastic hose, however, and thinking quickly, he pressed it into the narrow space between two ceiling beams, kinking it and squeezing it shut. Some gas might get through, but the flow would be reduced by ninety percent. Enough, he hoped, to foil NTRP's plan. Then he lowered his head and turned to see who had joined him in the basement.

Naturally, he was dressed in a shark-gray suit that perfectly matched the color of his hair. His gun, pointed at Silas's heart, was the same cold gray.

"Come on down from there," said St. John de Spere. "That's good. Hands where I can see them. No reason for anyone to get hurt here. Now have a seat over there on the floor, with your back to those pipes." He placed a hand on Silas's shoulder and gave a gentle push.

Instinctively, Silas recoiled from the touch, moving forward and out of reach.

De Spere laughed. "Oh. *Riiight*. I forgot. You don't like to be touched. Sorry about that. Here, you can put these on yourself." He tossed a couple of heavy-duty plastic ties to

Silas. "Slip those on your wrists and pull them tight. I'm afraid I may have to touch you again." He used a third tie to strap Silas to a two-inch steel pipe.

"Now, your phone. Where is it?"

"Coat pocket. Right side."

De Spere reached in and took the phone, examining it carefully before asking, "Password?"

"I forget."

De Spere laughed aloud. "Fine. We'll talk later. I'll keep this safe for you in the meantime, in case you suddenly remember."

"You won't get away with this. We know who you are. James Thorneside. Grootman College, Cambridge, class of . . . Oh, right, you didn't graduate. You were expelled. For conducting unauthorized experiments, which you're *still* doing. The only difference is that instead of laboratory rats, now you're experimenting on human beings."

"Bravo. Shall I tell you everything I know about you? You might be surprised. You see, I know things about you that even you don't know. To tell you the truth, though, you're quite boring—you and your zebra finches. I even know the reason for your special interest in them. It seems there's no end to your idealism. Your protégé, on the other hand, young Mr. Llewellyn, is another story. Ah, I see that you're surprised that we know about him. That, in a nutshell, is why you pathetic Agents of the Glass will fail. You're constantly underestimating us. Well, that ends today. And good riddance to all that mumbly-jumbly piffle about altruism and compassion. That's all so . . . twentieth century."

He strode toward the door, turning back with that coy I-know-something-you-don't smile that infuriated Silas. "Talk to you later, *Roger*. No point in calling out for help— it's like that line from the movie. This place is like space: No one can hear you scream."

◆ ◆ ◆

Meanwhile, Andy and Winter continued their reporting of every behind-the-scenes moment they could stick their noses into. Every chance she had, Winter stopped by the concession stand for a soda refill.

"As long as NTRP is paying for it, we might as well take advantage of it," she said.

Andy stared uncertainly into his cup of root beer, his third. "You didn't say that NTRP was paying for it. You just said one of the sponsors."

"What difference does it make? Do you really think it matters if two more kids get some free stuff? Those kids who won the contest—they're all getting brand-new tablets, along with bags of cool gear. So drink up."

A check of his watch told him that it was time to meet Silas backstage. "I, uh, need to, uh, you know . . ."

"You are *adorable*," said Winter. "It's okay. You can say you have to go to the bathroom. I understand. As a matter of fact, I need to go, too. Let's take a little break. Meet me in the back of the auditorium in . . . say, ten minutes."

He ran to the bathroom and then to the stage, looking for Silas. When he still hadn't shown up five minutes later, Andy sent a text—which, of course, Silas didn't receive because his phone was in St. John de Spere's pocket. Andy had no choice but to contact Mrs. Cardigan, so he sent this text: *Checked in on time, but S didn't show up.*

She responded immediately: *Don't worry. He contacted me. Everything is under control.*

And then Andy got his first real surprise of the day.

He left through the wings, started up the center aisle of the auditorium, and stopped in his tracks. Standing a few feet inside the swinging doors at the main entrance to the auditorium was Jensen Huntley, wearing, to Andy's surprise, a sweatshirt with the NTRP logo plastered across the front.

"Jensen!"

She turned, her face emotionless. "Oh. Hey, Andy. How are you?"

"How am *I*? Where have you *been*? First I thought you were arrested, then kidnapped, then I hear that you're in California. And now you're here. Wearing . . . *that*. What is going on?"

She shrugged. "I dunno. All that was . . . It's *over* now. I just wanna see the concert. You know, I'm actually starting to like Karina Jellyby. I didn't think I'd be able to get in, but your friend Winter . . . I guess she has some good connections, 'cause she got me this," she said, holding up a VIP pass.

Andy was seething. "Wait a minute. Nothing is 'over.' You *hate* NTRP. Do you even know what's happened since the night I saw them dragging you away? Remember Ilene Porter? The woman from the Halestrom Conference? Well, she's *dead*. We found her . . . right after *you* interviewed her. Even the police don't know that she's . . . They just think she's missing."

"*C'est la vie*. Nothing to do with me."

"Are you kidding me? It has *everything* to do with you. It was *your* story—the library books and the fire at that warehouse where they burned all those books, including *Jane Eyre*! And then you gave me the Porter interview. You clipped the flash drive to Penny's collar. Do you even remember that?"

Jensen continued to look completely uninterested, which aggravated Andy to the point of making him want to take her by the arms and shake her.

"Come on, Jensen! Don't you get it? You were right about NTRP. They're doing things . . . things I can't tell you about. That Halestrom Conference ? They were there. They made it all happen. Your interview with Ilene Porter helped *prove* it."

"Dude, chill. It didn't prove anything. So what if a bunch of rich people decided to stop giving away their money? Can you blame them? The past few days, I've had a lot of time to think, and you know what? Nothing ever changes. Rich people, poor people. Winners, losers. That's the way it goes. Except that now I get the best seats in the house. I'm in the same section as your dad. That reminds me—did you hear his show this morning? He is *hilarious*. God, you're lucky. My parents are so boring."

Andy shook his head. "They got to you, didn't they? They brainwashed you, Jensen. How did they do it?"

"Oh, cut the *drama*, Andy. Brainwashing. As if. This isn't some cheesy sci-fi movie, Andy. This is the real world. The same old boring world it was a couple of days ago. And I'm still the same old Jensen."

But she wasn't, and Andy knew it. He reached for his Lucian Glass to see if she had suddenly sprouted a *lumen*, but Winter was fast approaching, calling his name, so he let it fall back under his shirt.

The new, criminally apathetic Jensen had rattled Andy; any existing doubts about NTRP's ability to tinker with the human mind were erased the moment she'd said, *Cut the drama, Andy*. The old Jensen would have pulled out her own fingernails before uttering those words.

YOU'RE PROBABLY WONDERING ABOUT THE ZEBRA FINCHES. WELL, THERE'S A SIMPLE REASON I KEEP THEM, A REASON THAT ST. JOHN DE SPERE WILL NEVER TRULY UNDERSTAND. BIOLOGISTS ARE BAF-FLED BY THEM BECAUSE THEY DO SOMETHING INCREDIBLY RARE IN

THE ANIMAL KINGDOM: THEY ENGAGE IN COOPERATIVE BEHAVIOR. IN AN EXPERIMENT THAT IS A FORM OF THE VERY FAMOUS PRISONER'S DILEMMA, ZEBRA FINCHES HAD A CHOICE: IF THEY PRESSED ONE BUTTON, THEY GOT A SINGLE SEED. IF THEY PRESSED A DIFFERENT BUTTON, THEIR MATE GOT THREE SEEDS. GUESS WHAT? THEY CHOSE TO HELP OTHERS, EVEN THOUGH THEY GOT NO BENEFIT. PRETTY AMAZING, HUH?

SO, THE NEXT TIME SOMEONE TELLS YOU THAT COMPASSION IS A HUMAN-ONLY CHARACTERISTIC, TELL THEM ABOUT ZEBRA FINCHES.

46

Silas's watch alarm buzzed. Mrs. Cardigan was expecting an update, but at the moment, his hands were tied—literally—ensuring that he would miss his second consecutive check-in. When she didn't hear from him, the backup plan would go into effect. He felt foolish for sending that text message prematurely, but he consoled himself with the knowledge that at least he'd kinked the plastic hose to slow down the flow of gas into the auditorium. If he was lucky, that would be enough to cause NTRP's plan to fail.

St. John de Spere paid him another visit, checking the ties and propping up a tablet in front of him. He typed in a few commands, and a live video feed from the auditorium appeared on the screen.

"Now you'll be able to see and hear what's going on,"

he said. "After all the work you've done, I would hate for you to miss it, *Roger.*"

"That's the second time you've made a point of calling me that and then flashing that creepy smile of yours. Is there something you want to tell me?"

"I'm just being friendly. Ask anybody—I'm the nicest guy around."

"Except when you're killing lab animals or brainwashing a bunch of kids."

"Somebody's been watching too many movies from the fifties," said de Spere. "Brainwashing? *Please.* Give me a little credit. We are so far beyond that—"

"So you don't deny that you're planning permanent damage to those kids out there?"

"Tomato, tomahto. You say *damage*, I say *improve.* Clearly, you haven't been paying attention to the NTRP publicity. Don't you know that we are all about envisioning a better world? It's finally becoming a reality. Well, I need to get back upstairs. Are you sure you don't want to tell me your phone password? That way, I could respond to these rather serious-sounding messages you're receiving and let your friends know that you're all right."

"No thanks, I think I'll keep it to myself."

"Suit yourself, Roger. Enjoy the concert." And he disappeared again.

◆ ◆ ◆

Kids began arriving at Wellbourne between five-thirty and six. Fueled by an endless supply of free food and soda, their energy level spiked upward for the next hour and a half, the atmosphere in the auditorium growing more electric by the second. With each announcement counting down the time to the start of the concert, the crowd grew louder and louder.

Winter was the first to spot Andy's dad as he came through the doors, and she ran to greet him. "Mr. Two-penny! You actually came! Is this the coolest thing ever, or what? Did you come by yourself? Can I show you to your seat?"

Howard, eyeing her warily, considered her questions for a second. "Yes, yes, and yes."

"I'll take him up," said Andy, taking him by the arm to the side stairs that led to the balconies above the stage. "Look, Dad, I can't tell you why right now, but I need you to be Howard Twopenny tonight."

Howard examined his son's face closely, searching for signs of trouble. This was a side of Andy he'd never seen—confident, taking charge—and he liked it. "All right, then. I'll take your word for it. Howard Twopenny is officially . . . in the building. Of course, he's only here so he can make fun of the whole experience on Monday's show." He winked at Andy. "Before you go, can I give you some advice?"

"Uh, sure."

"Stay away from that Winter girl. I don't care how

pretty she is. There's something not quite right with her. Don't know what it is. Those eyes . . . you can just tell."

"Okay. I will. After tonight . . . well, things will be different. I hope."

"Is that someone you know?" Howard asked, pointing down at the main entrance. "I think he's waving at you."

"Detective Cunningham, the cop I met when I turned in the money. And that's . . . Huh, I wonder how they know each other? Zhariah Davis. She's a reporter."

Winter escorted them to the same balcony where Andy and his dad were and showed them to their seats. "This is you, A5 and A6. Right next to Mr. Twopenny. I'm sure you've both heard of him."

Introductions followed, followed by some uncomfortable laughs as Howard told an inappropriate joke about a priest, a rabbi, and a policeman.

Andy was finally able to pull the detective off to the side and point out Jensen, sitting in a balcony seat across the auditorium from them.

"What the . . . Is that who I think it is?"

Andy nodded. "She's acting like the whole thing was no big deal."

"She say where she was or what she's been doing?"

"Not really anything that makes sense. She's like a different person."

"I guess we should be happy that she's safe and home. In my business, that counts as a win."

◆ ◆ ◆

At seven-thirty, the kids were finally allowed to take their seats in the auditorium, where they found their new 233dot-com e-readers, fully charged and pre-loaded with a selection of classic novels. Karina Jellyby, dressed in jeans and a two-sizes-too-small Wellbourne blazer, ran onto the stage and shouted, "How's everybody doing?"

The screamed response was so loud that Andy covered his ears and, in the basement, Silas felt the wall behind him shake.

Karina continued, "Well, that's good, because you are in for one very special night. Those people out there who still don't believe in global warming haven't met you yet. The world is a *much* warmer place, thanks to all of you. We challenged you to help 'thaw' things out by donating two hours a week of your precious time, and you not only met that challenge, you exceeded our wildest dreams."

Lots more wall-shaking screaming as the four members of the band ran onstage. "There are a few people we all need to thank for making this possible," said Karina. "First, a big hand for Deanna Decameron from NTRP. Stand up, Deanna! There she is. Deanna is the director of NTRP's brand-new education broadcasting division, and she has promised to knock all our socks off tonight during our break. You are going to be the first to see some new technology that is going to change the way you learn and watch

TV and play video games *forever*. And, of course, Wellbourne's own Dr. Everly! When she heard about our contest, she reached out to us and . . . here we are! Thank you, thank you, thank you!" As the lights dimmed, she added: "And now . . . let's get this show on the road!"

47

Back in the basement, Silas listened and waited, wondering how long it would take de Spere to realize that something had gone wrong with his master plan.

On the floor in front of him, the tablet streamed images of the stage and, occasionally, the audience as Karina launched into her first set. She opened with "Save Yourself," an old-school rock anthem from her first album, which got all two hundred and fifty kids on their feet at the sound of the opening chords.

Across the basement, a door squeaked on its hinges, then clicked shut—the unmistakable sounds of someone trying very hard to be quiet. Footsteps getting closer. Silas held his breath and waited for the final blow. Like Ilene Porter, he was a loose end, and her fate was proof that NTRP didn't like loose ends.

"Fallon Mishra," he said. "I should have known you'd be here."

She stopped short when she saw him, shrinking back half a step.

It made perfect sense, Silas admitted. Who better to tie up a loose end than a ninth *dan* black belt in kendo? She probably knew fifteen ways to kill without leaving a mark. He couldn't stop himself from smiling at the irony of being killed by the woman who once occupied the Discipline chair.

Instead of snapping his neck like a twig or yanking out his heart by reaching down his throat, however, she did something even more surprising as they made eye contact: She put her finger to her lips. Then she reached out and turned the tablet facedown on the floor. Silas tensed as she moved behind him—*This is it*, he thought—but she surprised him again by cutting the plastic ties that bound him to the pipes.

He climbed quickly to his feet and faced her, looking completely dumbfounded. "What—"

"Shhh. De Spere may have this place bugged. We need to get you out of here. Quietly. Come on."

"How do I know I can trust . . ."

Fallon bent down and lifted her jeans a few inches so Silas could see her socks. Wool, of course. Dark green with two narrow purple stripes. The very ones that Mrs. Cardigan had been knitting the night of Andy's first visit to the Loom.

"But . . . all this time . . . you *betrayed* us."

She shook her head. "I've never been disloyal. Mrs. Cardigan orchestrated the whole thing to get me inside, to get me close to St. John de Spere. I had to do a lot of things, including following you the other night, to maintain the illusion. If de Spere walks in right now, it's months of work gaining his trust down the drain. Look, I don't have time to explain it all right now, but there's one more thing that might help to convince you. Remember the day Andy was at the NTRP building and he dropped his pen in the screening room? Didn't you wonder how it ended up back in his bag? I knew it was a camera from my own training."

"I did wonder, actually," Silas admitted. "That was you, too? So, how much do you know about this Operation Tailor?"

Fallon shook her head. "It's de Spere's pet project, and he won't let anybody completely inside. A lot of people know bits and pieces—kind of like the recipe for Kentucky Fried Chicken—but nobody knows *everything*, except de Spere himself. He's a lunatic, an absolute control freak. I wouldn't be surprised if you know more than I do."

"We have managed to make some interesting discoveries. He's using gas—something he's been working on since college—and combining it with lights that have some kind of hypnotic effect. Somehow, the combination of the two changes people—and not for the better."

Fallon squinted at him, chewing on that bit of information for a moment. "When you say that it *changes* people, you mean . . ."

"The *lumen*. Suddenly, it's just . . . there. Think what it would mean to NTRP—and to the Agents—if those good kids upstairs were all 'flipped.' But we don't have to worry, because I took care of the gas line."

"Where is it?"

Silas looked up. "Right there. I'll cut it, just to be certain."

Fallon helped get the ladder in place and held out a pocketknife to Silas, who sliced through the plastic hose in one quick motion. Expecting to feel the gas escaping, he pointed the end of the hose at the back of his hand.

"That's strange," he said, waving it in front of Fallon's face. "What do you feel?"

"Nothing."

Above them, the kids screamed and stomped and, encouraged by Karina, sang the chorus of "Don't Blame Me."

"Maybe he hasn't turned it on yet," Fallon said.

"I guess that's poss—" Silas stopped, his heart suddenly in his throat. "Oh, no. We have to go. Now. This isn't the gas line. It's a decoy. De Spere played me. He just wanted me to think that it was, that I had figured it all out. He knew I'd sent the message to Mrs. Cardigan saying that I had everything under control." He rushed for the door, with Fallon right behind.

"Where are we going? What are you talking about?" she asked.

"It was the burp."

"Excuse me?"

"Andy. Burped. Loud."

"What?"

"The gas—it's *in* the soda. And those kids up there are drinking it by the gallon." That final word was punctuated by the screams of a bunch of kids having the time of their lives.

"What do we do?"

"We have to cut the power . . . somehow. Follow me! And keep your eyes open for de Spere and . . . is there anyone else from NTRP here with him?"

"Not that I know of. But that doesn't mean anything. He's paranoid, so there's no telling who else he has involved."

"Well then, just shout if you see anyone you recognize."

◆ ◆ ◆

When Karina announced that she and the band would be taking a short break, the heavy curtain fell and the auditorium went black, illuminated only by the exit signs and a giant screen that hung from the ceiling. Every eye was glued to it as a camera focused on a mysterious figure in a black cape and wide-brimmed fedora standing a few feet behind the curtain. As he stood there, a pair of stagehands rolled a table toward him. On it was an enormous computer terminal with a console that looked as if it belonged in a fighter jet. Its hundreds of buttons, knobs, and keys formed a semicircle wrapping halfway around the monitor screen. Then a single spotlight switched on, illuminating the man, who bore an incredible likeness to the Phantom of the Opera, sitting at the console with his back to the audience.

He reached up dramatically and pressed a single button, and the first eight notes of Beethoven's Fifth Symphony boomed from every corner of the building: *dun dun dun DUN . . . dun dun dun DUN.*

Andy fidgeted nervously. "Something's wrong," he said under his breath. "This shouldn't be happening." Where was Silas?

Winter leaned in close to him. "Sorry, I didn't hear you."

"Nothing," said Andy. "I was just saying that I like this music."

She nudged him and nonchalantly slipped her arm through his. "Me too. This is so exciting. I can't wait to see this show."

Andy tensed when she touched him, but he didn't look at her, and he didn't respond. Instead, he sneaked a peek at his phone, still waiting for a message from Silas or Reza or Mrs. Cardigan—*anybody.*

"What's wrong?" Winter shouted over the music. "You seem upset."

Andy turned to face her, his eyes searching hers for signs of anything unusual, but every inch of Winter was as cool and unruffled as a newly frozen pond.

"Look!" she said, pointing at a giant beach ball floating just over the heads of the kids in the center of the auditorium.

It took Andy a few seconds of staring at it to realize that it wasn't real; it was an illusion, nothing more than light and air, and not like anything he'd ever seen before.

Winter smiled. "It's like I could reach up and touch it."

The Phantom pressed another key, and instantly birds of every color and species appeared—a thousand or more, flying in unison round and round the auditorium. After a few laps, a window materialized on the wall and swung open, and the birds all flew through it into the New York night. Except that neither the birds nor the window was real.

The kids were absolutely spellbound, cheering their hearts out, but Andy had more practical considerations: He was looking for the source of this sinister "magic." His eyes scanned the ceiling until he found the device that had been covered by the NTRP tarp backstage before the show—a steel and glass globe about five feet in diameter, with lenses poking out in all directions, spinning wildly. It was partly hidden behind a banner from one of Wellbourne's championship soccer teams, so Andy started to move toward the stage for an unobstructed view.

"Where are you going?" Winter asked, grasping at his arm. "Don't you want to see what's next?"

"I'm going backstage," answered Andy. "I need to see . . ." He shook himself loose of her grip and headed for the steps at the side of the stage, with Winter right on his heels. He had just hit the first step when the crowd gasped again. He turned to see the *Mayflower* crashing through a huge wave, sending a wall of spray that seemed so real that the crowd ducked.

As he reached the top step behind the curtain, he saw Silas—the actual human being, not a hologram—rushing toward him on the other side of the stage. He, too, was so preoccupied with looking for the source of the illusions that he never noticed Andy—and certainly not the length of iron pipe that connected with his head, making a *thud* loud enough for Andy to hear over the sound of the *Mayflower* surging through the Atlantic. Andy had seen it, but not in time to warn him. He and Winter recoiled in unison as Silas, his legs crumpling beneath him after the blow, dropped, stonelike, to the floor with another, even louder *thonk*.

For a moment, Andy was frozen in place, mouth agape, but he recovered quickly, shaking off the initial shock and pulling away from Winter. He was halfway across the stage when Fallon Mishra appeared, almost stumbling over Silas's limp body. She stopped, kneeling next to him to make sure he was still breathing. Based on everything he had heard about Fallon, Andy jumped to the logical conclusion that she was Silas's attacker.

"Hey! Leave him alone!" he shouted, his words drowned out by the pounding beat of the hologram version of Karina Jellyby (so lifelike that the audience thought it was actually her) playing his favorite song, "Do the Shake

Me Up!" He rushed to Silas, pushing Fallon aside, and felt his insides flip-flop when the hand he placed under Silas's head came back bloody. He checked for a pulse and listened to his chest for several breaths before directing his anger at Fallon.

"What is wrong with you? He's unconscious. You could have killed him."

Fallon quickly figured out what was going through Andy's mind. "I know how it looks, Andy, but it's not what you think. *I* didn't touch him—I swear."

Meanwhile, Winter moved back to the terminal where the Phantom was madly pushing buttons and turning knobs, and touched him on the shoulder. When he turned and saw Silas on the floor with Fallon and Andy standing over him, St. John de Spere smiled and rose to his feet.

"Listen to me, Andy," said Fallon. "I know what you're thinking, but you have to trust me. I'm on your side." She glanced over at the unconscious Silas. "He came here to shut down the system. We have to hurry. He was wrong. The gas—it's not being pumped into the air. It's in the soda that everyone has been drinking for the last two hours. It's too late to do anything about that, so we were coming to cut the power to the terminal. It's the only way to stop them."

"No. I don't believe you," he said. "I *know* who you are. *He* warned me about you, told me how dangerous you are, but I don't care. Besides, if you really were on my side, somebody would have told me, but the only message I got was to tell me that everything was under control. You just can't admit that you lost. There is no gas. We spoiled your big plan."

"You should listen to her, Mr. Llewellyn," said St. John de Spere, surprising both Andy and Fallon with his sudden appearance. "She's telling the truth. About everything. Come on out, Nicky."

A gangster-for-hire in a too-tight black suit and matching black shirt and tie stepped out from behind the curtain, eighteen inches of steel pipe still in his hand.

"Everything okay, boss?"

"Oh, yes, we're all just getting to know each other. Carry on with your duties just the way we planned, but don't go far—I still may need you with *this* one," de Spere said, pointing at Fallon.

Andy recognized the gangster instantly; he was the guy in the spandex shorts who had chased him in Central Park after he'd used his Lucian Glass for the first time.

Winter's eyes burned with anger as she faced Fallon. "You mean she is . . ."

"Devious? Dangerous? A traitor? I'm afraid so," said de Spere. "I have to admit to having mixed feelings at this moment. On the one hand, I can't tell you how *disappointed* I am, but on the other . . . bravo! You nearly had me convinced that your defection was real. But this . . . *Betrayal* is such an ugly word, don't you think? I hardly know where to begin when it comes to punishing you."

Fallon stared at him, defiant. "What I did, I did for the

good of humanity. Can you say the same thing, Mr. de Spere?"

He scoffed. "Ah, the humanity card. How quaint. How *obsolete*. Look around you, Ms. Mishra. Humanity is *over*. It had a nice run of what, five or six thousand years? It's time for a new world order. It's time to give up on ideas like charity and morality and compassion. They don't work. They never have. It was all a fantasy. People are only truly happy when they're doing what they *want* to do, not what someone else tells them is the *right* thing to do."

"According to whom? You?" Fallon pointed at Winter and scoffed. "Her? You're going to put mankind's future in her hands?"

De Spere shrugged. "And why not? She can't do worse than the troglodytes in office now. Democracy! Another idea whose time is long past. Lucky for us, it's as dead as the people who dreamed it up in the first place." He then turned to Andy. "Ah, Mr. Llewellyn. Sorry about your friend here." He kicked Silas in the ribs for emphasis and then stood with one foot on his back, like a big-game hunter with his trophy. "It's a pity, really. So close. Ah, but what is it they say? Close only counts in horseshoes and hand grenades. Well, now that we're all gathered here, I say we carry on with the show. Winter, what do you think?"

Winter's pale eyes turned frigid. "Yes. It's time."

De Spere pulled a revolver from his jacket pocket. He pointed it at Fallon, waving her next to Andy so he could keep them both covered. "I apologize for the gun—it's a bit melodramatic, don't you think? Then again, I've seen what you can do to a concrete block with your feet, so it's a necessary precaution. By the way, *Andover* . . . how much root beer did *you* drink today?"

Andy's mind raced, recounting the stops he'd made at the concession stand, and he suddenly felt ill.

Winter moved to de Spere's side. "He had three or four big cups at least. I made sure he took advantage of those free refills."

"Perfect. Because something tells me that Mr. Llewellyn knows more than he lets on. He and Miss Huntley have been sticking their noses into all sorts of pies. Of course, now that I've helped her see the error of her ways, I feel *so* much better. In fact—" He stopped mid-sentence, his jaw falling wide open.

"James Thorneside," said a woman's voice. "It's been a long time."

48

"Mom!" cried Andy.

Forgetting for the moment that a gun was pointed at him, Andy rushed into his mother's waiting arms. "What are you doing here?" he said, fighting back tears. "You weren't supposed to be home till tomorrow."

"Abbey Newell," said de Spere, shaking his head in disbelief. "The first time I talked to Howard, he mentioned a wife named Abbey, but I never would have dreamed that it was you. I have to admit, I'm still having a hard time getting my brain wrapped around *that*. You—and Howard Twopenny?" He threw his head back, laughing obnoxiously. "Of course, it helps to prove my theory about opposites."

"Wait—you know his mother?" said Winter. "What's going on?"

"Abbey and I are old friends," said de Spere. "From back in my Cambridge days."

"We were *never* friends," corrected Abbey. "I was your advisor. I gave you advice, which you ignored. You killed a woman. And thousands of animals."

De Spere laughed off those deaths with a wave of his hand. "Tsk, tsk. You're still lecturing me about *that* old news? You haven't changed a bit. Seriously, you have to learn to let things go, Abbey. Twenty years later and you're still shedding tears for a few lab rats and one under-achieving girl who was never going to amount to anything. The only difference is that now you have your son to join in the singing. Too bad no one's listening."

"That's where you're wrong," said Abbey. "The kids sitting out there are all the proof I need."

A few feet away, Silas stirred, raising his head groggily. "Wha—" He winced, then felt the back of his skull, where a lump was growing.

Abbey went to him. "You're going to be okay. Just a nasty bump on the head. Don't try to move yet."

"You just can't help yourself, can you?" said de Spere. "You see someone suffering, and you have to swoop in like some kind of comic-book superhero and save them. What have you been doing for the past twenty years? No, let me guess: You run a soup kitchen." Then, with a smirk, he added, "Give me your tired, your poor, your huddled masses."

"Something like that," said Abbey.

"And you're married to *Howard Twopenny*. Sorry, I can't seem to get past that. It is just so incredibly *ironic*. Don't get me wrong. I like Howard. In fact, I *almost* feel guilty for what is going to happen to the boy wonder here in a few minutes. But not quite."

Abbey held Andy close to her. "You're wrong about something else, James: I *have* changed. The last time, I was alone in standing up to you, and I didn't do enough to make sure that you couldn't carry out your experiment. I'm not alone anymore. I have a circle of friends who are just as committed to stopping you and your misguided followers." She then spun Andy so he was facing her as she pulled a black cord from beneath her blouse and held up her own circle of Lucian Glass.

"This stands for Compassion," she said. "And don't you believe for a second that it is dead. It's never been more alive—and not only here. Everywhere."

"Y-you're one of the Agents?" said Andy, utterly perplexed. His mind reeled; there was so much he wanted to ask her, so much he wanted to *tell* her.

"She is. For nineteen years, Andy," a woman's voice chimed in from a catwalk thirty feet above them. "I warned you that I still had some surprises in store."

Everyone tilted their heads back to take in the figure of Mrs. Cardigan peering down at them.

"My, my. *Another* unexpected pleasure," said de Spere.

"Mrs. Cardigan, I presume? I'm so thrilled that you're here. I can't wait to see the look on your face when you realize that you are finally, completely, and utterly *beaten*."

"Prepare to be disappointed, *James*," she retorted. "You see, no matter the outcome today, we will not be defeated, and we will fight you from the shadows no longer."

"Yes, yes," said de Spere impatiently. "But all this talk, talk, talk has gotten tiresome."

Fallon Mishra, glaring at Winter and twitching like a cobra about to strike, drew de Spere's attention. "Don't even think about it," he said, aiming his pistol at her through his jacket pocket. Without another word, he pointed a small remote control at the terminal and clicked.

The curtain began to rise slowly, and the silver globe in the center of the auditorium went dark and stopped spinning. Andy held his breath, praying that the system had failed. In those moments of darkness, his mind turned back to the explosion at the bank, to Jensen and Ilene Porter, to all the amazing people he'd met over the past two months—Mrs. Cardigan and Silas, Reza Benali and the other Agents—and what they stood for, and he realized that he wasn't the same person he'd been. He was *involved*, and there was no going back.

But then everything changed.

All eyes turned upward, focusing on the steel and glass globe, which began to glow red from the millions of watts of light struggling to escape. Now spinning slowly, it dropped lower and lower from the ceiling until it was hanging in the very center of the room.

It remained there for a few seconds, its motors humming quietly while everyone held their breath. Then came a flash of blue light from deep within it, like a spark, and the ball was spinning at high speed, the whirring becoming louder. Another spark of blue, then one of green. Then red. Yellow. Orange. Violet. Strobe lights stabbed through the blackness, all coming from that one source. It was beautiful, terrifying, and impossible to look away from.

And that was just the beginning.

Meanwhile, Silas was still sprawled on the floor, his head aching and groggy. Even though he was seeing them through closed eyes, the lights were so intense that he knew that it was St. John de Spere's moment to show the world what he had spent the last twenty years developing. He willed himself to sit up. "Andy!" he screamed. "Close your eyes!"

But Andy couldn't—it was all too incredible, too wonderful.

The lights were still increasing in intensity when de Spere turned a series of knobs on the console. Suddenly, every inch of the room was filled with the sounds and life-like three-dimensional images of suffering and despair— hundreds of them, brought to life (and, in some cases, death) through the magic of de Spere's infernal machine. Mere inches away from Andy, a dog that looked remarkably like Penny lay injured in a ditch, whining in pain. Behind him, a starving child, her eyes runny and pained, held out a fragile hand. Andy turned ninety degrees and was confronted by an elderly man crying over the body of a loved one. Andy's face was expressionless, lost in the power of the scenes unfolding before his eyes.

Winter laughed as he stood there, soaking up image after image—hundreds of them every second—as they were imprinted forever on his subconscious mind. "It's hard, isn't it?" she whispered. "You can't bear to look away, even for a second."

Fallon struck out at her, missing her face by millimeters.

"No, no, no, Ms. Mishra," said de Spere, waving his pistol at her. "On the floor. Now move away from Mr. Llewellyn. That's much better. Now, everyone else. On the floor." He glanced up at Mrs. Cardigan, still standing on the catwalk, twenty-five or thirty feet away from the globe, and decided that she posed no threat to the machine. "Looks like you have the best seat in the house, Mrs. Cardigan! Enjoy the view. Don't worry, this won't take long. Those adorable kids out there won't feel a thing. Then Ms. Carmichael can get on with her concert and her pathetic attempts to save a world that doesn't want to be saved. Of course, she won't have *quite* as much help as she had a few minutes ago."

Abbey shouted at her son. "Shut your eyes, Andy. You can do it. You have the strength."

De Spere grinned with devious delight. "He can't hear you. His mind is . . . occupied at the moment."

Andy looked as if he had been turned to stone, and his mother's heart sank, along with everyone else's. Silas knew it was up to him to do something, but when he tried to move, his legs betrayed him. From where he sat, he could see the audience behind Andy, and what he saw scared him more than anything he had ever seen: two hundred and fifty kids, staring, zombie-like, into the space above them, their faces illuminated by strobe lights of every color and tens of thousands of images flicking past.

I have failed, he thought. *Failed Mrs. Cardigan, who saved my life. Failed the Agents and their eight-hundred-year history of fighting evil. Failed those kids sitting in the audience, and all the people who would have benefited from their work in the future.* But what hurt most was that he had failed Andy, who had trusted and depended on him.

After flipping a few more switches and typing in additional commands, de Spere noticed that Silas was sitting up, his eyes wide open. "Well, well. Look who has rejoined the living. Sorry about that knock on the head. A shame, really, that you have to witness this," he said, pointing at Andy. "I know what the kid means to you."

"Y-you couldn't possibly know," stammered Silas. "You've never—"

"How much longer?" Winter asked.

"A few more seconds," said de Spere. "He's a strong

one. It's a good thing he had so much of the gas. Still, it's imperative that he see the complete cycle."

"Come on, Andy," his mother implored. "Don't give in. You can hear me, I know you can. This isn't real, Andy. The world isn't all bad. There is beauty. And love . . ."

Silas squeezed his eyes shut, hoping to avoid having to watch the inevitable conclusion to the tragedy playing out onstage under the direction of de Spere, who had cast away his cape and fedora.

But this play didn't end the way it was supposed to: One of the actors decided to improvise.

"Hey!" cried Winter. "What are you—"

Silas opened his eyes in time to see Andy shove Winter directly at Fallon, who caught and held her. He then grabbed Karina's prize guitar, a 1967 Fender Stratocaster, from its stand behind the terminal and ran toward the back of the stage. He threw the strap over his shoulder as if he'd done it a million times and started climbing the steel ladder on the back wall.

"Get him!" screamed Winter, thrashing to break free of Fallon's viselike grip.

"There's nothing he can do," said de Spere, training his gun on Fallon. "Let him go."

"He'll ruin everything!" Winter screamed. "Shoot him!"

De Spere took his eyes off Fallon long enough to catch sight of Andy clambering up the last two steps of the ladder and leaping five feet through the air to grab hold of a rope hanging from the ceiling, the Fender still strapped across his back.

"Be careful!" shouted his mother.

"That a boy, Andy," said Mrs. Cardigan as he swung back and forth on the rope until he got enough momentum to reach the catwalk, where she was waiting. She reached down and helped him climb up.

"Shut up!" said de Spere, suddenly looking concerned. "Everybody!"

"You never could handle pressure, James," said Abbey. "Go, Andy!"

Standing on the rail of the catwalk, Andy hesitated. There was another rope—one that might get him close to the globe—but it was farther away than he had hoped. Without ever looking down, he turned to Mrs. Cardigan. "I have to do it."

"I know," she said, nodding.

Meanwhile, the bleak images kept coming, pouring out of the globe like water from a faucet, and the kids in the audience were catatonic—blank expressions, eyes unblinking, mouths open. On the stage, Fallon held tight to Winter while de Spere frantically sought a solution. He moved to Silas, pointing the gun at him.

"Let the girl go, Fallon," he ordered. "Or I shoot your friend."

"Don't let her go," Silas said calmly.

Thirty feet above them, Andy teetered on the rail of the catwalk, his eyes fixed on the rope hanging near the globe.

"Damn that kid!" said de Spere.

Andy coiled his legs and launched himself across the chasm as de Spere aimed and fired.

49

The bullet missed its target, ricocheting into the metal rafters, and Andy's arms and legs flailed wildly as he fought to maintain his grip on the rope. The coarse hemp scorched his hands as he slid down. When he finally came to a stop at a knot, he smelled his skin burning.

"Is he shooting at me?" he asked Mrs. Cardigan as he started to swing back and forth on the rope.

He got an answer in the form of a second shot, which missed him by inches, once again bouncing off the ceiling.

"Go, Andy!" cried his mom. "Hurry!"

"One more swing!" he shouted. He gripped Karina's guitar in his right hand and the rope with his left as he willed himself closer to the machine. Making his final approach, he pulled the Fender back behind his head and, with a war cry, swung it in a picture-perfect forehand that drained every last bit of energy from his exhausted body.

Below him, de Spere took careful aim. "Got you this time, kid." He put his finger on the trigger and squeezed . . . as Penny did a little flying of her own, hitting him square in the chest with all four paws, catching him totally off guard and knocking him off his feet.

Andy expected, naturally, that the guitar would seriously damage the globe, which would have been a fine, dramatic-enough ending to the show. Instead, he got the Death Star scene from *Star Wars*. The globe *exploded* in a blue-green flash that blinded everyone on the stage for several seconds and sent Andy flying once more—only this time there was no rope to grab at the end of his flight.

He was prepared for the worst, and a lot went through his mind on that short, fast trip across the auditorium as he braced himself for the impact: *Maybe I can get out of this with a few broken bones. Man, this is going to hurt. I'm not ready to die. I haven't finished my model yet.*

Instead of slamming into the floor at forty miles an hour, though, he found himself looking up into Billy Newcomb's eyes, the football player's massive biceps cradling him as if he were an egg.

"Hiya, Andy," said Billy. "Sorry I'm late. Traffic was murder."

◆ ◆ ◆

For three long seconds, the auditorium was deathly silent, and the only light came from the emergency lights that kicked on when the explosion shut down the power to the entire building. Smoke alarms began to screech from every corner of the room, and the smell of an electrical fire hung in the air.

The first person to speak was Abbey: "Andy! Where's Andy?" She couldn't see Billy from where she was standing, and based on the magnitude of the explosion, she feared the worst.

"Over here, ma'am," said Billy. "I've got him. He's okay. A little cut up, but he'll be fine."

Actually, considering how little remained of Karina's guitar (nothing but a few inches of the neck and six dangling strings), Andy was in remarkably (*miraculously*, thought Silas) good shape.

Abbey ran to him, crying out for a towel when she saw his face. A shard of glass had struck him on the forehead, just to the left of the scar from the bank explosion, and blood was flowing from the cut at an alarming rate.

"Where's Dad?" he asked, delirious. "Tell him not to drink the soda."

"It's okay, Andy," said Abbey. "Your dad is fine. Everyone is safe."

"Listen to me!" he insisted. "It's really important. Don't let him drink it!"

"Here, you can tell him yourself," said Silas, making room for Howard to squeeze in next to his son.

"Dad! Whatever you do, *don't* drink the soda."

Howard looked up at his wife quizzically. "What is he talking about? What happened here? One second, I'm watching beach balls and a giant ship sail around the room—I still don't know what to think about that—and the next, alarms are going off and I hear you screaming for Andy. And now he's telling me not to drink the soda." He then noticed the group of strangers surrounding Andy—Silas, Fallon, Billy Newcomb, and even Mrs. Cardigan, who had climbed down from the catwalk. "Who *are* you people?"

"We have a lot to talk about," said Abbey. "There are some things . . . It's a bit complicated to get into right now. For the moment, you should be proud of Andy—he just prevented a catastrophe."

Howard looked around at the damage from the explosion. "That . . . was him *preventing* a catastrophe? Geez, what does it look like when one actually happens?"

Out in the seats of the auditorium, no one moved for a long time—two hundred and fifty catatonic kids, frozen in place. Finally, they began to stir, although they looked as if they were coming out of a long, deep sleep, murmuring and glancing this way and that, completely in the dark about what they had been through. When Karina's Fender struck the globe, the cycle of lights and colors and images was mere seconds from completion, and their brains were too preoccupied with the dismal details of the holograms to take notice of anything else.

"We really should get him to a hospital," said Silas. "Have him checked out. He could have a concussion." He felt the back of his head where the pipe had landed. "And I should probably join him," he added, sinking slowly to the floor.

"It's just a good cut," said Billy, gently setting Andy down into the chair that Karina carried to him. "The glass is still in there. I can just see the end of it."

"Let me see," said Abbey. Using her fingernails, she pulled out the shard of glass and held it out for Andy to see.

Andy smiled.

Karina looked horrified. "Why are you *smiling*? You could have been killed."

Andy marveled at the crescent-shaped glass in his hand, immediately noting its resemblance to the piece taken from the same spot on his forehead after the bank explosion. He slipped the glass into his shirt pocket. "I'm starting a collection."

"This had better be the *end* of your collecting," said Abbey, pressing a clean Karina Jellyby concert T-shirt onto the wound.

Howard agreed: "Two pieces of glass pulled out of your head is *more* than enough."

Andy suddenly sat bolt upright. "Penny!"

"She's here. She's fine," said Fallon, so pale that she was almost unrecognizable. "The two of you saved the day. I still can't believe . . ." Her voice trailed off as she collapsed, her fall broken by Billy, who caught her a millisecond before her head hit the floor.

"She's been shot!" he said. He held up a hand, covered in her blood.

"What! Where?"

"Looks like it's her shoulder," said Billy.

"I didn't even hear the shot," said Abbey.

"Me neither," said Silas. "Penny must have knocked de Spere's arm at the exact moment Andy was hitting the machine. She probably saved his life."

Fallon opened her eyes briefly. "De Spere . . . Winter . . ."

"They're long gone," said Mrs. Cardigan. She stepped gingerly over the broken glass that lay scattered all around and pointed at the floor. "Trapdoor."

Silas pulled it open and peered down into the blackness. "Like rats. Which is fitting, I guess."

"No point in going after them," said Mrs. Cardigan. "Make sure nobody else needs help, and then we'd better get Andover and Fallon to the hospital to get stitched up. And you—let's get that bump looked at. Don't worry. I'll take care of the sticky details with police and doctors and so on." With a quick wave, she opened the exit door at the back of the stage, holding it open for Billy Newcomb, who was carrying Fallon in his arms.

"What's this?" Abbey asked, reaching down for a small

manila envelope with *Roger* printed on it in neat letters. "Who's Roger?"

Mrs. Cardigan's eyes widened in surprise. She turned to Silas. "I believe that is intended for you."

Silas looked confused. "He called me Roger. . . . How did you know . . ."

"Perhaps it's time you knew the whole story about yourself," she said. "But not now. I must be going."

Abbey handed the envelope to Silas, who turned it over in his hands several times before sliding his thumbnail under the flap and opening it. Inside was a yellowed photograph, no more than three inches square, cut from an unidentified newspaper. Two children, a boy and a girl, stood on the deck of a fishing boat, their faces a bit too thin, their ribs a little too prominent. The boy seemed to be daydreaming, gazing at something off in the distance. The girl, however, stared boldly into the camera lens, a somehow familiar smile revealing a gap between her front teeth. Silas shivered as he recognized her as the little girl from his dreams. All the air went out of his lungs as he realized that he knew the boy. He was staring at a picture of himself— the first photograph of him as a child he had ever seen.

The caption read: *On Sunday, these two children, approximately six years old, were found adrift on a makeshift raft in the North Atlantic, three hundred miles west of Scotland. Nothing else is known about them, as they have declined to speak.*

"What is it?" Abbey asked. "You'd better sit back down. You look terrible."

"It's nothing," Silas said, shoving the clipping back into the envelope. "Let's get out of here before the police show up and start asking questions. Karina, do you have a story ready?"

"Looks to me like an amplifier blew up," said Karina. "Speaking of police, look who's here. I completely forgot about him."

"Is everything okay up here?" asked Detective Cunningham, climbing the steps to the stage, with Zhariah Davis beside him. Their eyes had a glazed-over look to them.

"What happened?" Zhariah asked. "Looks like something blew up."

"Amplifier," said Karina. "Only one minor casualty. A Wellbourne student who was helping out backstage took a piece of shrapnel to the forehead. He's going to be okay, though. Someone's bringing a car around, and they're going to take him to the hospital to get checked out."

"Hi, Detective," said Andy, removing the blood-soaked T-shirt from his forehead.

"Andy—holy cow! That is some cut. Is that the—"

"Same spot as the last time? Yeah. Weird, huh?"

"You definitely need stitches," said Zhariah. "That looks pretty deep."

"So . . . you didn't see . . . anything?" Andy asked Detective Cunningham.

"What do you mean? We saw the concert. Great show, by the way, Karina."

"But after the . . . when the lights started . . . you didn't notice anything strange?"

Cunningham looked at Zhariah; they both shrugged. "Nothing that I recall," he said. "The band was playing, and then . . . they weren't." As the words came out of his mouth, he knew they didn't make sense, but he couldn't understand why. "Well, I'm glad everybody else is okay. Take care of yourself, Andy." He spun around and went back down the steps, more bewildered than when he had arrived.

Howard and Abbey got Andy to his feet and started guiding him to the door.

"Andy, can I have a minute?" Silas asked.

"It's okay, Mom," Andy said, in response to her worried look. "It really doesn't hurt that much."

Silas looked him up and down, shaking his head in wonder. "I don't understand. How did you do it? You drank a gallon of that gassed-up soda. The flashing lights, the holograms . . . Everyone else who had the soda was completely catatonic. Why didn't it affect you? I know there's more to you than meets the eye, but . . . *how?*"

Andy grinned at him, a line of blood still running down the side of his face. He wiped some on the back of his hand and held it out. "I'll bet you didn't know my blood was green, did you?"

"What are you talking about? Your blood is red. Just like mine."

"To *you*, maybe. I'm color-blind. Red looks kind of greenish to me. And green stuff looks brown. Blue and yellow are okay, I guess. The way I understand it, those two look the same to me as they do to you."

"How long have you known?"

"I don't know—a long time. It's not like I notice it—I've never seen anything different. Remember when you and Reza and Mrs. Cardigan were showing me all those pictures, and you were talking about all the colors? I thought about saying something, but it didn't seem that important. The funny thing is, I'm pretty sure Mrs. Cardigan knew all along." He pulled up his pant leg to show Silas the wool socks she knit for him . . . in blue and yellow.

"I'll be darned. How'd she know?"

Andy pointed across the stage at his mom. "She's color-blind, too."

"But . . . I thought it was strictly a male thing."

"Nope. Girls, too. Only not as often. But here's the best part: I'm about ninety-nine percent sure that's why Ilene Porter wasn't affected. When Jensen asked her about the images she saw, do you remember how she answered?"

"She said they looked like an old black-and-white movie," said Silas.

"Exactly. I didn't think anything about it at first, but after what I saw in the Loom, I started to put it together."

"It makes sense. I'm sure we can find out for sure. Someone in her family must know. Does anyone else know about you? You didn't tell anyone? Good, let's keep it that way. We may be able to use that. One more question: When you were in a trance—was that real?"

He laughed and then winced in pain. "Just pretending. I was waiting for the right moment. It was more exciting that way, don't you think?"

50

On Friday, exactly a week after the concert, Andy sat in the school library, staring at the 233dotcom terminal that had been installed on Wednesday afternoon.

Mr. Brookings, the librarian, paced around the room, muttering under his breath. "They take away all my books and give me this monstrosity. No one knows how it works. For all I know, the damned thing is plotting to kill me, like the computer in *2001: A Space Odyssey*. Look at it. Every time I get close, the lights go crazy—like it doesn't like me. Well, the feeling is mutual, pal."

A senior girl opened the library door and stuck her head in. "Excuse me, Mr. Brookings? Is Andy Llewellyn here? Dr. Everly is looking for him."

The librarian looked toward Andy. "Mr. Llewellyn,

you're being summoned for an audience with Her Majesty. Better look sharp, young man."

Andy ran his fingers through his hair and tucked in the half of his shirttail that was hanging out.

"Oh, much better," said Mr. Brookings.

Andy followed the girl to the reception area and was ushered immediately into Dr. Everly's office. Detective Cunningham was there, along with the reporter Zhariah Davis, a man he didn't recognize, and his parents—all of them looking very serious.

"Andover, please come in. Sit down," said Dr. Everly.

"W-what's going on?"

"We want to talk to you about a very serious matter," said Detective Cunningham. "A *police* matter."

Andy tried to swallow but couldn't. Suddenly, his blazer felt extremely tight around his shoulders and he had difficulty breathing. He turned to his mom for support, but his stomach flopped when he saw the disappointed look on her face.

Cunningham stood directly over him, glaring angrily. "Did you really think we were going to let you get away with it? Did you?"

"What are you . . . I didn't do—"

"Don't try to deny it, kid. We've got you *cold*."

The unknown man handed an envelope to Andy. "Maybe he'll know what you mean when he sees *this*."

Fingers trembling, Andy opened the envelope and took

out a single piece of paper: a check, made out to Andover James Llewellyn, for ten thousand dollars.

"I don't get it—"

Everyone in the room burst into laughter, with Detective Cunningham's eruption almost breaking the window glass.

"Andover, I'd like you to meet Mr. Upshaw, the president of the First Mutual Bank," said Dr. Everly. "I'm sorry if we frightened you."

Mr. Upshaw took Andy's hand in both of his and shook it long and hard. "Andy, on behalf of the bank and myself, thank you. Thank you, thank you, thank you. With your father's permission, Detective Cunningham told me the whole story—how you returned the money after the robbery but didn't want anyone to know. The check is a reward, a token of our appreciation. We will continue to honor your request not to go public with the story, but we insist that you take this . . . with our eternal gratitude."

Abbey smothered him with hugs and kisses, and Howard clapped him on the back.

"You're sure you don't want to be in the papers?" Zhariah asked. "The city—heck, the *world*—needs stories like yours. I could make you famous. I thought that's what every kid in America wanted these days."

"Not me," said Andy. "I'm fine just the way I am."

◆ ◆ ◆

The next day, a drizzly fall Saturday afternoon, Andy reached into the cooler at YouNeedItWeGotIt! and pulled out a bottle of GoodTimes root beer.

"That stuff will kill you," Silas said, standing behind him.

Andy didn't even flinch. "I've been expecting you. You want one? I was thinking of switching to cream soda, but I feel . . . I don't know, *loyal,* I guess, to root beer. Do you know what I mean?"

"As a matter of fact, I do. Do you have a little time? Let's take a walk. And maybe I will have a root beer—thanks. I guess you can afford it."

"You heard, huh?"

"Of course. What are you going to do with the money?"

Andy twisted his lips to the side in his favorite expression. "Don't know yet. For now it's in the bank."

"The one—"

"Yeah. Funny, isn't it?"

They stopped at Andy's building to pick up Penny and then wandered into Central Park, north of Ninety-Sixth Street, chatting about school, the best places for pizza, and how the model of the *Indefatigable* was coming along (the hull was nearly complete, thanks to some expert advice from his grandfather, but lots of work still remained) before Andy finally blurted out, "So, are we ever going to talk about what's going on with NTRP? Or am I done with all that?"

"You're not done with it unless you want to be done

with it," Silas said. "After the concert, Mrs. Cardigan and I had a lot to talk about, and we decided it would be best to leave you alone for a few days, until things settled down. I'm sure you and your mom—and your dad—had plenty to discuss, too. But if you're ready to talk . . . that's why I'm here."

"I'm ready."

"Good." Silas pointed at a park bench. "Let's have a seat. First, tell me about Winter. What's the latest news? She's back in school, right?"

When de Spere's machine exploded, it sent a sliver of glass flying into Winter's left eye. Silas had used all of his contacts in the hospital but had not been able to determine what damage had been caused. No one knew or was willing to tell him whether the doctors had been able to save the eye.

"She has a patch over her left eye," said Andy. "When she saw me, she looked right at me with her other one. She didn't say anything. She didn't even look mad. Like nothing had happened."

Winter, Silas knew, would never waste time and energy on being angry. She *would* want revenge, and she had the resources of NTRP and St. John de Spere himself at her disposal. Silas didn't want to tell Andy *that,* so he reassured him that the Agents were keeping a close eye on her.

"NTRP is already expanding her role at the network. That first segment she did, the interview with Karina, was a huge ratings hit for them, so they're going to sit her down with all kinds of big names. In a few weeks, she's going to be one of the most famous teens in America. After that, who knows? De Spere, I'm sure, has big plans for her. Her own show. A website. Political office. With her abilities and his help, the sky's the limit. I've seen the two of them together, on a park bench not far from here, laughing and talking as if they didn't have a care in the world. At this point, God only knows what they're planning."

"I'm not afraid," said Andy. "We'll be ready for them."

"That's right. We will. And you know why? Because there are some things in life that just *are* black-and-white. Maybe you see that more clearly than most because you're color-blind, but the truth is simple: We're *right* and they're wrong. What you did at the concert was a real victory for our side, but that was only one battle. The war goes on. NTRP will be back; you can count on that."

"I don't think we'll have Jensen. She's dropped out of the Broadcast Club, and the other day she even told me about something that happened on *How Far Will You Go?* that she thought was hilarious. She used to *hate* that stuff."

"Don't give up on her. Mrs. Cardigan likes to say that nothing lasts forever. If there's a way to get Jensen back, to reverse the process, we'll find it. I promise."

"And we'll be even stronger now that we have Fallon back, right?"

Silas smiled. "You know, I think today is the first day you've said *we* instead of *you* when you were talking about the Agents. You really are one of us now. But to answer your question, yes, we will be stronger with Fallon back at the table, even though she was never actually gone. We've had another change that I should tell you about. Benson Siraji, the Agent who sits in the Humility chair, has gone missing somewhere in southern Tanzania, near where your mom was working. We haven't heard from him since the day after the concert. He sent a message that he was on his way to Arusha, his home city, for a few days and would fly back to New York. Somewhere, somehow, something went wrong. So until we find out exactly what is going on, I'll be sitting in for him in meetings."

"Will . . . you . . . and me . . . will we still be a team?"

"Afraid so. You're stuck with me, kid. Unless I end up in jail for the murder of Ilene Porter. Your friend Detective Cunningham is still snooping around the hotel where she died, and it's only a matter of time till he finds a security camera with *this* face on it."

"Funny thing about him," said Andy. "After the thing at school where they gave me the money, we all went out for pizza. Mom and Dad invited him up, just to thank him, I guess. Well, Penny did not like that at all. He was trying to be friendly with her, but she wouldn't go near him. She sat across the room and just stared, showing her teeth. I never got the chance to look at him with my glass, but . . . Penny knows what she's doing."

"Good girl, Penny," Silas said, rubbing the spot behind her ears. "That's *very* interesting news. A little disturbing, maybe, but I'd rather know it now than later."

They walked back across the park without saying much more, pausing outside Andy's apartment building. The sun had dropped below the buildings to the west, and the temperature had fallen with it. Directly above them, a streetlight came on, and Silas reached out to shake Andy's hand.

Andy hesitated. "Are you sure? I mean, I know you—"

Silas stood firm, moving his hand closer until Andy grasped it.

WELL, THAT'S ANDY'S STORY—AT LEAST THE PART THAT WE'RE ALLOWED TO SHOW YOU FOR THE MOMENT. IF YOU'RE READY TO JOIN US, DON'T TELL A SOUL ABOUT WHAT YOU'VE READ HERE.

IN THE MEANTIME, GO HAVE A ROOT BEER.

I'LL BE IN TOUCH.

ACKNOWLEDGMENTS

Call me naïve and an idealist (I've been called worse!), but I believe in the Andy Llewellyns of the world. They're out there, I remind myself daily—though some days I have my doubts, as any New Yorker who has ever taken the 6 train must. For every Andy and Silas and Mrs. Cardigan doing good, however, a Winter Neale or a St. John de Spere or an NTRP (resemblance to any actual company is a product of your imagination) can't be far behind, eager to restore the balance with a little evil. With the fog of (gasp!) optimism circling my head, I hope that this book finds its way into the hands of a few of those would-be Andys, who, like him, are willing to stand up to the Winters of the world.

My heartfelt thanks go out to:

Laura Grimmer, the love of my life: At long last, here it is—the superhero book that you coaxed, inspired, cajoled, and, in so many ways, *helped* me to write. I hope it exceeds your (great) expectations. (You knew I'd slip a Dickens allusion in there somewhere, didn't you?)

Nancy Hinkel, my brilliant editor: Part cheerleader, part psychologist, and altogether wonderful human being, you guided, pushed, and pulled me through six—count 'em, *six*—books! I've said it before, but it bears repeating: I can't even *imagine* a writer having a better experience. I am *so* going to miss you!

Rosemary Stimola, my agent: Eight years and seven books later, I still have to pinch myself to make sure I didn't merely dream that you took me on as a client. Two words: You rock.

And finally, a hearty shout of thanks from the rooftops to everyone at Knopf Books for Young Readers, Random House Children's Books, and Yearling Books. Your talents, hard work, and enthusiasm inspire me to work a little harder every day.